You Are
One of Them

You Are
One of Them

❊

Elliott Holt

THE PENGUIN PRESS

New York

2013

THE PENGUIN PRESS
Published by the Penguin Group
Penguin Group (USA) Inc., 375 Hudson Street,
New York, New York 10014, USA

USA · Canada · UK · Ireland · Australia
New Zealand · India · South Africa · China

Penguin Books Ltd, Registered Offices:
80 Strand, London WC2R 0RL, England
For more information about the Penguin Group visit penguin.com

Grateful acknowledgment is made for permission to reprint excerpts from the following
copyrighted works:
Endgame by Samuel Beckett. English translation copyright © 1957 by the Estate of Samuel
Beckett. Used by permission of Grove/Atlantic, Inc. Any third party use of this material,
outside of this publication, is prohibited.
Eloise in Moscow by Kay Thompson. Copyright © 1959 Kay Thompson, copyright renewed
1987 Kay Thompson. Reprinted with permission of Simon & Schuster Books for Young
Readers, an imprint of Simon & Schuster Children's Publishing Division.

ISBN 978-1-594-20528-6

Printed in the United States of America
1   3   5   7   9   10   8   6   4   2

BOOK DESIGN BY KATY RIEGEL

This is a work of fiction. Apart from the well-known actual people, events, and locales that
figure in the narrative, all names, characters, places, and incidents either are the product of the
author's imagination or are used fictitiously. Any resemblance to current events or locales, or to
living persons, is entirely coincidental.

For my mother,

who wasn't afraid of anything

⊕

Then babble, babble, words, like the solitary child who turns himself into children, two, three, so as to be together, and whispering together, in the dark.

—Samuel Beckett, *Endgame*

YOU ARE
ONE OF THEM

PROLOGUE

IN MOSCOW I was always cold. I suppose that's what Russia is known for. Winter. But it is winter to a degree I could not have imagined before I moved there. Winter not of the pristine, romantic *Doctor Zhivago* variety but a season so insistent and hateful that all hope freezes with your toes. The snow is cleared away too quickly to soften the city, so the streets are slushy with resentment. And I felt like the other young women trudging through that slush: sullen and tired, with a bluish tint to the skin below the eyes that suggests insomnia or malnutrition or a hangover. Or all of the above. Every day brought news of a drunk who froze to death. I saw one: slumped over on a bench on Tverskoy Boulevard with a bottle between his legs and icicles decorating his fingers.

Distilled into something so pure and solid that I didn't recognize it as death until I got up close. The babushka next to me summoned the police.

I cracked under the weight of the cold. My only recourse was to eat. I inhaled entire packages of English tea biscuits in one sitting. They came stacked in a tube, and when I found myself halfway through one, I decided I might as well finish it. I polished off a whole tube every night after work and then pinched the extra flesh around my hips in the bathtub and thought, *At least I'm warm.*

It was 1996. At the English-language newspaper where I worked, the other expats were always joking. Russia, with all its quirks, was funny. There was a sign at Sheremetyevo Airport, perched at the entrance to the short-term-parking lot, which had been translated into English as ACUTE CARE PARKING. It was a sign better suited to a hospital, where everything is dire. And at the smaller airports, the ones for regional flights, the Russian word for "exit," *vykhod,* was translated into English as GET OUT. A ticket to Sochi, for example, said you would be departing from Get Out #4. I laughed with them, but I knew that eventually these mistranslations would be corrected, that Russia would grow out of its awkward teenage capitalism and become smooth and nonchalant. You could see the growing pains in the pomaded hair of the nightclub bouncers, in the tinted windows of the Mercedes sedans on Tverskaya, in the garish sequins on the Versace mannequins posing in a shop around the corner from the Bolshoi Theater.

At the infamous Hungry Duck, I watched intoxicated Russian

girls strip on top of the bar and then tumble into the greedy arms of American businessmen. American men still had cachet then; as an American woman, I hugged the sidelines. ("Sarah," said the Russian men at my office, "why you don't wear the skirts? Are you the feminist?" They always laughed, and it was a deep, carnivorous sound that made me feel daintier than I am.) Everyone in Moscow was ravenous, and the potential for anarchy—I could feel its kaleidoscope effect—made a lot of foreigners giddy. Most of the reporters at my paper spoke some Russian. But among the copy editors, many of whom were fresh out of Russian-studies programs and itching to put their years in the language lab to good use, the hierarchy was built on who spoke Russian best. They were not gunning for careers in journalism; they just wanted to be in the new post-Soviet Moscow—the wild, wild East—and this job paid the bills. The Americans with Russian girlfriends—"pillow dictionaries," they called them, aware that these lanky, mysterious women were far better-looking than anyone they'd touched back home—began to sound like natives. They were peacocks, preening with slang. In the office each morning, they'd pull off their boots and slide their feet into their *tapochki* and head to the kitchen for instant coffee—Nescafé was our only option then—and they'd never mention their past lives in Wisconsin or Nevada or wherever they escaped from. *"Oy,"* they said, and *"Bozhe moy,"* which means "my God" but has anguish in Russian that just doesn't translate. A little bravado goes a long way toward hiding the loneliness. You can reinvent yourself with a different alphabet.

On Saturdays at the giant Izmailovo Market, tourists haggled for Oriental rugs and *matryoshka* dolls painted to resemble Soviet leaders—Lenin fits into Stalin, who fits into Khrushchev, who fits into Brezhnev, who fits into Andropov, who fits into Gorbachev, who fits into Yeltsin. History reduced to kitsch. While shopping for Christmas gifts once, I stopped by a booth where a spindly drunk was selling old Soviet stamps. And there, pinned like a butterfly to a tattered red velvet display cushion, was Jenny. Her image barely warped by time. *"Skolko?"* I said. The man asked too much. He had the deadened eyes of a person who hasn't been sober for years, and I didn't feel like bargaining, so I handed him the money. He could smell my desperation. He put the stamp in a Ziploc bag, and on the way back home on the Metro I studied her through the plastic. My best friend, commemorated like a cosmonaut. Her name had been transliterated into Cyrillic: ДЖЕННИФЕР ДЖОНС, it said above the smiling photo of her freckled face. A five-kopeck stamp from the postal service of the USSR. I had just paid ten dollars for something that was originally worth next to nothing.

Conspiracy theorists will tell you that Jennifer Jones's death was not an accident. They will tell you that her plane crashed not because of mechanical failure, not because the pilot was suffering from dizzy spells, but because the CIA shot it down. She had become a Soviet pawn they say, too sympathetic to the party. Others say that the KGB was responsible, that after the press took pictures of her smiling at the Kremlin and quoted her saying how nice the Russians were, they needed to quit while they were ahead. I've read the official reports. I heard the pundits spew their Sunday-morning-talk-show ire. But I don't recognize the Jennifer Jones I knew in their versions of the story.

Some people will tell you that all of it was propaganda, that she was just a pawn in someone else's game, but the letter—the original letter—was real. It came from a real place of fear. The threat used to be so tangible. I was prepared to lose the people I loved best. My mother, with her fuzzy hair and lemon-colored corduroys; our dog, Pip; and Jenny. Always Jenny, whose last act must have been storing her tray table in its upright and locked position. Yuri Andropov wished her the best in her young life. Maybe this blessing was a curse.

Or maybe her luck just ran out.

PART 1

1.

THE FIRST DEFECTOR was my sister.

I don't remember her, but I have watched the surviving Super 8 footage so many times that the scenes have seared themselves on my brain like memories. In the film, Isabel (Izzy, for short), four years old, dances on a beach. She is twirling, around and around and around again, until she falls in the sand. There is grace in her fall; she does not tumble in a heap but composes herself like a ballerina. She wears a bathing suit with the stars-and-stripes design that the U.S. swim team wore in the 1972 Summer Games in Munich. It is the same suit that Mark Spitz wore when he swam to gold seven times. On Izzy the Speedo bunches near her armpits but is taut across her stomach. Her body has already lost most of its toddler pudge. Her legs are long and lean and are beginning to show muscle definition. My parents were both athletes; Izzy's coordination and flexibility suggest that she, too, will win many races. But her belly still protrudes slightly like a baby's, and there are small pockets of fat on her upper thighs. Her hair is startlingly blond and tousled by the wind. Her eyes are green and transparent as sea glass. Behind her the ocean is calm. Her expression betrays—already!—a hint of skepticism. She is the sort of child who is universally declared beautiful. She looks directly at the camera, unafraid of meeting its gaze. My mother hovers at the right side of the frame in sunglasses and a wide-brimmed straw hat. She wears a pink paisley bikini, and she holds me, a juicy nine-month-old with a half-gnawed banana in my right hand, on her lap. The camera rests for a moment on my face, but I am blurry, and before the focus can be adjusted, the lens turns abruptly back to Izzy, who is kneeling in the sand, strangely reverent and, judging from her moving lips and rhythmically tilting head, singing something. The camera pans to my mother once more. She is laughing, head thrown back.

Three minutes of footage, shot in August of 1973, exactly one year before Nixon resigned. There are several notable things about this short film: (1) My mother looks relaxed and happy. Half of her face is obscured by the hat, yes, but the smile she wears is an irrepressible one. She is laughing at her older daughter, squeezing her younger one. She is all lightness and joy. (2) The camera lingers on her lovely legs for at least four seconds, which suggests that my father the auteur was, at this point, still very much in love with (or at least attracted to) my mother. (3) My sister is alive.

Just three months after this scene on the beach, Izzy died of meningitis. It was the sort of freak occurrence about which every parent has nightmares: a sudden fever that won't go down, a frantic call to the pediatrician—supposedly one of the city's best— and six hours later, despite said pediatrician's reassurances that "it was nothing to worry about," a visit to the emergency room at Georgetown University Hospital, where my sister's meningitis was diagnosed too late to save her. It had already infected her spine and her brain.

This happened on November 7, 1973: my first birthday. Forever after that it was tainted. My parents could never bring themselves to celebrate it convincingly. During every subsequent birthday, they would excuse themselves at various points and disappear into their own private corners to grieve. At my fifth birthday party—the first one I remember—I could hear my mother's wails from the laundry room in the basement. The sound was so alarming that the clown who had been hired to make balloon animals kept popping her creations. She seemed skittish. "Why is your mom crying?" the kids from my kindergarten class wanted to know. "I had a sister, and then she died," I said. I used to deliver this information matter-of-factly. It was no more weighty than the fact that our house was stucco or that my father was British. I was three when my parents told me I'd had a sister, and it was a relief to know that there was an explanation for the absence I'd felt for so long in my limbic memory. I'd reach for a baby doll—a doll I later learned had belonged to her—and picture it cradled in another set of arms. Sitting beneath our dining-room table once when I was four—I liked to crawl into private spaces to play—I was overcome with déjà vu. I was sure I had sat in the same spot with Izzy. It must have been just before she died. I must have been eleven months old. I could almost hear a breathy, high-pitched voice urging me to "smile, little Sarah, smile!"

And soaking in the tub, even now as an adult, I sometimes sense the memory of bath time with my sister. My foot touching hers under the water as the tub filled, the sight of her leaning back to tip her blond head under the faucet. Letters of the alphabet in primary colors stuck on the porcelain sides of the tub, arranged in almost-words, and my mother crouched on the floor beside us, her sleeves rolled up so that her blouse didn't get wet as she washed our hair. And after we were pulled from the water, did we wriggle free of our towel cocoons and chase each other around the house naked? Did I make her laugh? I have no proof that it didn't happen. I feel certain it did.

Intuitively I knew that something was missing long before I knew how to articulate it. Long before I knew that most people's parents slept in the same bedroom, that most people's mothers weren't afraid to leave the house, that some children had never seen their parents cry, I knew that something was off in my family. "Your poor parents," people would say to me when I was older and I told them the story. But no one seemed to understand that I felt the loss, too. My sister was in heaven, my mother said, with my mother's parents, who also died too young for me to meet them. I mourned the sister I didn't get to know. I longed to share secrets and clothes. I wanted a co-conspirator. I was jealous of the kids with siblings, who rolled their eyes at each other behind their parents' backs, who counted on the unconditional loyalty only a sister or a brother can provide.

I loved watching that film of my sister. My parents had bought the camera right before that beach trip, so there is no earlier footage of her. There are some photographs, of course, but it was a thrill for me to see her move. Her right hand ebbed and flowed through the air, replicating the motion of the waves behind her. Her body language was like a tide pulling me in; I recognized it somewhere deep inside myself. If she had lived, I know that we would be the kind of adult siblings about whom people say, "Their mannerisms are the same."

My mother liked to watch our home movies every Saturday night, but screening them was a labor-intensive process. You had to set up the projector on the end table we used as a base, thread the reel through the machine—"Careful, careful!" my mother would say to my father—and sometimes, when the projector overheated, the film would burn and darkness would spread across the image on the living-room wall. It was terrifying to watch the dark blot fill the screen, as if our past were being annihilated right in front of us. It happened so quickly: one moment bright with life and then, suddenly, nothing but darkness. We lost many precious moments in this way—"Stop it, stop it, turn it off!" my mother would cry as my father fumbled with the projector, trying to save the rest of the reel from being fried—including the establishing shots of Izzy on the beach. A zoom into her cherubic face and then we watched that face melt. "My baby girl!" my mother whimpered while the loose strand of film flapped hysterically and my father struggled to turn off the machine. The manic whirring stopped, and then we were all quiet as my father put the reel away in its gray steel case.

"Sometimes I think we should just let it burn," he said one evening.

"It's the only one we have of her," said my mother.

"But we've got to let go, Alice. We've got to look forward."

She launched her iciest stare at him. "Is there something better on the horizon?"

I could tell he wanted to erupt. I don't know if he locked up his rage because I was in the room or because he had already given up on my mom.

We didn't watch the Izzy footage again after that—my mother was afraid the rest of the reel would be destroyed, so she hid it inside a hatbox in her closet. But when I was old enough to operate the projector, I sneaked late-night viewings of my sister. I would wait until I was sure my mother was asleep and then creep into her dressing room. She kept the hatbox on the top shelf, and as I reached for it, my hand would graze the silks of the dresses my mother had long ago stopped wearing. She retired her glamour when my sister died. ("You may not believe this," my father said, "but at Radcliffe your mother was always the life of the party.")

In the dark of the living room, where I set up the projector in the same place we always watched home movies, Izzy's sequence of movements—turn, turn, fall, kneel—became a sort of meditation. I realize that I see all my memories this way. Everything I remember unspools in the flickering silence of Super 8 film. Each scene begins with the trembling red stripe of the Kodak logo and ends with the sound of the reel spinning, spinning, spinning until someone shuts it down.

2.

I MET JENNIFER JONES in 1980.

It was the summer of the Moscow Olympics, and I was devastated that the American athletes were denied the chance to compete because of the boycott. I was a gymnast then, and although I was not good enough to be an Olympic hopeful—I was too tall and too scared of turning somersaults on the balance beam— there was an older girl named Amanda at my gymnastics club who had made the U.S. team. She was sixteen; by the time the L.A. games rolled around, she'd be twenty and past her prime.

Why, I remember asking my mother, did the Soviet athletes have "CCCP" on the backs of their uniforms instead of USSR? She explained that the Russians had a different alphabet, that in Cyrillic what looked to us like a *C* sounded like an *S* and what looked like a *P* sounded like *R,* and the Russian name for the Soviet Union—the Union of Soviet Socialist Republics—was abbreviated as CCCP. This was a mind-blowing concept for an eight-year-old. It had never before occurred to me that there could be other alphabets, that somewhere out in the world people were arranging entirely different shapes into words. Like most American children of my generation, I had learned the alphabet watching *Sesame Street.* When episodes were brought to us by the letter *S,* I always smiled, because *S* was my letter, and now my mother was telling me that in the Russian alphabet the *S* looked like a *C.* She might as well have told me that I didn't exist. It was like money, she said. Different countries have different currencies, and you have to exchange them. Different coins and different letters sometimes. I knew about foreign currency. My father had given me a few English pounds.

The Olympic boycott was one of many signs that 1980 was a turning point in the Cold War: tensions between the United States and the Soviet Union were escalating. Whenever my mother said this, I thought of escalators. For years escalators had scared me, a phobia caused by the steep ones of the D.C. Metro, which plummet straight into darkness. Riding down into the stations induced such panic in me that for several years we didn't ride the Metro at all. *What are you so afraid of?* my father asked me when I was six, as if I could rationally analyze my fear. He wasn't afraid of anything, my father, or didn't seem to be, and until my phobia of escalators developed, he thought I was like him. *You're turning into your mother's child,* he said to me.

We were on the steamy July sidewalk outside the Dupont Circle station. He had promised to take me to the Air and Space Museum if, and only if, I agreed to ride the Metro to the Mall. Now we were at an impasse. We stood at the top of the station entrance, looking down the short flight of stairs that led to the main escalator. I wasn't afraid of these steps, but I knew that if I descended into the station, I would be trapped. My father would drag me onto the escalator, he would tug me like a stubborn dog on a leash. I didn't want to turn into my mother's child. I knew that she was not normal, that her anxiety was crippling.

What are you so afraid of? my father asked again. This time his tone was frustrated, patronizing. *You are my flesh and blood,* he seemed to be saying. *Isn't it time you acted like it?* To my father, fear was weakness. To my mother it was preparation. I looked at him. He was so tall. Six foot four in bare feet. He was wearing a sport coat and a button-down shirt. Even on weekends, even in the heat, he dressed up. He never wore jeans. They were, he thought, too American. This dapper, impatient Englishman seemed, suddenly, like a stranger. He crossed his arms. *Sarah,* he said. *You used to ride the bloody things all the time.*

I know, I said. I could remember stepping gingerly onto the top step, careful to make sure my shoelaces didn't catch in the spinning belt. Then clutching the handrail and looking forward, not down, as my stomach sank. The D.C. Metro has an earthy, mineral smell that reminds you you're plunging straight into bedrock. The cavernous stations are so deep and cold that you half expect to see stalactites dangling from the stone ceilings. The New York and Moscow subways hum with civilization; they smell of human exertion and alcohol-saturated despair. But in Washington, where the trains are not as crowded, where the walls are not tainted with advertisements, the Metro feels almost organic. It's as if the stations were hollowed out by some primal force. Even the platforms used to scare me. The lights at the edge flashed to warn that a train was coming, then turned a threatening red as the train pulled in to the station. I was always afraid I'd fall onto the track.

I can't, I said to my father. *I just can't.*

Fine. I give up, he said. *Let's go home.*

We trudged along Q Street toward our car. He walked ahead of me, let his back show his disappointment. I had failed. A month later he left.

So the second defector was my father.

There was another woman involved—there usually is in these situations—but my mother was so unstable that he probably would have left even if he hadn't met someone else. My mother had an anxiety disorder, and her panic attacks were triggered by a wide variety of daily activities: driving over bridges, flying (or any kind of travel, really), heights (she wouldn't go above the fourth floor of any building), crowds (tourist-riddled museums had to be avoided), and confined spaces of all sorts (Metro cars, movie theaters, and elevators were all off-limits). The panic developed after my sister died—a not-atypical response to such trauma, her psychotherapist said—and my mother no longer felt safe anywhere. She could be her usual charming self—she had a coquettish streak, and in those days she and my father still entertained people—but she was also capable of wild mood swings. It was not uncommon for her to disappear in the middle of a dinner party. My father would find her hiding in the bathtub, fully dressed, while her guests pretended not to notice her absence. Most people tolerated my mother's behavior as mere eccentricity; she was beautiful, so she got away with a lot. She insisted on keeping all the lights on at night; she couldn't bear the dark. She couldn't sleep without pharmaceutical aid. She became obsessed with preparing for disaster, as if vigilance alone could save us. She slathered my face with sunscreen even on cloudy days. She stockpiled batteries and medications and took my temperature every morning as a precaution.

My father was a pragmatist. My sister's death confirmed his worldview: that terrible things happen despite your best efforts and when you least expect them, so there was no point living paralyzed by fear. For my mother, Izzy's sudden death was a reminder that she could never let down her guard, that to relax even for a moment was to open the door to danger. My father took me to the places she wouldn't go: to the dentist, whose office was on the seventh floor of a Bethesda high-rise; to my gymnastics classes that were located in Virginia and required a trip across Key Bridge. He did his best to compensate for my mother's agoraphobia. But the more neurotic she became, the less time he spent at home.

And then one day he'd had enough. He was exhausted, he said. He couldn't do it anymore. This was 1979. In the wake of Watergate, every institution—including marriage—seemed to be falling apart. ("Of course your parents split up," college friends said to me later. "Statistically speaking, it's incredibly likely for a marriage to end after a child dies.") My father had moved to Washington to work for the IMF as an economist, and when he left my mother, he went back to London to join an investment bank. He said he was leaving my mother, not me, but after that I was lucky to see him once a year. The first year he flew in for a long weekend, took a suite at the Mayflower Hotel, and escorted me around like a tourist. He watched me scramble over the giant bronze dinosaur outside the Museum of Natural History. We went paddleboating in the Tidal Basin. We climbed to the top of the Washington Monument and took in the broad expanse of Constitution Avenue from above. When people asked my mother about her husband, she said, "He repatriated." But he defected. Once he left, he was gone for good.

HE'D BEEN GONE for about a year when Jennifer Jones moved into the house across the street from us. It was Labor Day weekend. On that Saturday I watched the movers unload a couch, covered in plastic, from the truck. As the men unloaded other furniture, our dog, Pip, was on his hind legs, pressed against the narrow window above the mail slot, frantically barking. "What's he looking at?" said my mother from the dining room. The table was covered with paper—she had turned the room into a make-shift office.

"Someone's moving into the Goldmans' house," I said.

"I'm glad it finally sold."

The house was a stately Queen Anne in white clapboard with black shutters and a wraparound front porch that was typical of Cleveland Park. I always thought of our neighborhood as a community of giant dollhouses.

"Maybe they'll let us use their pool," I said. Several houses on our street had pools, but we were not well enough acquainted with the owners to have access to them.

"Don't get your hopes up," she said.

But my hopes were never up. Our house had no room for hope.

A brown Chevrolet station wagon with suitcases strapped to its roof pulled up in front of the house. Before the motor was off, a back door opened and a girl tumbled out. She had two neat braids that reached her shoulders. She was wearing blue shorts and a blue-and-yellow-striped polo shirt and carried a cage of some kind (later I'd learn that it contained her cat, Hexa). Pip couldn't hold himself up anymore and dropped to all fours, but he continued to bark as he paced back and forth behind me.

"Pip, quiet," I said. Silencing him was useless; he continued to yap. Like most herding dogs, he had a brittle nervous system. He was like my mother that way. The irony is that my parents got Pip because my mother thought she would feel safer and calmer with a dog. Instead his anxiety fed off hers and then his barking made her more anxious.

A man and a woman—presumably the girl's parents— emerged from the front seats of the car. The woman had short, feathered hair and wore a white blouse with tiny red flowers embroidered around the collar. The man had glasses with thick tortoiseshell frames. The houses on that side of the street were on a hill, so they looked down on us. I watched the girl scamper up the long flight of steps to the front door. Later I'd count those steps; there were twenty-one. The sloping lawn on either side of them was impenetrable with ivy. The girl tried the door, then spun around impatiently to check her parents' progress. "Come on!" I heard her shout. When her father reached the porch, she stepped aside to let him open the door. And then they were inside, out of sight. The movers were lugging stuff up the steps.

"There's a girl," I said. "She looks like she's about my age."

"You should go say hello."

"Now?"

"Not now. Tomorrow maybe. Let them get settled."

It wasn't until Monday—Labor Day—that we actually met. I was walking Pip down the street when I heard a promising voice say, "Can I pet your dog?"

I turned around, and there she was. My new neighbor. "Sure."

She came closer and crouched to extend a hand for Pip to sniff. "Like Lassie," she said.

"Lassie was a collie," I said. "My dog's a Shetland sheepdog."

"Mini-Lassie," she said. "Boy or girl?"

"Boy. His name's Pip."

Pip allowed her to scratch him behind his ears. "I want a dog," she said. "But my dad won't let me get one."

"I live across the street from you," I said, and pointed at my house. It was pebbled stucco, charcoal gray with white shutters and a mansard roof. From the outside it looked normal.

"I'm Jenny," she said. "I'm from Ohio. The Buckeye State."

"Sarah," I said. "I've never lived in a state."

"What do you mean?"

"This isn't a state," I said.

"My dad says Washington, D.C., is the most important city in the world." She had the zeal of a convert.

I shrugged. Washington was always more impressive to new-comers: the aspiring politicians at Georgetown University, the freshman representatives who traded state legislatures for the U.S. Capitol, the idealistic reporters determined to be the next Wood-ward and Bernstein, the tourists who sweated outside the White House hoping to spot the president. For those of us who lived there, Washington was not glamorous. It is a swampy city of wonks, a factory town where everyone—the lawyers, consultants, think-tank strategists, journalists, and diplomats—works in the same business. And the languid pace of life in the leafy enclaves of northwest Washington is so far from urban bustle that it's hard to believe you're in a city at all. Even then I knew I wanted to live in New York. I'd been there just once, but before my father had even hailed a taxi outside Penn Station, I remember thinking, *Now,* this *is a real city.*

Jenny had turned eight in June; I would be eight in November. We were both entering third grade at John Eaton. And when school started the next day, Jenny and I were in the same class. Our teacher, Mrs. Haynes, was a woman in her fifties who wore a pearl choker and blew her nose into monogrammed handkerchiefs. When she discovered that I had already met "the new girl," she let us colonize adjoining desks. Jenny and I spent that first recess on the swings, where we exchanged information about our lives as we flew higher and higher.

Your sister died? she said as she moved through the air, her white kneesocks extending straight out over the blacktop.

Why did you move? I asked as I pumped my legs as hard as I could.

We covered the basics: Her father had been transferred from his consulting firm's Dayton office; her mother was a nurse who hadn't found a job in D.C. yet. Jenny had always wanted a sister; I had been cheated of mine. And so that's it: we were friends. Jenny invited me to her house after school.

The Joneses had moved in only three days before, but already the boxes were unpacked. Books were on shelves, paintings were on walls. At my house there were boxes that my mother had not opened for years. Her dressing room was so cluttered that she had to climb over stuff to get to her closet. Our house was like a museum, filled with relics. She kept all of Izzy's clothes stored in a trunk in her bedroom. There were piles of paper on every surface. The floors were covered with Oriental rugs that trapped dog hair and dust. My mother kept the curtains drawn—she felt safer that way—so our house was like a tomb. And the slightest provocation (a ringing phone, the arriving mail) was enough to send Pip into a frenzy.

Jenny's house was bright and modern. Although it had been built at the turn of the century like ours, it had been renovated in the 1960s, and the kitchen opened into a spacious family room with lots of windows and skylights. The ceilings were high, and the rooms were sparsely furnished with midcentury pieces. It was a house that seemed to look forward, not back. The floors were polished wood, and Jenny slid around pretending to surf.

We went swimming that afternoon, and I can still remember my first glimpse of Jenny underwater. We sank beneath the surface in unison and sat cross-legged on the bottom of the pool in a breath-holding contest. She wore a canary yellow bathing suit and green goggles, and I could see her eyes open wide and staring at me, her rival. I had no goggles, but I forced my eyes open despite the sting of chlorine. From above, the pool looked glassy and hard, a surface that must be broken with force, but below, it was soft and beckoning, a membrane through which light sieved like sugar. The sunlight webbed across Jenny's skin and through her hair, giving it a reddish tint, and the bubbles of air streaming from her nose added to the impressionistic effect. Suddenly she stretched her mouth open in a ludicrous way and stuck out her tongue. My laughter forced me up for air. "I win!" Jenny announced as she triumphed from below.

For the next two weeks, I swam at her house every day until the pool had to be closed for the season. They had a diving board, and Jenny and I took turns executing tricks and giving them ridiculous names. It wasn't a cannonball when I folded my body into a tight tuck, it was a "popcorn kernel," and when I did backflips— thanks to gymnastics, diving came easily to me—I dubbed them "rewinds." Mrs. Jones was our lifeguard. She watched us from a lounge chair at the shallow end and clapped whenever either of us completed a dive.

"It's so nice to meet you," said Mrs. Jones the first afternoon I was there. She had the perky delivery of a cheerleader. She made us a snack—peanut butter on celery sticks—and asked about my family. What did my dad do? she wanted to know. Her flat midwestern *A*'s made it sound like "Daaad."

"He lives in London," I said.

"London, England? Gosh, that's far away," she said.

"They're divorced," I said. And though divorce was common in our Washington circles, Mrs. Jones looked shocked. I liked her innocence: troubled thoughts rushed across her face like clouds and were gone just as quickly. She was a clear sky.

"What a shame," she said. "What a terrible shame."

"It's okay," I said. "Some people just aren't meant to live together."

"What about your mom? What does she do?"

"She works for nuclear disarmament," I said.

It was only after my father left that my mother had begun to worry about nuclear war. She learned to channel her anxiety. The good thing was that she started leaving the house to attend disarmament-movement meetings. She got over her fear of the dark so that she could turn our basement into a fallout shelter.

My mother mapped out scenarios, calculating the reach of the radioactive fallout if the blast hit Kansas City, say, or Washington. She drew ominous red circles in our Rand-McNally to mark the circumference of destruction. At the kitchen table, the hanging lamp created a tunnel of light under which she envisioned doom. She'd press her slide rule across swaths of U.S. territory. The fifty states were rendered in pastels—yellow, orange, and green—but as I squinted at them, the crimson lines that my mother etched around their innocent metropolises gave the whole nation a fiery hue. "Look," she'd say, pointing at the Midwest of her childhood. The corn-soaked plains where her hopscotch squares had been overshadowed by stories of Hiroshima.

"What," I'd say, moving into her orbit. It was not a question when I said it, because I knew the answer. She always wanted to show me the same things. Missile silos dotting the prairies. Air force bases with nuclear weapons stacked neatly underground, ready to violate the vast blue skies. She marked the location of these Russian targets with black stars. My mother wouldn't look at me, but she took my arm, pulled me close. And then, with one cool hand, she guided my stuttering finger across the page. For a moment she was still. Unusual for a woman who was generally so high-strung. Who fretted through rooms, who would often shake her hands—as if spattering water—when she was thinking. She never realized she was doing it. Sometimes I'd call her from a friend's house and hear the flutter in her voice. "You're shaking your hands, aren't you?" I'd say. "No," she'd say, and then pause, and I knew she was startled by the sight of her own manic fingers.

I liked to flip the atlas to the Soviet Union, its borders drawn in a muted red. I couldn't even fit the top of my pinkie inside Luxembourg but could press both my palms onto the Soviet sprawl. The Russians fascinated me. My mother and I watched clips of Brezhnev on the evening news—his chest clotted with medals, his eyebrows bristling under his fur hat—but it was ordinary Russians I was curious about. Moscow, as the capital of the other superpower, struck me as Washington's twin. Was there an eight-year-old girl somewhere in Moscow whose sister had also died, whose father had also left? "They live in communal apartments," my mother said. "So that eight-year-old probably shares a bathroom with nine other people."

Some parents might have hesitated to expose their children to the gloomy realities of the hydrodynamic front, but I was six when my mother explained the concept of half-life. I was seven when she began stocking our basement with canned goods. Baked beans and tuna fish. Creamed corn. Beef jerky. Whole peaches in syrup. My mother did not hide anything from me. I knew that Khrushchev had promised to bury us. I knew that Carter had ordered the Olympic boycott because the Soviets invaded Afghanistan. In those days I'd squint at the sun, knowing that it could vanish, that

omnivorous darkness could descend at any time. That a mush-
room cloud could swallow us whole or leave us to shrivel in an eter-
nal winter. In my nightmares the landscape was as barren as a
photographic negative, the reverse of everything I knew. A world
silent and still. Was I scared? Yes, but the fear was so constant that
it was like a hum barely audible below our daily chatter. I went to
school, I came home. I went to gymnastics. I practiced the piano. I
did my homework. But the bomb was always on my mind.

Jenny and I settled into a rhythm that fall. We walked the two
blocks to school together—we'd meet outside our houses at exactly five minutes past eight and arrive before the opening bell
rang at eight-fifteen. After school, on the three days I didn't have
gymnastics, we'd go to her house and do our homework and, more
often than not, bake brownies. There were always Duncan Hines
mixes in the cupboard. Mrs. Jones was always there to ask about
our day. She smiled a lot. At first it made me nervous—there was
something unsettling about all that grinning—but my mother
said that people smiled more in Ohio.

We rode our bicycles around the oak-canopied streets of our
neighborhood. There were a lot of kids in Cleveland Park. They
congregated on the Macomb Street playground or at the community club on Highland Street. We were all allowed to roam without supervision until dusk, when a chorus—mostly the accented
voices of nannies and housekeepers—summoned everyone home
for dinner. For years I had lingered on the fringes of the other kids'
society—I would occasionally be drafted into kickball when their
numbers were uneven—but now Jenny was with me. She could

have picked anyone to be her friend. I've come to understand that some people are suns that pull others into their orbit. The first time we went to the Macomb Street playground together, the others swarmed around Jenny like mosquitoes around a light. She dictated the terms of the interaction. Before they could ask her name, she announced it. Before they could ask where she was from, she told them. "Do you call soda 'pop'?" asked one of the older boys when he found out she was from the Midwest. His name was Josh, and he was in sixth grade. He and his younger brother lived two blocks away from me but had never acknowledged my presence. "I do," Jenny said without apology. "Pop is way more fun to say. POP!" Josh invited her to join their soccer game. But Jenny chose me. We ignored the others and created our own world.

The National Cathedral was just a few blocks away from us, and the Bishop's Garden—with its labyrinth of hedges—became our favorite place to play. In the garden we were princesses and fairies, we were orphans and spies. The gargoyles towering above us became monsters we had to escape; the cathedral bells chimed to celebrate make-believe weddings. We held summits in the gazebo. And in a crack that we discovered in the ten-foot wall that encircled the garden, we began to leave each other secret messages. An average piece of ruled paper could be folded into sixteenths and squirreled in the masonry's hole without detection. The messages lacked consequence: since we saw each other almost every day, we didn't need them to communicate. But it was exciting to slip across Woodley Road and up the hill—the cathedral is on the highest point in Washington—to check for messages. She'd leave notes for me on the afternoons I was at gymnastics; I'd retrieve them on Sunday mornings while she and her parents were at church. My mother was agnostic, so my exposure to God was limited to the cathedral police (the "God Squad") who periodically mazed through the Bishop's Garden on patrol. Eventually I'd end up at a school that was nominally Episcopalian, but it was only really religious about getting its alumnae into the Ivy League. Jenny and I never signed our notes in case a stranger found them. *"This message will self-destruct,"* I wrote. Or *"Burn after reading."* Sometimes Jenny's notes were in pig latin. *"Athmay omeworkhay uckssay,"* said one.

At dinnertime—the Joneses sat down promptly at six-thirty with cloth napkins and everything—I scuttled back to my house, where we usually ate in front of the TV so my mother could watch the news. We didn't yet have a microwave, but my mother favored dishes that were easy to prepare; we had spaghetti sauced with Ragú at least twice a week. For vegetables she relied on bags of frozen peas.

"It's strange that the Joneses bought a house here," my mother said not long after they moved in.

"Why?"

"Because most people in our neighborhood are Democrats. Cleveland Park is a liberal stronghold. You'd think they'd want to be in McLean or Arlington. All those Pentagon types are in northern Virginia."

"Mr. Jones doesn't work at the Pentagon," I said.

"No," she said. "But his company's out there in the suburbs somewhere. They consult for the government. Strategy for defense agencies, that kind of thing."

"Are they Republicans?"

"They claim they're independents," she said, "but Linda is so smitten with Nancy Reagan. You should have heard her talking about Nancy's hair."

Reagan's campaign against détente infuriated my mother. She couldn't bear to get out of bed the day after the election, and she remained depressed two days after that, on my eighth birthday. It was customary for kids to bring cupcakes to school on their birthdays, but I was empty-handed as Jenny and I walked down Lowell Street that morning. I tried not to feel sorry for myself. "You're privileged," my mother always said to me when self-pity creased my face. But when we got to school, Mrs. Haynes said, "Happy birthday!" and there was a tray of twenty-four cupcakes, half of them frosted in chocolate, half in vanilla. Jenny's mother had baked them.

"For me?" I said.

"Yes, silly," said Jenny. "It's your special day."

I knew that my mother was skeptical of Mrs. Jones's motives. ("She's baked cookies for everyone on the block. It's like she's running for office," my mother said once.) But I was grateful. I spent more and more time at Jenny's house. It seemed immune to the anxiety I tuned in to everywhere else. Jenny's parents always looked like they were coasting downhill. They had the thrilled flush and bright eyes of alpine skiers. They were never fearful or fazed. They sang while they loaded the dishwasher. They wore matching sweaters on their annual Christmas card. While my mother went to disarmament meetings, the Joneses initiated tennis round-robins at the neighborhood courts. I think my mother's activism amused Jenny's father. "If one of those godforsaken Russians is crazy enough to push the button, there's nothing we can do about it," he said.

I thought that if something happened to my mom—a car crash or a fallen tree limb—I could live at Jenny's house. That I could sleep on the top bunk in her green-and-white-flowered Laura Ashley paradise, that I could store my toothbrush next to hers in the yellow ceramic cup in her bathroom. That I could wake up to Mr. Jones's pancake breakfasts. The Jones household was neatly made with hospital corners. I took comfort in their routines. Mrs. Jones was always ordering things from catalogs; I got used to hearing her recite item numbers and colors *(One in watermelon, one in lime)* into the phone. Mr. Jones went for a run at six-thirty every morning, and the sound of the glass door in the kitchen sliding open marked his return. I loved my mother, but she was always exhausted. She was too tired to bother to fix her hair anymore, so she wore scarves on her head all the time, tucking away the unruly frizz so that people wondered if she had cancer. Mrs. Haynes asked me more than once that fall if I was really sure my mother was all right. And when I said "Yes, why?" she tilted her head in that pitying way reserved for people who don't yet understand the pain they are going to face.

"Let me braid your hair," Jenny used to say. I'd sit in her desk chair while she used her fingers to get my tangles out. "Don't you love having your scalp scratched? My mom always used to scratch my head when she did my hair." I did love it. Her fingernails sketched gentle patterns as she separated strands, prepared to plait. My mother had never braided my hair. I couldn't even remember her brushing it. When she was done, Jenny pushed me into her bathroom to confront the mirror. "What do you think?" she'd say. I always thought it looked perfect.

Jenny and I were best friends. That title mattered then. We didn't throw the term "best" around lightly. You had to earn it. I'd never had a best friend, but I didn't tell Jenny that. I didn't tell her that until she came along I'd never felt like I belonged anywhere. I knew that the other kids at school thought I was strange. I was the first kid whose parents got divorced. I was quiet and pensive. They could smell the sadness on me, rank and stale. Jenny and I exchanged friendship pins—safety pins decorated with tiny colored beads—that we fastened onto the laces of our L.L. Bean Blucher moccasins. We pricked our fingertips with one of her mother's sewing needles and became blood sisters. Our bedrooms faced each other across the street. The houses were too far apart for us to actually see into each other's rooms, but at bedtime we exchanged good-nights, flicking our flashlights on and off three times: blink, blink, blink. I couldn't fall asleep until I saw her light winking at me. With Jenny I felt safe.

———

SOMETIMES I THINK of the three of them—my sister, my father, Jenny—nesting inside one another, like a *matryoshka* doll. Each loss has to be unpacked to find the loss that came before. My sister is the smallest doll, the kernel of pain. My father is the next one, and then Jenny. And if there are bigger dolls, the hollow shells that contain the others, they represent various boyfriends who abandoned me, usually because I was too serious, too "intense." Their departures were just echoes of a much earlier grief.

If "defection" seems too strong a word—"A defection is a deliberate betrayal, is it not?" said my college shrink. "It's not as if your sister or Jenny *chose* to die"—you have to remember that I came of age during the Cold War. When I was a kid, the United States and the Soviet Union were always keeping score. Each defector claimed by the other side was a point. If your country is so great, why did so-and-so leave?

I was one and a half when Mikhail Baryshnikov defected while on tour with the Bolshoi Ballet in Canada. And seven in 1979, when another Soviet dancer, Alexander Godunov, slipped away while the Bolshoi was in New York. ("Those dancers sure are good at sneaking around," my father said. "Must be the ballet shoes. They can walk without making any bloody noise.") KGB officer Vitaly Yurchenko defected in August of 1985—just eight months after Jenny died—and then escaped from his CIA handler at Au Pied de Cochon in Georgetown and marched up the street to the Russian embassy to redefect. In high school my friends and

I used to go to Au Pied de Cochon for croque-monsieurs after we'd been drinking at house parties. The restaurant was open all night and was a good place to sober up before curfew. On those boozy nights when I tried to mimic the carefree behavior of my peers, I always thought of Yurchenko, who missed his homeland enough to return and risk execution. So yes, I said to my shrink, maybe Jenny's death wasn't deliberate, but she betrayed me *before* she died, and besides, when you've had as many people disappear from your life as I have, you start to wonder if you're defective. You start to wonder if there's somewhere better to go.

3.

"THERE ARE GANGSTERS IN MOSCOW," my mother said when I told her I wanted to go to Russia.

It was 1995, six years after the fall of the Berlin Wall, and I had just graduated from college. My classmates set off for New York and San Francisco—several of them went on to make millions at Internet start-ups—but now that the Cold War was finally over, I wanted to see the former Soviet Union. I'd also begun to harbor romantic notions of journalism, and I'd heard that it would be easier to break into a newspaper there. A new English-language daily was hiring expats. I even argued that my trip would help my mom's foundation—it had been exactly ten years since Jenny's death, and a commemorative journey to Russia would be good PR.

What I didn't tell her is that I had another reason for wanting to visit Moscow. A month before graduation, I'd received a strange letter. It arrived inside a manila envelope from my mother, who periodically forwarded mail that came to Washington. It drove me crazy that my mom never added a note of her own. She had never been the kind of parent who sent letters or care packages, but I would have settled for scribble on a Post-it: *"See you at graduation!"* This package, though, contained only a white envelope addressed to me in a broad sweeping hand:

Sarah Zuckerman
c/o Jennifer Jones Foundation
P.O. Box 408
Washington, D.C. 20008
USA

The envelope had a corporate logo, but it was not one I recognized. DDBD in orange block letters and beneath it, in gray, MOCKBA. I'd fulfilled my foreign-language requirement with two years of Russian, so I knew that MOCKBA (pronounced "Moskva") is "Moscow" in the Cyrillic alphabet. I turned the envelope over. The return address was printed in the same corporate orange: Petrovka Ulitsa 26, Moscow, Russia.

Dear Sarah, the letter said,
You are Sarah which is friend of Jennifer Jones? You organize Jennifer Jones Festival? I am Svetlana which is friend of Jennifer in

Russia. We with Jennifer spend much time together when she came to USSR. We were on the pioneer camp. She often talked about you. I always want to meet with you.

I know that you lives in Washington, in USA. Many people thing that "grass is always greener on the other side of the fense" but I am not agree. Moscovites really love their city. This is why I invite you to Moscow. It is capital city like Washington. Since perestroika, it is easy for traveling here. I can organize for you special tour. I can tell you many thing about Jennifer.

Please to write to me. My address in web: Svetlana.Roma nova@ddbd.ru

Sincerely yours,
Svetlana

Officially, my mother organized the annual Jennifer Jones Festival, but she always forced me to say a few words at the opening ceremony—a ceremony that had seen increasingly lower attendance over the years. The year before, my remarks were addressed to sixteen people, and most of them had wandered into the room by accident. But the writer obviously had a problem with her verb tenses in English. I *was* Jennifer Jones's friend. My mom started the foundation right after Jenny's death, and now she was already hard at work on plans for the tenth annual Jennifer Jones Festival. In fact, I had already ignored several frantic calls requesting my input. My mother's voice-mail messages were delivered as if through a bullhorn: *"JENNY'S LEGACY IS IN YOUR HANDS!"* she said in one. She did not seem to understand that most people had stopped worrying about nuclear war. The Cold War was over, and anxiety about a hot war ended with it.

I looked at the letter again. How bizarre, I thought, that someone all the way in Moscow could be reached instantly by electronic mail. E-mail was still a novelty in 1995. My high-school friends and I used it to correspond from our various college campuses, but our messages retained the formal conventions of letters. They were long, began with proper salutations and closed with "Yours truly," and betrayed our collective uncertainty about this new technology. *"Did you get my last message?"* we wrote, or *"Write back to let me know you received this."* We often telephoned each other to verify that e-mail had arrived. Cyberspace was so mysterious. This was pre-Google, so we weren't yet relying on the Internet to answer our every question; in fact, we weren't consciously using the Internet at all, just our various college e-mail servers. I had never heard the term "Web site," let alone seen one. One of my friends tried to tell me about the seemingly mythical "Internet," and I nodded indulgently, certain it was something that would only capture the imagination of Dungeons & Dragons enthusiasts. Most e-mails I received were from on campus, many of them completely inane. You could target the whole student body by addressing an e-mail to ALL:STU and these "all-stus" ranged from announcements about various a cappella performances (*"Tonight in Kirkland Hall: Scott Hardy solos on 'Africa' by Toto for the last time before he graduates!"*) to drunken nocturnal confessions (*"Yes, I'm gay. Are you happy now?"*) to prank messages sent from the accounts of those who had failed to log out of public computers. (*"I'm proud to be a Psi-Uterus!"* was a message that came from the account of a woman who spent a lot of time at Psi U frat parties.) I still felt a shiver of surprise when messages appeared in my in-box, especially when they had been sent from another city or state. And now it was possible to write an e-mail to another *country*. Not just any country either, but to our former Cold War nemesis. When Sting wondered if the Russians loved their children, too, he could not have imagined that we'd be e-mailing those Russian children.

I don't know how Svetlana found me, but I recognized her name from Jenny's book. She was the girl plucked by the Kremlin to travel around with Jenny and her parents.

After Jenny returned from the Soviet Union, a New York publishing house gave the Joneses a lot of money for a book detailing her travels. *My Trip to the Soviet Union* consisted mostly of photographs of Jenny smiling outside various Soviet monuments and tombs of unknown soldiers. A ghostwriter was hired to tell Jenny's story. It began with this sentence: "It all started when I decided to write a letter to Yuri Andropov." There is no mention of the fact that it actually started when *I* decided to write a letter to Andropov. There is no mention of me in the book at all. The book was rushed into production for holiday sales in 1983. Jenny gave me a copy for Christmas. It had a giant picture of her smiling on the cover. Inside, she'd written, *"I wish you could have come with me!"*

Look at the cover photo and you'll see the Jenny I remember. She was pretty in a wholesome, unthreatening way. Her cheeks dimpled. Her glossy brown hair was always parted in the middle and pinned back with tortoiseshell barrettes. Her eyes were blue. She had a light dusting of freckles on her dainty nose. Her expression tended to be open and warm. She had long, graceful arms and legs. She was unfailingly polite. She wore classic American clothes: polo shirts and crewneck sweaters in primary colors. Central casting could not have found a more ideal candidate to represent American childhood.

Pictures of me at the same age—we were ten when she was invited to the USSR—reveal a wan, wary child. Jenny and I were always about the same height (her mother measured us every six months against a wall in their kitchen, and our pencil marks climbed in tandem, never more than a few centimeters apart), but while she was thin, I was so bony that I looked emaciated. If I had been born just a few years later, I could have capitalized on the heroin-chic trend. Even in photos of supposedly happy occasions—Christmas morning, my birthday—I am not smiling. This is partly because I had braces at the time and was reluctant to open my mouth in front of the camera, but mostly because I was a serious child. It's a good thing that I wasn't the one who went on the tour of the Soviet Union. My sullen face wouldn't have won over the media or the Russians. Jenny was a natural diplomat. And she was so photogenic that when she returned to the States, she was offered roles in several films. She might have grown up to be a movie star, like the other Jennifer Jones. The one who married Selznick.

The cover photo was taken at a Soviet Pioneer camp on the Black Sea. Jenny was invited there to meet the Soviet youth, to witness their loyalty to the party and their devotion to friendship and peace. The Pioneers were like Girl Scouts with a political agenda. They marched in formation, they sang the praises of the motherland, "the country of happy childhood." In the picture Jenny wears one of the Pioneer uniforms: a white blouse with a Peter Pan collar, a scarf knotted around the neck, a crisp blue cotton kilt, and white kneesocks. Slightly out of focus behind the smiling Jenny is Svetlana—also uniformed as a Pioneer with a red kerchief. The caption inside says, *"Svetlana Romanova and me at Artek."* She had been recruited by the Kremlin because she spoke some English. And probably because she was as ideal a representative of Russia as Jenny was of America. She had blond hair, tawny skin, and a wide-eyed Slavic face—and although she was only twelve, you could see outlines of the feline beauty she would become. When Jenny returned from the USSR, she would not stop talking about her new friend. "Svetlana is so good at ballet," she would say, or "Svetlana gave me this lacquered Russian box." I never responded to these comments. I felt like I was being replaced. It was bad enough to have been left out of the trip. Our friendship was already on shaky ground, and by the spring of sixth grade we were often passing each other in the halls at school with little more than a nod. It might have been awkward if Jenny didn't travel so much, but she missed fifty days of school that year because of media appearances.

I didn't e-mail Svetlana right away. I wasn't ready to dredge up the past. For years I had kept a file box of Jenny memorabilia under my bed. I even brought it to college with me, because I worried my mother would confiscate it for her own collection. She was still petitioning the Smithsonian to create a Jennifer Jones exhibition at the Museum of American History. But I hadn't opened the box since I arrived on campus. After years of being known as the best friend of the girl who died ("Such a *tragedy*," everyone always said to me), it was a relief to finally be viewed as my own person. In college I was Sarah Zuckerman, not Jennifer Jones's best friend. I made a point of telling no one that I knew her. And, to be honest, no one remembered Jennifer Jones. She had been reduced to a footnote in the history of the Cold War. Once during my freshman year, I asked the people at my dinner table if they knew who she was. "Is she that girl in our psych seminar? The one who always wears her field-hockey jacket?" asked one. "Was she on that TV show?" said another. "The one about the girls' boarding school?" A few people mentioned Jennifer Jones the movie star, but most people responded with blank stares.

As graduation loomed, I worried more and more about what I was going to do next. I felt qualified to do absolutely nothing, and the real world filled me with dread. In those days résumés were supposed to include a list of all the computer programs you knew, as if Adobe proficiency were a predictor of success, and the fact that I knew only Word seemed proof that my liberal-arts degree was worthless. I had no job and no plan. College was comfortable—so comfortable that I had stretched out my time there, going abroad for so little academic credit that I had to remain on campus for a fifth year. I had always been young for my class; now I would graduate, like most students, at twenty-two. I liked the pattern of my days. Midmorning lectures in imposing Gothic buildings, afternoon seminars in quaint clapboard houses, late nights in the library, where friends were never more than a few carrels away and could be easily coerced into coffee breaks. It was a picturesque campus on a hill, and even in winter, with several feet of New England's snow on the ground, the place seemed to be bathed in warm light. It was a nostalgia factory; we were being trained to be sentimental about the school so that we'd respond to their relentless appeals for money after we left. But I couldn't be cynical about the place. I was happy there. I liked formatting my life around a syllabus, checking off assignments at each due date. I liked hunting and gathering for my meals with orange plastic trays in the dining hall. The parties were appealingly predictable: the supply of drinking cups always dwindled long before the kegs were dry, so it behooved you to snag one early or bring your own. I even liked the dorms. Sure, the furniture was institutional, but not having to decorate took the pressure off. I'd been lucky to live in a single room all four years, and every fall it was so easy to settle in. You just needed to unfurl your bedding, plug in your fan, shelve your books. No IKEA assembly, no grocery shopping, no cooking, no grieving mother. I knew I'd never have it so good.

So I found myself thinking about Svetlana. I had been waiting for a letter from Moscow since 1983. Now that I'd finally received one, could I really ignore it?

I went to the library computer lab and e-mailed Svetlana a week before graduation:

From: swzuckerman@merton.edu

To: Svetlana.Romanova@ddbd.ru

Date: May 17, 1995

Dear Svetlana,

Yes, I am the Sarah Zuckerman who helps organize the Jennifer Jones Festival. She was my best friend before she died. I've wanted to visit Moscow for many years. What do you mean by "special tour"?

Best,

Sarah

It was her reply that made me determined to go to Russia:

Dear Sarah,

How do you know Jennifer Jones is dead? Because you saw on the television? You must believe also that your American cosmonauts walked on moon! Americans are like the kindergarten. You believe every thing you see. Here in Russia we know that news is not truth. When trouble happened, television here showed Swan Lake on all channels. Everywhere you look, it was Swan Lake. The last time Swan Lake was on the TV was during coup in 1991. There were tanks in the street but on television, ballet.

If you come to Moscow, I can organize for you to visit churches, theatres, Kremlins. Is very interesting time here.

Sincerely,

Sveta

Of course Jenny was dead. Her demise was part of my curriculum vitae. Her name was chiseled into me, as if I were a memorial wall, so that even a blind person could feel the impression she'd made. Death had restored our friendship, like varnish on a weathered floor, and given me an easy explanation for my elegiac strains. I had a knack for grief.

Reading Svetlana's e-mail made suspension of disbelief awfully tempting, though. I'd always loved magic shows as a kid: how wonderful to watch things disappear and then—presto!—reappear again, good as new. Jesus's resurrection? Hocus-pocus, I thought, but what an irresistible story. Roll back the stone, Mary Magdalene, and tell us about the empty tomb.

Svetlana's insult about Americans seemed especially stinging since she had used (incorrectly, and all the more pointedly) a definite article. There are no articles in Russian, so the difference between "a" and "the" can be perplexing. *"The kindergarten,"* Svetlana wrote, as if it were the only one, as if everyone in the United States were going down for an afternoon nap at the same time.

"Dear Svetlana," I wrote. *"American astronauts did walk on the*

moon. Perhaps you have not seen the footage of Neil Armstrong in 1969." I had been to the Air and Space Museum enough times to know the legend of the Apollo missions. *"And as for Jennifer Jones, I was at her funeral."*

It was at the National Cathedral to accommodate the hundreds of mourners and press. The service was for all three of them—Jenny and her parents, who died with her—but it was Jenny that the news crews were interested in. "Jennifer wanted peace," the bishop of Washington said. "And now she has found it." My mother rolled her eyes.

I still have copies of the obituaries that ran in all the papers. *"Jennifer Jones, 12; Peace Ambassador Killed in Plane Crash,"* said the *New York Times.* It was a charter flight, scheduled to fly from Boston Logan to Waterville, Maine, because Jenny had been invited to address students at Colby College. She made a lot of appearances at schools around the country in those days. She'd narrate a slide show of her trip to the USSR and then take questions.

"Your moon landing was Gollywood special effects," said Svetlana's reply. (Because there is no equivalent of the letter *H*, Russians say "Gollywood," not Hollywood.) *"Staged spectacle to win Space Race."*

I was angry now. This person was comparing one of my country's greatest achievements to the likes of a Jerry Bruckheimer film. I was about to type a flip response—*"Did you read that in* Pravda?"—when the doubt crept in. Could I *prove* that we had actually landed on the moon? It was theoretically possible, I realized with a queasy feeling, that Neil Armstrong had taken those famous steps across a stage on a Hollywood back lot. It had never before occurred to me that we hadn't actually walked on the moon. It was one giant step forward for mankind. Wasn't it? Was the supposed moon rock embedded in one of the stained-glass windows of the National Cathedral just detritus from a local construction site? I felt like I did when I finally learned the truth about Santa Claus. It was humiliating to have been so naïve, so full of faith. My second-grade classmates scoffed at me. *Why was I the last to know?* I remember asking my mother.

The thing is, they never actually found Jenny's remains. The plane that crashed was a twin-engine, unpressurized, fifteen-seater (though only four passengers—Jenny, her parents, and her manager—were on board that day), and it went down off the coast. When the plane disappeared from the radar screen, a search went out, and the wreckage was found the next day, but the bodies were never recovered. And the cause of the crash remains mysterious. The plane was a Beechcraft 99, a model that was not large enough for the FAA to require a black box. So in the aftermath the investigation was hindered by the absence of a cockpit voice recorder and flight data information. And the nearest airport—Portland, Maine—had no radar data to show exactly when and where the plane had disappeared. According to the airport, the flight had been chartered by Edmund Jones, but there was no forensic evidence that Jenny and her parents were on board. So technically Svetlana was right: it was possible that Jenny didn't die.

Who did this Svetlana think she was? You can't just write to someone out of the blue suggesting that her dead best friend is still alive. It was a cruel joke. I imagined my antagonist halfway around the world. She was almost certainly wearing too much makeup. The Russian girls I'd seen on TV looked like they were living in a funhouse mirror reflection of the 1980s: blue eye shadow applied with so little discretion that the effect was grotesque. Their garish, painted faces were a distorted and terrifying image of capitalism.

"Come to Moscow to see truth," Svetlana wrote.

What was the truth? Jenny's death was front-page news in at least thirty countries. If she was alive, where was she? How could she disappear without a trace? And did Svetlana actually know something, or was she just trying to be provocative?

"Moscow?" said my friend Juliet when I told her my plans. "Don't you want to go somewhere warmer? Somewhere with palm trees, maybe? Don't you know that the Cold War is over?"

"Moscow's the new Prague," said my friend Sam.

The three of us were stretched out in the quad, plucking blades of grass as we spoke, vaguely aware that we would never again have so much time to kill. Our graduation was the next day. "A lot of expats are moving there," I said. I didn't tell them that I'd been waiting to go there since 1983.

"Russian girls are hot," Sam said. "At least until the babushka drop-off."

"What makes you such an expert on the life cycle of Russian women's looks?" I said.

"The babushka drop-off is well documented. Russian women are insanely hot when they're young, and then, at like twenty-six, they turn into these fat old women wearing head scarves. There's no in-between phase."

Sam's opinions came courtesy of his cousin Corinne, who had recently moved to Moscow to launch the Russian edition of an American fashion magazine. When I e-mailed her, Corinne offered me her guest room until I could find housing of my own.

"I have a place to stay," I told my mother. "With an American. I'll be safe."

4.

1982

My MOTHER SAYS we're going to have an adventure.

Where are we going? I want to know.

It is a Saturday morning in the middle of March. The cherry blossoms have started to bloom, and I hope that we are going down to the Mall to see them. This is something we do every spring. The cherry blossoms are so beautiful that it surprises me every year. So delicate, so auspiciously pink.

No, not to the Mall, my mother says. *We are going to be detectives.*

Like Harriet the Spy? I like Harriet the Spy so much that for two months when I was eight, I would eat nothing but tomato sandwiches.

Or Miss Marple, says my mother. She puts on her trench coat—in which she looks like a spy, or a glamorous Hollywood version of a spy—and fastens Pip's leash. Her hair is tied up in a striped scarf. She hands me my yellow windbreaker—it is unseasonably chilly and damp—and we set out from the house.

What are we looking for? I ask as my mother begins walking briskly down our street toward Connecticut Avenue. Pip can tell that my mother's on a mission. He falls into step on her left, mirroring her determined gait.

I like playing detective. After I read *Harriet the Spy,* I wandered the neighborhood with a pocket notebook and wrote down the license plate of any car I didn't recognize.

Fallout-shelter signs, she says. *The shelters are closed now, but some of the signs are still on the outsides of the buildings. Let's see how many we can find.*

I am nine years old. At my school we do 1960s-style duck-and-cover exercises, as if a classroom desk could protect any of us from nuclear bombs. I ask my mother why they closed the fallout shelters. She says they were expensive to maintain. She says that disarmament treaties in the 1970s made people relax. I don't remember détente; all I know is dread.

We find our first sign on the back wall of my old elementary school. The sign has three cautionary yellow triangles, turned upside down, their tips pointing toward the basement. I was corralled out this back door during fire drills for years and never noticed the sign before, but now that I see it (*This is the closest shelter to our house—this is where we would have gone if we'd lived here in the 1960s,* my mother says, her voice breathy with fear or excitement or both), it gives me the creeps. I can't bear the idea of pressing into a dark basement with hundreds of neighbors. My mother says the shelters were stocked with supplies—food and water and medicine. You wouldn't know how many days you'd have to stay down there, away from the radiation. The fallout could be deadlier than the explosion itself. But even if you survived the bomb, would you want to live in the wreckage left behind? To emerge from that dark space not into light but into a wasteland?

She snaps a picture of the sign. I stand beside her as she shakes the Polaroid, waiting for the image to emerge. It is, I think, the opposite of the overheated projector: instead of being melted away, the picture rises out of darkness like a figure out of the fog. There is something hopeful about watching the Polaroid develop. *Look,* she says, holding it out for me to see. Pip yaps. The fallout-shelter sign and the doorway it marks look faded and ineffectual. How could something so small save us?

Once we find our first sign, we start spotting them everywhere. In our neighborhood of Cleveland Park, we find ten signs that day. They are on the outsides of apartment buildings, mostly. There is one on a church. My mother notes their locations in a small blue book. *Civil defense,* she mumbles like a mantra. She says there are hundreds of deserted shelters all over the city, including one below Dupont Circle. *A few years ago,* she says, *they excavated all the food from that one and sent it to starving people in*

Pakistan. Recently I went back to Washington and discovered that most of the signs—at least in neighborhoods like ours— are gone. Reminders of the nuclear threat were probably bad for real estate prices. I never asked my mother why she wanted to document the location of the shelters. I learned long ago not to ask *why.*

＃

DURING THAT SPRING OF 1982, Jenny and I spent a lot of time in the woods. Just a few blocks away from our street was a tributary of Rock Creek Park. Around the stream was a wooded haven with a trail through the middle of it. We weren't supposed to go there alone, but we told her mother we were off to the playground on Macomb Street and then we kept going to Rodman Street, where the woods began. Sometimes I brought Pip with us. We'd go after school and stay until the light started to fade and shadows filled the hollows under the trees. We teetered across the fallen trunks that bridged the stream. We collected stones from the sandy creek bed and arranged them in sculptural mounds. Sometimes we just sat on a mossy stump and pretended we were camping. We could see the tops of the houses on Rodman Street through the trees—we felt safe because we were so close to home.

"What if we got lost in the woods?" Jenny said once. It was April. The trees were still half bare—their new leaves were coming in, shimmering in chartreuse, not yet thick enough to block out the sky—but the underbrush was vibrant and lush. There were little yellow flowers in bloom in the ivy along the creek. There was still a chill in the air, but the sky was the true blue of spring.

"We won't," I said. "We know the way."

"We could leave a trail of bread crumbs," Jenny said. "Like Hansel and Gretel."

"Squirrels would eat the crumbs," I said.

"Or Pip," she said.

But Pip wasn't with me that afternoon.

"Let's play hide-and-seek," Jenny said. "I'll hide first."

We were too old for hide-and-seek, but we often played it in the woods, where the stakes seemed higher. I counted to twenty, sent my voice far and wide. When I opened my eyes, there was no sign of Jenny. I listened for a rustle in the trees, trying to discern in which direction she'd gone. She had managed to slip away in silence. I looked behind the thick bushes near the stream's head. I checked the cavities in rotting tree trunks. I walked all the way to the end of the trail—just half a mile, but at nine years old it seemed like a long way—to see if she was lurking there. I found stepping-stones to the other side of the creek. The underbrush was so dense on that side that I couldn't see my feet. I was afraid I'd step on a snake. I knew they came out of hibernation in the spring.

"Jenny!" I called. I didn't realize I was scared until I heard the plaintive wail in my voice. It was hard to believe she'd come to this side of the stream. We always stayed near the trail. I tiptoed along the creek bed, trying not to get my sneakers wet. "Jenny!" I shouted again. "Tell me if I'm hot or cold!" But my lonely voice boomeranged back to me.

I didn't have a watch, but I could feel the heavy approach of dusk. I wondered if Jenny had been kidnapped. There were a lot of missing children in the news. The six-year-old boy in New York City, the one who disappeared on his way to school in 1979, still hadn't been found. Jenny would be a face haunting me from lampposts. It would be my fault. "You told me you were going to the playground," her mother would say.

As it grew darker, the trees lost their crisp outlines and blurred into menace. The woods seemed bigger, less familiar without light. I couldn't see the houses on Rodman Street. The air turned cold, and I didn't have a sweater. I found my way back to the path, gnarly with roots, and stumbled toward our entrance to the park. "Jenny!" I cried, but fear tamped my voice to a whisper. I dared not make noise in the dark. I crept through the encroaching black, brambles clawing at my arms. I knew I was almost home when I saw the streak of headlights on Reno Road. The cars rushed past, oblivious to my plight. As soon as I reached the sidewalk, I started running. My mother could come back and help me look for Jenny. I sprinted the rest of the way.

But when I finally made it back to our street, I heard Jenny's voice call out to me. "Slowpoke!"

She was on her front-porch swing, a silhouette against the inviting yellow lights in the windows. "It's seven-thirty," she said. "We've already had dinner." I had been gone for two hours.

"Where were you?" I said. "I looked everywhere."

"I left the woods right away. I wanted to see how long it would take you to find me. I can't believe you stayed there so long." She seemed amused by my stupidity.

"I was afraid you were kidnapped."

"Nope."

I paused at the bottom of the steps to her house. She remained on the swing, moving back and forth, steady as a pendulum.

"Weren't you worried about me?" I said.

"I knew you'd figure it out. I didn't think you needed someone to hold your hand every second."

"Weren't your parents worried?"

"I told them you went home," she said.

"My mom didn't call looking for me?"

"No. Why are you so upset?" she said. "You know your mom is a total space cadet. She probably has no idea what time it is."

"Something terrible could have happened." We were so young. Even now I can't believe she didn't see the danger.

"Jeez, it was a test," she said. "It was only a test. Don't be so dramatic. You're a nervous freak like your mom."

"It's not funny," I said. "And she's not a freak." I knew I was starting to cry. It was humiliating. I was too sensitive. Why couldn't I let things roll off my back?

The door opened, and Mrs. Jones leaned out. "Jennifer," she said. "Time to come inside." Then, sensing my presence, she looked down at me. "Sarah? What are you doing on the street in the dark? Did you have a good dinner?"

"Yes," I said, choking back tears. "Thank you. We had chicken pot pie."

"See you tomorrow!" Jenny said as she trotted after her mother into the house. After the door closed behind them, the porch swing continued to sway. I stood there frozen, watching it. When it finally came to a standstill, I went home.

#

ONE NIGHT NOT LONG AFTER THAT, Jenny got her mother's old Ouija board out of the wooden chest where the Joneses kept games. It was late; her parents had already retired to their bedroom. She took one of the candelabra from the dining room and a box of matches from over the living-room fireplace and told me to follow her. In her room she locked the door behind us and lit the candles. Then she turned out the light. She sat down cross-legged on the floor and opened the box.

"We're going to contact Izzy," she said.

"Izzy my sister?"

"Don't you want to talk to her?" she said.

Of course I wanted to talk to her. I would have given anything to hear Izzy's voice. My mother said it was sort of hoarse and made her sound older than she was. "It's just a game," I said. "You can't actually talk to dead people."

"Have you ever tried?" Jenny said. "Come on."

I took my seat beside her. She guided my hands to their place on the pointer next to hers.

"We have to be quiet," she said. "And we have to be patient. She will come to us when she's ready. Focus."

She closed her eyes and took a deep breath. I watched the candlelight flicker on her face. The pointer moved a bit under my fingers. Startled, I looked down.

"Is there a spirit here?" Jenny said. She opened her eyes and addressed the empty room.

The pointer moved again. I wasn't pushing it; Jenny seemed as surprised as I was. The pointer hovered over the letter *Y*. Then moved to *E*. Then *S*.

"YES," Jenny hissed. "There's someone here. Tell us your name," she said. And I swear the wind howled.

The pointer moved to *I*. Then to *S*.

"Stop!" I said, and jerked my hands away from the board.

"She wasn't done spelling," Jenny said. "You scared her off." She looked around as if trying to locate the presence. "You wrote 'IS,'" she said softly to the invisible ghost. "'IS' what? Can you give us the next word?"

"Isabel," I said. "It's Isabel. You moved the pointer. You're spelling her name."

"I did not," Jenny said. "I am not a faker."

"She's my sister," I said. "You don't know anything about her."

I blew out the candles in a huff. We sat fuming in the dark. I wanted to go home, but it was too late to leave the house without upsetting her parents. Mr. and Mrs. Jones always turned on the burglar alarm at ten o'clock, so there was no way to escape without deactivating the system. I knew the code, but the beeping keypad would disturb them. From their bedroom across the hall, I could hear the faint laughter of the studio audience on *Saturday Night Live*.

Finally Jenny said, "I was just trying to help. I didn't mean to upset you." She stood up and switched on her desk lamp. She was wearing a lavender nightgown trimmed with white ribbon. "Want to sleep in my bed tonight?"

This was not the first time she'd let me squeeze into her bottom bunk. It was something I never asked for, but she seemed to know when I needed an extra degree of closeness. We had already brushed our teeth, so we scooted into bed. I took the inside, near the wall.

"Isn't it funny that married people share the same bed every night?" she said.

"Until they get divorced," I said.

"I'll never get divorced," she said.

"I don't know if I'll ever get married," I said.

"You're so weird," she said. Then, after a few minutes, she said, "Do you think your parents had sex before they were married?"

"I don't know. Did yours?"

"Probably not," she said. "But one time I heard them having sex."

"Ew," I said.

"My mom kept saying 'Oh, oh, oh, oh' really fast, like she was breathing really hard. My dad wasn't saying anything, but the bed was squeaking."

"Why were you listening?"

"I didn't mean to," she said. "I had a bad dream and woke up. I went to their room, but then I heard all the noise before I knocked."

"You're sure they were having sex?"

"I didn't see them, but they must have been doing it."

"I don't want to think about it," I said. But I couldn't stop thinking about it. After Jenny fell asleep, I lay beside her and wondered if my mother missed having sex. Did she make those noises in bed with my dad? When my father had an affair, did his mistress make those noises in a hotel room? Would Jenny make the same noises someday? I listened to her breathing: mouth open, every exhalation throaty and extreme, as if she were entitled to more air than the average human. There was no one I felt closer to in the world, but someday I knew that we would be in bed with other people, that nights like this would take on the foggy quality of dreams.

※

WHAT ELSE DO I REMEMBER? Jenny and I on our backs in her yard on a summer night, our heads touching, our hair intertwined, pinpricks of light from the fireflies, and the day's swelter draining from the air as the sky blackened and the stars came out. The whole neighborhood smoky with barbecue. Our skin itchy with chlorine, our fingers sticky with watermelon, bits of corn lodged in our teeth, and her mother's voice, like a wind chime from the patio, telling us it was time for bed.

⁂

ALL THE ARTICLES about Jenny described her the same way. She was "precocious" and "charming" and even "brilliant." Everyone wanted a piece of her. I once made a list of things you wouldn't know about Jenny even if you read every single published word about her:

1. She was fussy about the texture of her food. She wouldn't eat anything mushy (no avocados, no oatmeal).
2. When we played Clue, she insisted on being Miss Scarlet.
3. When we played Monopoly, she was always the shoe.
4. At night while she brushed her teeth, she would pretend she was in a toothpaste ad. She slicked her tongue across her enamel and said, "Now, that's what I call clean!" I said her mother was like a mom in a commercial because she smelled the laundry while she folded it. Jenny thought that was funny.
5. She may have been precocious, but she wasn't the genius the press made her out to be. Every night she called me so I could walk her through our math homework. And she also needed my help with grammar. The subjunctive confused her.
6. She wanted to have three children when she grew up. She intended to name them Amy, Lucy, and Troy. Troy because of the Trojan Horse, which was her favorite story in our studies of ancient Greece. "What if you don't have any girls?"

I said. But she refused to indulge this line of questioning. Jenny was always certain that things would work out.

7. She planned to live in a "mansion"—so many dreams in the eighties involved mansions. We played that game called MASH (Mansion, Apartment, Shack, House) in which possibilities for the future were limited to four categories scratched on a pad. Four names of boys we might marry, four careers we might have, four places we might live.

8. Jenny talked in her sleep, although she never said anything coherent. *I didn't!* she said, or *NO!* Sometimes she'd start laughing so hysterically that I was sure she was awake. I'd lean my head over from the top bunk and shine the flashlight in her face to verify that she was really asleep.

9. She had a birthmark on the front of her left thigh. It was a small caramel-colored stain, so high on her leg that it wasn't visible when she was dressed.

5.

IT ALL STARTED WHEN I DECIDED to write a letter to Yuri
Andropov.

I was at Jenny's house on a Saturday afternoon in November of
1982. We were in private school by then. In the fourth grade, we
had both started at the nearby girls' school, so now our morning
walk took us in the opposite direction on Lowell Street. We had
been in our new school for a year and were still adjusting to the
absence of boys. A boycott, we called it. The school started in
the fourth grade, but most of our classmates had been together at
the same private, coed elementary school, so Jenny and I felt like
foreigners among them. We were trying to decipher their refer-
ences and translate the inside jokes. Mrs. Jones had begun dress-

ing like the other mothers—with cashmere sweaters draped over her shoulders—and was looking for sponsorship to join the exclusive Sulgrave Club. She asked my mom if she knew any women who were members, and my mother laughed. "I used to be," she said, "but I gave it up."

It had been raining all day. We'd spent the past few hours restlessly searching for ways to fill the time. We played three games of Connect Four. We played five games of Spit—I can still hear the impatient snap of the cards as Jenny shuffled. We made chocolate-chip cookies and licked most of the dough out of the mixing bowl instead of baking it. We took turns dialing Q107's request line— we wanted to hear our voices on the radio—but it was always busy.

"If you get through, what will you request?" Jenny said.

"I don't know," I said.

I didn't need to ask her what she would choose. Her favorite song was "867-5309," since it was about "Jenny."

There were girls at school who knew which bands were cool, who knew all the lyrics to the right songs, but I was always out of sync. On more than one occasion, I'd made the mistake of nodding knowingly at the mention of a band only to be humiliated when grilled about its discography. If you weren't careful, you could be tricked. "You like U2? What do you think of *November*?" a classmate named Lisa said to me. "It's okay," I said diplomatically. "There is no *November*!" she said. "Just *October*. And *Boy*." Jenny was almost as clueless about music as I was, but she listened to Casey Kasem's *Top 40* and took notes.

Jenny's room was in a turret, so one wall was round, like a

gazebo, with large windows that faced my house. I liked the shape of her bedroom—it usually made me feel like I was in a castle—but in dreary weather the fishbowl shape added to the sense that we were trapped. And because the room jutted farther out than the rest of the house, we seemed especially vulnerable to the storm. Every gust of autumn wind sounded dangerously close. The rain was furious on the windowpanes.

Jenny was on the bottom bunk, flipping through the yearbook from the previous school year. Each graduating student got a whole page of the yearbook and got to choose who was on the page opposite her. We were connoisseurs of those senior pages; in them we hoped to find clues about how to navigate preppy culture. We studied the photos of girls bracketed by friends, smiles perfected by orthodontics, and memorized their senior quotes. I still remember the page of a Caroline Winslow Corcoran, class of 1982. She was pictured with her black Lab and quoted David Bowie *("Time may change me / But I can't trace time")* and Eleanor Roosevelt *("No one can make you feel inferior without your consent.")*

Jenny was already thinking about our pages. "If I have a boyfriend then," she said, "I won't put a picture of us together, because what if we break up by the time the yearbooks come out?" Seniors had to turn in their pages in September, but the yearbook was published in June.

"We won't be seniors for seven years," I said. I wasn't sure we'd still be alive then. I sat on her plush pink carpet, scribbling.

"What are you writing?" Jenny wanted to know.

"A letter."

"To your dad?" In those days I often wrote to my father. He rarely wrote back. He had recently remarried. His new wife, Phillipa, was a barrister and an equestrienne.

"To Yuri Andropov," I said.

"Who?"

"The new head of the USSR." Brezhnev had recently died, and my mother was already worried about his successor. Andropov used to run the KGB; his shadowy past made him seem especially sinister.

"Why?"

"I want to know if he's going to start a nuclear war."

My mother subscribed to *Time* and *Newsweek,* to the *New Yorker* and the *New Republic.* But also to *Mother Jones,* and the September/October issue was devoted to disarmament. When it arrived that fall, I was the one who picked it up from the floor where it landed under the mail slot. THE RACE AGAINST DEATH, screamed the cover. And below those ominous words, four faces in four separate photos, arranged like the frames in the opening sequence of *The Brady Bunch.* But these were not smiling faces. In fact, when I looked closer, I could see that the faces in the bottom panes were not faces at all but masks. A bloodred skeleton on the left, with an expression so infernal it seemed possessed, and on the right a Picassoesque profile painted on papier-mâché. It reminded me of a KKK hood. The top two images were equally frightening: a wounded woman (or was it a man?) whose head was wrapped in a bloody bandage and whose expressionless gaze made me wonder if she'd rather be alive or dead. And on the left, a face stiff with white pancake makeup, the hair covered by a shroud. I didn't know the context of these gruesome photographs. But the faces had been haunting me. For the last two months, it was those faces and that horrible headline, THE RACE AGAINST DEATH, that had dominated my dreams. It was more terrifying than any horror flick. I had to do something.

"Can Andropov read English?" said Jenny. This was an astute question. I'll admit I hadn't considered it before.

"I'm sure he has people to translate stuff."

"Even if he is going to bomb us, do you think he's going to admit that to *you*? My dad says they have way more nukes than we do."

"That's true. They do," I said. What I didn't say was that it didn't really matter who had more nukes. Thanks to the space-based detection technology developed in the 1970s, the United States would know about a Soviet strike as soon as the missiles launched and would immediately retaliate. If there were a launch on warning, we would destroy each other simultaneously.

I didn't expect Andropov to reply. But I wanted him to know that regular Americans—people like my mother and me—were scared. If he listened only to Reagan, he might think of us as enemies, but if he heard from regular citizens, he might understand how many innocent lives were at stake. That was my mother's logic. She'd been writing letters to American members of Congress for years. I don't know exactly what I said to Jenny—probably something I parroted from the Nuclear Weapons Freeze campaign rally in New York that my mother had dragged me to in June.

Nearly a million people had descended on Central Park to hear Helen Caldicott preach about civic responsibility. Bruce Springsteen sang also, but my mother and I were too far away from the stage to see him. Whatever I said to Jenny was persuasive, because she announced that she was going to write a letter to Andropov too. She sat at her desk and flourished a purple pen with a pompom on top.

"'Dear Mr. Andropov,'" she said as she bent over to write in her notebook. "How do you spell 'Andropov'?"

I told her.

"Thank God this pen has erasable ink." She fixed her mistake. Then she said, "This is like writing to the Wicked Witch of the West."

"Except he's in the East."

"He can't be as bad as he seems."

"I hope not."

"'Dear Mr. Andropov,'" she repeated. "'My name is Jennifer Jones. I am ten years old.'"

How long did it take her to write the letter that made history? I'd say she worked on it for twenty minutes. I knew she was concentrating hard, because she was sucking on a strand of hair, the way she did during math tests, her saliva releasing the unmistakable scent of Prell. And then in a burst of energy, as if breaking through a finish line, she said, "I'm done! Are you?"

"It's not a race," I said.

We sealed our letters in envelopes we took from her father's rolltop desk.

"What are you girls up to?" he said when he found us in his office. "You know you're not supposed to be in here without permission."

Sometimes Mr. Jones spoke a little too loudly, as though addressing a courtroom. If I hadn't known better, I would have guessed he was a litigator. Most people we knew in Washington were lawyers, though there were also cabinet members and senators among the parents at our school. I didn't know exactly what Mr. Jones did every day—his work was as nebulous to me as that of every other adult. I assumed that every office was like my dad's old one at the IMF, where the occupants' names hung on placards outside their office doors, where the copy machines were segregated in a room down the hall, where page-a-day *Far Side* calendars were exhibited on desks as proof that long hours spent restructuring loans for developing countries couldn't dilute the employees' sense of humor.

"We needed envelopes," said Jenny.

"We had to write some letters," I said.

"To Yuri Andropov," said Jenny.

"What do you know about Yuri Andropov?" said Mr. Jones.

"We wrote to ask him for peace," she said.

"Well, that's an idea," he said. I couldn't tell if he was laughing at us.

"We need to know his address," said Jenny.

Mr. Jones was one of the adults who seemed to know everything. It was reassuring to be in the company of someone who always had answers. We addressed the envelopes under his supervision. "I'll tell you what," he said. "I'll take these to the post office on my way to work Monday morning and make sure they have enough postage to get all the way to the Kremlin." Mr. Jones exuded competence. And unlike everyone else I knew, he had actually been to the Soviet Union. He and some of his college friends traveled to Moscow in the 1960s for a basketball tournament. He still had the poster—with huge red letters in Cyrillic—hanging in his home office.

I've tried many times to remember what Mr. Jones did with our letters. Did he leave them on a corner of his desk? Did he put them in his briefcase? I only remember handing mine to him. Mr. Jones's face was unremarkable and bland—the sort of face that blends into crowds—but his hands were strangely graceful, with the long fingers of a piano player, and he wore a gold signet ring. My mother made cracks about men in jewelry, but on Mr. Jones the ring seemed like proof of something solid in his character. I can still see my letter in his hand; it was authoritative and substantial.

We mailed the letters in the middle of November, and after that we were distracted by the holidays: Thanksgiving (for the second year in a row, the Joneses invited my mother and me to join them; I was grateful to sit at a candlelit table with a perfectly roasted turkey and homemade pies); Christmas (the Joneses went to Vermont to ski, and my mother and I stayed in Washington— she was still afraid of flying—and I feigned enthusiasm about the gift of vintage *Encyclopaedia Britannica* my father sent me); and New Year's Eve, when the Joneses hosted their annual party (thirty or forty people, lots of champagne) and let Jenny and me stay up and watch the ball drop on TV. *Time* magazine's 1982 Person of the Year was the computer.

And then it was 1983.

At school we were diagramming sentences and slaving over fractions. We joined a swim team and went to practice two afternoons a week. We spent snow days sledding at Battery Kemble Park—it was not uncommon to see Teddy Kennedy there with his Portuguese water dogs. We carved construction paper into valentines and were careful to hand out only the most innocent candy-heart messages. Giving someone a "Be Mine" could complicate things. We rehearsed for our class play. We were doing *The Wizard of Oz,* and Jenny was cast as Dorothy. I had only one line—I was a Munchkin, which required me to shuffle around the stage on my knees—so I helped Jenny memorize hers. I knew her part so well that our teacher, Mrs. Gibson, made me Jenny's understudy. I had terrible stage fright, but I knew I'd never actually have to perform: nothing short of apocalypse could keep Jenny from the stage.

In February, U2 released their third studio album, *War.* On March 3, President Reagan delivered his famous Evil Empire speech. Three weeks later he announced the Strategic Defense Initiative. The Cold War was getting colder, and my mother was staying later and later at her office downtown. Her disarmament efforts had begun as a hobby, but by the time Reagan was inaugurated, she was working for WAND, Women's Action for Nuclear Disarmament. She found friends among the fellow acolytes of Helen Caldicott and Randall Forsberg. Occasionally one of them would stop by to strategize over coffee. Knowing that my mother was not alone made it easier for me to leave her behind and escape to the serenity of Jenny's house. So I was at the Joneses' house on the afternoon at the end of March when the first reporter called.

"Jennifer, come down here!" her mother shouted up the stairs.

The urgency in her voice made me think Jenny was in trouble. I followed her down to the kitchen to find out what she'd done.

"Honey, you're famous," said Mrs. Jones.

"That was the *Washington Post* on the phone," said Mr. Jones.

They had asked her parents to comment on Jenny's letter to Andropov. It had just been published in *Pravda,* and the Western news media were picking up the story. The next day the headline of the *Post* read, AMBASSADOR FOR PEACE IS 10 YEARS OLD.

I told my mother that I had written a letter to Andropov, too.

"The Russians probably chose to publish her letter because her name sounds so quintessentially American," my mom said.

"My name doesn't sound American?"

"It sounds German," she said. "Or Jewish."

"But we're not Jewish," I said.

"I know that," she said. "But Zuckerman could be a Jewish name." My mother wasn't a Zuckerman. She'd kept her maiden name, Whitney. "And the Russians are notoriously anti-Semitic. Besides," she said, "it doesn't matter which letter they published. The exciting part is that they published it at all. This is good for the cause. It puts the focus on ordinary people instead of politicians. Everyone's sick of reading about summits with the Soviets."

The American embassy in Moscow arranged to have copies of

Pravda sent to Jenny via diplomatic pouch. Looking at her missive translated into Russian made me tired: every letter was capitalized, so the print was uninvitingly dense. "I'm sure they'll publish yours next," said Jenny.

But the next letter published was Yuri Andropov's response. Because he wrote back, of course. That's what made Jenny really famous. She showed me the letter when it arrived from Moscow—it was typed in English on official stationery. And it was long. "Propaganda!" said my mother when she read the text of it in the newspaper. "My God, look at this. He compares Jenny to a Mark Twain character. Jesus, they're turning her into an American archetype."

"The Soviet people," wrote Mr. Andropov, *"are for friendship and peace. The Soviet Union will never use nuclear weapons first. We would never start a war. We are occupied with exploring space and reading poetry and growing wheat. I invite you and your family to come to our peaceful country and see for yourself."*

The next morning four news vans jockeyed for position outside Jenny's house. The cameras aimed at us as we set out for school. "Jennifer, did you think Mr. Andropov would write back?" a reporter shouted.

Jenny parried with a humble smile. "I didn't know what to expect," she said. "I just wanted him to know that regular kids like me are worried about nuclear war. I'm just a girl from Ohio who wants peace."

"You didn't tell them about my letter," I said when we reached school.

"Sorry, I was nervous," she said.

But she didn't seem nervous. She was remarkably poised. Her sound bite made it onto all three networks that night. *I'm just a girl from Ohio who wants peace.* ("That's savvy," my mother said. "Playing the heartland card.") Jenny was a natural. If my letter were published, I knew I'd freeze up in interviews. My mother was right. Jenny was good for the cause.

Letters began arriving for Jenny from all over the world. *"Dear Jennifer,"* they wrote. *"You were brave to write to Andropov."* Sometimes I'd see the postman carry an overstuffed sack up the steps of her house, as if he were delivering mail to Santa Claus. The envelopes made unruly heaps on the Joneses' front porch. Jenny invited me over to help open them. I sat on the porch swing and watched her. "Listen to this one," she'd say, trying on different accents as she read them aloud. Then her mother whisked them away, filed them in labeled boxes. Mrs. Jones loved her label maker.

Jenny said Andropov would write to me. Every day for weeks, I checked the mail as soon as I got home from school. Pip always ripped the mail out of the slot with his teeth the minute the postman shoved it through, so the edges of our letters and magazines were often torn. I wondered if a letter from Andropov had arrived only to be eaten by the dog, but that was wishful thinking. Pip was not in the habit of consuming paper. While I waited for a letter, Jenny flew to New York to appear on *Nightline* and then to Los Angeles to be on *The Tonight Show.* My mother let me stay up late to watch her chat with Johnny Carson. "God, the camera loves her," my mom said. She rang the opening bell of the New York

Stock Exchange; she made a guest appearance on *Sesame Street* (Oscar the Grouch to Jenny: "What are you so happy about?"). She was on the cover of so many magazines that I lost count. My mother saved them all. She missed a lot of school, but Mrs. Gibson didn't care. "This is the most exciting thing that has ever happened to one of my pupils," she told the *Washington Post*. "I'm so proud of Jennifer. She's such a thoughtful girl."

And in the midst of all the television appearances and ribbon-cutting ceremonies, the Joneses, with the help of the Russian embassy in Washington and the American embassy in Moscow, were planning their trip to the USSR that summer. They would go for two weeks in July. They had an official invitation from Yuri Andropov, and their itinerary would be carefully controlled by the Kremlin: six days in Moscow, six days in Leningrad, and three days at Artek, the Pioneer camp on the Crimea. Meanwhile my mother was busy prepping for the International Day of Disarmament on June 20. There were protests scheduled at fifty sites around the world.

I helped Jenny pack before her big trip. "I wish you could come," she said. I wished I could go, too. I figured I'd earned it, since the letters were my idea. But I didn't tell her that. It wasn't her fault that her letter was picked. It wasn't her fault that she was photogenic and charismatic and named Jennifer Jones. I didn't want her to feel guilty. My mother and I went to Dulles Airport with the Joneses to send them off. I gave Jenny three granola bars for the flight.

"I've never been to another country before," she said to the flock of reporters. She held up her newly minted passport. I was right there beside her, but I was cropped out of all the published photos.

We watched their plane take off. My mother stood next to me, breathing deeply in an attempt to ward off a panic attack—the mere sight of planes was enough to make her nervous. If we had been invited to visit the USSR, I would have had to explain that my mother didn't fly.

For the next two weeks, my mother and I watched the coverage of Jenny's trip on the news. Orchestrated footage of her being greeted at Sheremetyevo Airport by the Soviet Friendship Committee—they gave her so many bouquets of flowers that she could hardly walk—of Jenny posing outside Lenin's Mausoleum in Red Square, singing folk songs with other girls at Artek, and strolling through the cavernous galleries of the Hermitage in Leningrad.

While she was away, I had agreed to feed Jenny's cat. Every afternoon I let myself into their house to fulfill my duty. I stacked their mail—mostly letters addressed to Jenny from her adoring fans—on the sideboard in the dining room. Hexa's bowls were in the kitchen, and while I served her Meow Mix and refilled her water dish, she studied me from her perch on the windowsill. Hexa was a fat gray cat with amber eyes so penetrating they freaked me out. Her default expression was a scowl, and she had the annoying habit of using the bathtub as her litter box. I was never much of a cat person, but I made an effort. I tried to stroke her under the chin the way Jenny did, but the cat just switched her tail and stared me down.

After I watered the plants, I often climbed the stairs to the second floor. I told myself I wasn't snooping—even as a child I had a profound respect for privacy—when I wandered into the master bedroom. I just wanted to examine the evidence of fatherhood: the cuff links in a silver box on the dresser; the wooden shoe trees on the floor of the closet, awaiting their next assignment; the Speed Stick deodorant next to the toenail clippers in the medicine cabinet. I am embarrassed to admit that I even pressed my nose into Mr. Jones's ties, hoping to inhale some paternal comfort. He had dozens of ties, hung in neat silk stripes from a rack, and his shirts were arranged by color: Oxford blue, white, a few pale pinks. His loafers had dimes in them, not pennies. *Everyone wears a uniform,* I thought.

In Jenny's room I'd put on one of her LPs and let the needle find the deepest groove, to see which songs she listened to most. Above her desk was a bulletin board on which she stuck various mementos and talismans: a picture of her old yellow house in Dayton, a ribbon from a swim meet, a black-and-white photo strip of the two of us. In the months since the Andropov letter, newspaper clippings had crowded out the photos I knew so well. One day I lifted up one of the articles ("Jennifer Jones is just a normal American girl") to see if our photo strip was still there, and I must have bumped the board, because it slid off its hooks and fell onto the desk. I checked to be sure the articles were still securely tacked, and then when I lifted the board to rehang it, I felt a wad of paper taped to the back. I turned the board over, and there it was, lodged in the lower left corner: the envelope addressed to Mr. Yuri Andropov in my handwriting. Inside was the letter I'd written in Jenny's room the previous November, the letter Mr. Jones had promised to post. There was no stamp in the upper right corner. It had obviously never left the Joneses' house.

"I'm sure Andropov will write to you," Jenny had said to me again and again, but she must have known that wasn't true. Did her father forget to mail my letter? Or had Jenny encouraged him to send hers alone? She was an only child and sometimes had to be prodded to share. We'd had petty squabbles over Smurfs and Barbie dolls. I once stomped out of her house when I believed she was cheating at Sorry. But I'd never doubted her loyalty. I've read that guilt can be detected by physical changes. You know someone's lying because the person sweats or blinks or can't make eye contact. Polygraph tests measure physiological changes—in your breathing, your blood pressure, the beating of your heart. But I'd never noticed anything unusual in Jenny, at least not before her trip.

I put the letter in my pocket, and then I sat on the floor of Jenny's room and cried. I couldn't understand why she had lied to me. It didn't make any sense. When we wrote the letters, we didn't expect a response from Andropov or the press. We never talked about the possibility of fame. It had never occurred to me. And it wasn't Jenny's celebrity I resented so much as the randomness of her cruelty. Such arbitrary meanness was common at school, where the alpha girls would turn on people suddenly and without reason. A person could be welcome at their lunch table one day and exiled to the other side of the cafeteria the next.

The ringleader of the group was Kim, a blunt, blond girl whose popularity had been established in kindergarten and who retained her tyrannical grip on the class. She liked to check the labels on everyone's sweaters. If you weren't wearing Benetton, she made sure you were shunned. I didn't own any Benetton sweaters. She once concocted a scheme in which all the girls talked about an up-coming bowling party at Kim's country club. I was the only one who was not invited. Even Jenny was going. In the end I learned it wasn't a real party at all: Kim just wanted to hurt my feelings. The fact that it was a phantom soiree did not alleviate the ache brought on by exclusion. Long after she moved on to her next victim, I still felt inadequate. Kim was already buxom at eleven, and my mother assured me that she would peak in eighth grade. My mother's words about Kim offered no consolation at the time, but at least I still had Jenny as a buffer.

Before they departed for the Soviet Union, the Joneses had in-vited me to join them on the Martha's Vineyard vacation they'd planned for August. A lot of kids we knew summered on the Vine-yard, and in her eagerness to fit in with the Washington estab-lishment, Mrs. Jones persuaded her husband to rent a house in Vineyard Haven. We were scheduled to depart a week after they returned from their Soviet tour. I'd been looking forward to the trip all summer. I'd never been to the Vineyard. Thanks to my mother's travel anxiety, I'd hardly been anywhere at all. I hadn't even been to London to visit my dad. I longed for a passport crowded with exotic stamps. After I found my letter in Jenny's room, though, I began to dread her return. I hid it under my mattress and waited. I remember passing much of the next week at the local tennis courts, hitting furiously against the backboard, alternating forehand and back-, changing my grip, and trying to keep my swing steady as I eyed the ball and listened to the *thwack*.

❈

JENNY CALLED ME the day after she returned at the end of July. "I'm back!" she said when I answered the phone.

"I know," I said. "I saw you on TV." Her arrival at Dulles was even better documented than her departure.

"Tell us about the Russians," the reporters said, and Jenny obliged them.

"Everyone in the Soviet Union is so friendly. They all want peace." It was a refrain she'd repeat until her death.

She was an effective Soviet propaganda tool, even if she was an unwitting one. It was as though the Russians were already looking for a photogenic American girl to ship off to Pioneer camp and promote Soviet values. Cynics—especially hawkish conservatives—argued that Jenny probably didn't write the letter herself. Some said her parents had put her up to it; others went so far as to suggest a Soviet conspiracy. My mother and I watched the pundits argue on TV.

"Issue one," said John McLaughlin. "Jennifer Jones: too good to be true?"

Maybe she was.

＃

I TRIED TO FIND a way to bring up my unmailed letter before we left for Martha's Vineyard. I rehearsed what I might say: *Can you explain why this was behind your bulletin board?* But I could predict her retort: *What were you doing nosing around my room?* I kept waiting for her to notice that my letter was missing from its hiding place. I was sure she'd call and demand an explanation. I hoped she'd broach the subject. There might be a perfectly good explanation. I tried to act as if nothing had changed. I've never been good at confrontation. I didn't want to lose her.

I climbed into the back of the Joneses' Volvo sedan for the long drive to the Vineyard ferry. They had traded in their Chevy wagon a few months before, and now the name of our school was stuck on the rear window of their new car, as on the Volvos of all the other parents. Mrs. Jones had ordered freshly monogrammed tote bags for the trip. Jenny's said JAJ. Her middle name was Anne. My mother and Pip watched the car as we pulled away from the curb. I could see her lips silently form a warning: *Be careful.*

It takes nearly ten hours—without traffic—to get to Woods Hole and four hours into the drive we were still creeping up the New Jersey Turnpike. Mrs. Jones worked on her needlepoint while Mr. Jones gripped the wheel. Jenny was never satisfied with the temperature. "Max high!" she cried when she wanted her mother to turn up the air conditioner, and when the icy blast became too much to bear, she whined, "It's *cold*." She also assumed an insufferable worldly pose. "You haven't tasted tea until you've had it from a samovar," she said. "There's no traffic in the USSR," she sighed later. "There are also no backyard swimming pools," said her dad. I tried not to laugh.

"Time for a pit stop," said Mr. Jones when he jerked the car into a rest area. Inside at McDonald's he ordered a nine-piece Chicken McNuggets for Jenny and me to split. "But it's not fair. One of us gets only four," said Jenny. She was especially concerned about fairness since falling under the Soviets' spell.

"Cut one in half," said her mother. So we used a flimsy plastic knife to divide one McNugget and then sat across from each other and hardly spoke as we ate.

"What's wrong with you?" she asked me.

"Nothing," I said. *Everything,* I thought.

Many of the details of the rest of the week are fuzzy. I know that we went to the lighthouse at Gay Head and ate lobster rolls at sunset in Menemsha. There were a few days with Mrs. Jones on the beach. Mr. Jones didn't like sand, so he whiled away his hours elsewhere. Jenny was recognized only once that week: in a store, the clerk grabbed my arm and said, "Is that the girl who went to meet the Russians?" I nodded. The woman asked for Jenny's autograph and then gave her a free hermit crab. "Something to remember the Vineyard," she said. The crab's shell had been painted an iridescent blue and it glowed as he clawed up and down the mesh walls of his small cage.

I still have a picture of us ferrying to the island: Mr. Jones snapped it as the boat neared the harbor at Oak Bluffs. We had scrambled up to the bow for a better view, and Jenny was pointing at the docks. The photograph has yellowed with age, so the sky is no longer the evening pink I remember. It was the start of our vacation, and we weren't yet sick of each other. By the end of the week, though, I couldn't wait to get home. Being with someone else's family can make you feel like a hostage, to their diet and schedule, their idea of etiquette, their variations on board-game rules. I was tired of straitjacketing my emotions.

One afternoon when Mr. and Mrs. Jones were playing tennis, Jenny said she had something to show me. I followed her into her parents' room. She lifted up the mattress and pulled out a copy of *Playboy.* On the cover a naked woman posed in a pile of jelly beans, with jewels of candy strategically placed over her nipples and between her legs. "It makes me think of Ronald Reagan," said Jenny.

"Why?"

"Because he likes jelly beans," she said. "Duh." This was true. At Christmastime the White House sent commemorative jars of Jelly Bellies to friends and donors. More than a few of our classmates' parents had received them.

"Look," said Jenny as she opened the magazine. "The centerfold."

I knelt beside her on the rug and looked at the woman. Her pout was at odds with the bubbly handwriting on her questionnaire. I don't remember her name, but I know that she dotted her *i*'s with hearts. Her skin was golden and waxy, like a piece of fruit. She was wearing lacy white kneesocks and nothing else. "Her boobs are huge," said Jenny.

I had never seen *Playboy* before. The generic shame it produced made me queasy. "Whose magazine is this?"

"My dad's," said Jenny. "He always hides them from my mom."

I didn't want to know this about Mr. Jones. "It's gross," I said. But it was also exciting, in the way that only secrets can be. "We should put it back."

So Jenny returned it to its spot under the mattress. And I almost asked her what *she* was hiding in her room at home, but we heard the car pulling in to the driveway and ran out to the porch to greet her parents.

On the last night, I couldn't sleep and overheard Mr. and Mrs. Jones fighting from their bedroom next door. I could hear the trilling, eager voice of Mrs. Jones, though her words were muffled. Then Mr. Jones barked, "Goddamn it, Linda, I'm tired of hearing about what you want. Want, want, want. Jesus. Do you have any idea how much moving to Washington has cost us?"

In some ways it was a relief to realize that Jenny's parents didn't always get along—it made my own family seem less screwed up—but it was also disturbing. It was like seeing a famous actress without makeup.

———

THE NEXT MORNING we rushed to pack up the car because Mr. Jones was worried we'd miss our ferry. The front doors were open so that he could stand on the running board to reach the roof. While her father strapped our bags onto the rack, Jenny lingered beside the open door, studying her reflection in the side mirror. "I think I have some new freckles," she said. "Just from this week." She did have new freckles. Four on her forehead, three on her nose. She also had a narrow stripe of sunburn down one leg, where the sunscreen had missed a spot.

"Come on, girls, get in the goddamn car," Mr. Jones snapped. It was the first time I'd witnessed his temper, and the flare-up scared me. His jaw locked, and he pushed his glasses up on his forehead to reveal an unforgiving squint. It was a glimpse of a man I didn't know. My nerves were still wobbly as I buckled myself into my seat.

We made the boat back to the mainland, but somewhere in the middle of Connecticut my suitcase fell off the roof. We heard the thump, and by the time Mr. Jones yanked the car to the shoulder, the contents of the bag had already scattered across the highway. My days-of-the-week underpants made a rumpled calendar in the far lane until a tractor-trailer ran them over.

"Ed," Mrs. Jones scolded, "you didn't tie them down tight enough."

"Get off my fucking back."

"You said the F-word, Daddy," said Jenny.

"And I'll fucking say it again," he said. Jenny, chastised, slid down in her seat.

Mr. Jones set up emergency flares, and as passing cars slowed to rubberneck, he darted out into the lanes to retrieve a handful of items.

"Oh, honey, I don't think anything survived," Mrs. Jones said sadly, as if I'd lost family members instead of articles of clothing. I could feel tears trembling on my lashes; I didn't care about the clothes, but I was tired of being the one to whom the bad things happened. No one else's suitcase fell off the roof. It wasn't fair.

We left the shredded garments on the pavement. The suitcase itself—it was black-and-white houndstooth and belonged to my mother—had come to rest near the guardrail. It survived the fall without damage but was smeared with axle grease. Mr. Jones secured the empty bag on the roof with extra bungee cords. For the rest of the long ride home, the only sound I remember is the unsettling tickle of the hermit crab moving around his cage.

Back in Washington that evening, Jenny decided that the crab deserved freedom. She released him from his cage and let him crawl around on the kitchen floor. "Just for a few minutes," she promised her mom. But hermit crabs move fast: we soon lost sight of him. Before we could figure out where he'd scampered off to, we heard Mr. Jones shout, "Goddammit." Jenny and I rushed to the front hall and found a cracked shell, a violent smear. The crab had met his end under Mr. Jones's shoe.

"My crab!" Jenny wailed. I realize now that it was the worst thing that had ever happened to her.

"Daddy didn't mean to," said Mrs. Jones.

"There's a moral here," said Mr. Jones.

But I can't remember what the moral was.

⌗

JENNY AND I BEGAN to drift away from each other that fall. She continued to smile benevolently at me in the halls, even after she fell in with Kim's crowd—her newfound celebrity made her an asset to the clique—and if she sensed any hostility or awkwardness from me, I'm sure it was attributed to envy. I still spent some afternoons at her house, but while I was there, she was usually on the phone. She had inspired a cult of personality. She twisted the telephone cord around her finger like a lock of hair. "We need to get another line," her mom said. "What if it's urgent and someone has to get through?"

Jenny and I used to joke that we needed a direct hotline to each other's house, like the red phone between Washington and Moscow. But now she was busy talking to other people. By second semester it was Kim who was going to the Joneses' house after school; from my bedroom I watched her saunter up the twenty-one steps to their front porch. Was Jenny telling Kim all the things I'd said about her? "I just don't think she's that smart," I'd said once. And "She's so fake." I'd confided in Jenny about so many things, and now I worried that my information was no longer safe. Were they laughing at me or, worse, feeling sorry for me? *Kim just likes you because you're famous,* I wanted to say. *You're just another cool brand.*

Jenny quit swimming and joined Kim's soccer team. "Isn't it boring going back and forth alone in a pool?" Kim said. "At least in soccer you get to talk to people on the field. It's a *team* sport."

In the cafeteria Kim led Jenny around like a trophy. And on the days when Jenny was out of school, she took charge of informing all the teachers of her whereabouts. At the start of every class, she raised her hand to announce her famous friend's schedule: "I just wanted to let you know that Jenny is in L.A. until Friday. I talked to her last night."

Social dynamics often shift in sixth grade. We weren't the only friends who grew apart that year. But I wasn't just losing a friend; I felt as if my whole life was unmoored. That fall my father called to tell me that Phillipa was pregnant. My half sibling was expected in January. "We hope you'll meet the baby," he said, but I knew that wasn't likely. I'd never even met Phillipa. At school I learned to catch the sorrow in my throat and then stick my head into my locker and let the tears slide down my cheeks without making any vibration at all.

I didn't tell my mother about finding my letter in Jenny's room. Of course she noticed that Jenny hadn't been around in a while, but she ascribed the absence to Jenny's relentless publicity schedule, and I didn't disabuse her of that notion. I needed an ally, but I wasn't sure my mother could be one. She was so fixated on disarmament that everything about Jenny's fame—and the attention it brought to the cause—thrilled her.

Jenny became a touchstone for nuclear anxiety. When *The Day After* premiered on ABC that November, various newspapers asked for her comment. "Are you going to watch the movie?" they asked. A stupid question, since we were *all* going to watch the movie. Our teachers had instructed us to watch it, with our parents. For most kids the depiction of mutually assured destruction was traumatizing, but for me the film just confirmed everything my mother had told me. Once launched, ICBMs could not be recalled. It would take just thirty minutes for those missiles to reach us. Enough time to retaliate, but not much else.

We were all doomed.

#

I WAS IN SEVENTH GRADE when the head of the middle school pulled me out of class to give me the news. It was January 1985. Jenny and I had hardly spoken in a year.

"There's been an accident," she said. She touched my shoulder, then thought better of it and extracted her hand. She wore a beige cardigan, the antiseptic color of a dentist's office. We were in the library; there was a blur of red encyclopedias behind her. My stomach growled. It was almost time for lunch. "An accident?" I said.

"Your friend Jennifer's plane."

I was allowed to leave school early that day. At home I found my mother in her bathroom. She was stretched out in the empty claw-foot tub, fully dressed, as if indulging in a good soak. She didn't even look at me as I entered the room.

"Now do you see why I hate flying?" she said.

"Plane crashes don't happen very often," I said, resorting to my father's old tactic, which had been to respond to her irrational fears with statistics. It never worked. I closed the toilet lid and sat down. I inventoried the expired bottles of sunscreen and painkillers on the bathroom counter. There was a graveyard of old lipstick tubes next to the sink. I was surrounded by rot and decay. My tears came fast and furious. Suddenly I was crying so hard I could hardly breathe.

"Come here," my mother said.

I knelt on the floor beside the tub. She cuffed my wrists and pulled me in like a convict. "I love you so much it hurts," she said.

"I know," I said.

She pressed her forehead to mine, and we were locked together like two magnets, the grief pulsing between us. I finally stopped crying. "It's our job to make the world a safer place," she said, and then released my wrists as if they were balloons that might lift into the sky.

⁂

THERE WERE MANY NIGHTS before her death when I'd wished for Jenny's comeuppance. We studied ancient Greek myths, and when we got to Narcissus, I remember deciding that Jenny was a narcissist. All that attention had gone to her head. Her ego was out of control. She deserved to be exposed as the mean, spoiled brat she had become. I imagined humiliating scenarios: a glimpse of her underwear on national TV; her diary, where she described her secret crushes on the boys at the school across the Cathedral Close, leaked to the press. In the winter of 1984, I wanted to pelt her with snowballs. *Cold War!* I imagined yelling, with the assertiveness I possessed only in my head. I hated her for being so lucky. I hated her for having a father, for having a mother who baked, for being named Jennifer Jones. People loved her because she was easy to love, I thought, and I prayed for a time when my complexity wouldn't scare people away.

But I also longed for détente. I would have given anything for someone to broker a treaty between us. I missed my friend.

The last time Jenny and I had a real conversation was a few weeks after my half brother was born. Phillipa sent a birth announcement: *"Sebastian Andrew Zuckerman, January 23, 1984, 7 lbs., 6 oz."*

"Too soon to tell if he's got his father's selfish streak," said my mother as she studied the baby's photo.

I hadn't called Jenny since the day after Christmas—when I thanked her for the copy of her book—but I dialed her number without thinking. I needed to hear her voice. Mrs. Jones answered the phone. "Sarah? Is that you?" she said. "You haven't been to see us in so long."

"No," I said. "Sorry." I wasn't sure what Jenny had told her mother about me. Had I become persona non grata?

"How are you doing, honey?"

"I'm fine," I said. "May I speak to Jenny, please?"

I waited for an impossibly long time. I wondered if Mrs. Jones was talking her daughter into taking the call. I imagined Jenny rolling her eyes in protest. But when she finally came to the phone, she sounded like her usual self. Distracted, but not hostile. I stood at the window of my room, looking at her house as I talked to her.

"My dad has a new baby," I said.

She wanted to know if it was a boy or a girl. And when I told her, she said, "So you're his only daughter. That means you're still special."

"I guess so," I said.

"Don't worry so much, Sar," she said. "You still matter. Everything's gonna be okay."

"You think so?" I wanted to keep her on the phone, to settle into our old habits. After just five minutes, I could feel myself starting to lean on her again.

"I've gotta go. Kim and I are going to Commander Salamander."

She hung up before I could say good-bye. Commander Salamander was a boutique in Georgetown that catered to punks, and though Kim was not the target demographic, she and her friends frequented the store to buy the black rubber bracelets that were sold next to the register. Even Jenny, the girl from the heartland who wanted peace, had begun to stack black rubber bands on her right wrist. I watched Kim's mother's silver Mercedes wagon idle next to the curb outside the Joneses' house. Then Jenny, swaddled in down against the February chill, was slinking to the bottom of the steps. Before she opened the back door of the car, she lifted her face in my direction, as if she knew I'd been watching the whole time.

When she died, I still had the keys to her house. I'd put them on my key chain while the Joneses were in the USSR, and they had never asked for them back. So for a whole year, even though Jenny no longer called me or invited me to swim in her pool, I kept her keys with my own. I knew that it was pathetic, but I couldn't bring myself to remove them from the key chain. As long as the keys were still attached to mine, there was hope. Maybe she'd come back to me.

After the accident I used those keys to let myself into their house. The place was still thrumming with their presence. The remnants of a tuna-fish casserole were preserved in Tupperware in the refrigerator. A notepad on the kitchen counter—it was always spotless—revealed a grocery list in Mrs. Jones's flowery hand: *"Tomatoes, ground beef, onions, bananas, milk, raisin bread, toilet paper, Windex."* There were clean plates waiting to be unloaded from the dishwasher. A tin of Mr. Jones's shoe polish had been left on the coffee table in the family room. I knew that he sometimes brought his wingtips downstairs to shine them while he watched sports. Hexa's water bowl was empty, so I filled it, but I didn't see the cat anywhere. Cats were sneaky, though. Hexa had been known to sit silently in a dark corner for hours at a time.

I went to Jenny's room one last time. Her school binder was on her desk; her Benetton rugby shirt was folded on her bed. I climbed to the top bunk, where I had spent so many nights staring up at the glow-in-the-dark stars on her ceiling. The stars were still there, but in the daylight they made a sad constellation, drained of magic. I tried to peel them off. The rings of Saturn came off easily, but my fingernails couldn't gain purchase on the others. They were stuck firm. In Jenny's underwear drawer, I found her diary. It was polka-dotted in pink with MY DIARY embossed in cursive on the front. I would have read it—death trumped privacy, I decided—but it was locked and I didn't know where she kept the key. The photo strip of us was still on the bulletin board. In all four images, even the one in which we had decided to "be silly," Jenny looks good. She couldn't take a bad picture. I pulled it loose and put it in my pocket. I took the rugby shirt, too, in hopes that its coveted label would ward off attacks from the girls at school.

Jenny's aunt flew into town to pack up the Joneses' house and put it on the market. I watched the movers take away the furniture I knew so well. And even when For Sale was replaced by Sold, I didn't take the keys off my key chain. The new owners would change the locks, I thought. I needed the keys for sentimental reasons.

The cameras finally pointed at me when my mother started the foundation in Jenny's name. "We'll keep her memory alive," she said. In addition to her general efforts to prevent nuclear war, my mother wanted to establish an annual Jennifer Jones Prize that would send a worthy American high-school student to the Soviet Union for two weeks.

My mother organized a press conference. The reporters descended on our street, where she stood outside our house and sold the narrative of the Joneses as neighbors and friends. She had done her hair and put on a dress. I was impressed that she could still pull herself together, even though she was doing so for Jenny, not me.

"How did you feel when your best friend died?" the reporters asked me. I quivered, couldn't speak. I'd waited for a chance in the spotlight, but now I was flubbing it. I felt like a fraud. I wasn't Jenny's best friend anymore, not really. History was being revised; Kim was written out. And I felt guilty. Guilty for all the times I'd begrudged Jenny's good fortune. Eventually, I thought, everyone has an unlucky break. She was the pretty one, and she had an alliterative American name. But I was alive. And that was something I could never take for granted in the nuclear age.

"Jennifer Jones's work had just begun," my mother said. "My daughter and I are going to finish it."

In the morning, news of the foundation made it into the *Washington Post*. There was a picture of Jenny, not my mother or me. But I was declared "Jennifer Jones's best friend" in print. Kim no longer had any claim. On the record, Jenny was mine.

Donations to the foundation poured in after Jenny's death, but within six months people were distracted by other Cold War stories. Nineteen eighty-five turned out to be the year of the spy. There was Yurchenko's defection. Edward Lee Howard sold secrets to the Soviets, then escaped into the New Mexico desert. And Vladimir Alexandrov, the Soviet scientist who helped develop the theory of nuclear winter, vanished from Madrid. The Soviets claimed he was kidnapped by the CIA, but he was never heard from again. Construction on the new American embassy in

Moscow was halted that year when the United States realized that the whole building was bugged. And then in 1986 the *Challenger* exploded our space program. There was no refuge from terror.

But then the disaster at Chernobyl renewed interest in the foundation. An anonymous donor sent the first American high-school student—a seventeen-year-old girl from Sacramento, who won the essay contest my mother judged—to Moscow in the summer of 1987.

Would Jenny and I have been friends in high school? Would she have been one of those girls who developed an eating disorder? There were a lot of them at our school. In the cafeteria the anorexics picked nervously at bowls of sprouts. The bulimics slithered to the bathroom after lunch and reemerged with eyes bloodshot from purging. One girl was famous for eating just one apple a day. It's hard to picture Jenny as a teenager. Her body still held its childish contours when she died. Some of the girls in our sixth-grade class needed bras; the most advanced were already whispering about tampons. But Jenny's skin was unblemished, her ears not yet pierced. Her mother told her that she could start shaving her legs at thirteen. She didn't reach that milestone.

In the locker room after high-school swim practices, I tried to imagine Jenny among the other girls. There were no doors separating the showers, and so we were forced to cluster like refugees, thirty of us rotating under three showerheads, passing around bottles of Ultra Swim shampoo while the blondes among us complained that the chlorine turned their hair green. The most self-conscious girls kept their suits on and soaped their bodies under the fabric with surreptitious hands. You could tell what body part they were most insecure about: the flat girls like me kept their arms folded in front of their chests; the bottom-heavy girls kept their backs to the walls. We saw one another in swim-suits in the pool every day, but in the locker room we turned shy. Only the team captains—confident in their lean, strong bodies—had no shame. My sophomore year the captain was a senior named Miranda who massaged soap into her unruly black pubic hair in front of all of us. Her nipples were large and dark, and there was a bristle sprouting from one, but there was something mesmerizing about how sure of herself she was. I was on the abashed end of the spectrum—I kept my suit on, only rolling it down halfway so that I could clean my bare chest—but I suspect that Jenny would have been unapologetic about her nudity. She would have turbaned a towel on her head and coaxed Jergens into her damp skin while everyone else dressed in quick, furtive strokes.

After she died, I found myself writing letters to Jenny. *"How could you lie to me?"* I wrote. *"How could you leave me?"* I furrowed the words I could never say when she was alive into handkerchiefs of paper and tucked them into our old secret spot in the wall of the Bishop's Garden. And even when I'd made new friends and discovered, in adolescence, that my sad stories were valuable cur-rency with the skinny New Wave boys I favored, I still wrote to her sometimes. The letters became a sort of diary in which I told her what she was missing. Every new experience was muted by her ab-sence; I needed to confide in her to make the colors pop. *"I tried pot. It made me sleepy,"* I wrote. *"I lost my virginity on a basement floor after the Super Bowl. The Redskins won."* I wrote, *"I didn't get into Harvard, even though I'm a legacy."* My anonymous confessions may still be there decomposing in our dead drop.

I've been told many times that I am too forgiving. Of the college friend who started sleeping with my boyfriend, of the boss who presented my ideas as his own, of the lover who made so many promises he couldn't keep. "You're too forgiving," they say, as if it's a character flaw. But I'm not sure I'm forgiving enough. And I have come to believe that forgiveness is the key to survival. It does no good to see everything as a struggle between opposing factions. Few things are that simple.

During my first month in Moscow, I visited Khrushchev's grave. The headstone is half black, half white, a compromise reached after Soviet leaders couldn't decide whether his tenure had been good or evil. It's a narrow marble monument, toweringly literal, with a bust perched on top. It is in Novodevichy, the same cemetery where Chekhov and Gogol are buried—along with countless other artists capable of nuance that Khrushchev was not—and on that October day there was already snow on the ground.

It would be a long winter.

Part 2

Here's what there is
absolutely none of in Moscow

Privacy

—Kay Thompson,
Eloise in Moscow

6.

JENNY WAS MET at Sheremetyevo Airport with smiles and flashing bulbs. But my arrival was more typical: I emerged from customs into a room of cold, leery eyes. Moscow was a furtive city. People were as closed and guarded as fists. Their faces hardened against possible scrutiny. The crowd lapped the door, waiting for arriving family members and friends, sizing up each passenger through a film of cigarette smoke. Being watched made me jittery, but the stares passed through me like X-rays. I was inspected and shunted aside. I wasn't the one they were looking for. I felt like a minor cast member exiting the stage door, ignored by the crowd waiting for the ingenue.

It was the middle of September. It took longer than expected to get my Russian visa, so I had spent the summer after graduation in my old attic bedroom where the garret window looked directly at the house that had belonged to the Joneses. An older couple lived there now, and I would see the wife in the front yard in the mornings, pruning her garden in yellow clogs. In June she tended roses and hydrangeas. As the summer ripened, she focused on the annuals, heliotrope and impatiens. I worked as a barista at a local coffee shop, and while I perfected the art of latte foam, my mother made lists of things I'd need for my trip. Traveler's checks. A tetanus booster. An HIV test. (The Russian government required proof that you weren't HIV-positive before you were allowed into their country.) My mother filled Ziploc bags with Band-Aids, vitamins, water-purification tablets. My visa was good for sixty days, so I'd be back home in time for Thanksgiving. But my mother was still anxious. She paced my bedroom while I packed.

"Even the icicles in Moscow are dangerous," she said. "I've read about it. Long icicles like daggers hanging off ledges of buildings. They fall and kill people. It happens all the time."

"I won't walk under any ledges," I said.

"The rates of HIV infection are alarmingly high," she said. "Lots of intravenous-drug users sharing needles."

"You don't have to worry about that," I said. I feared losing control so much that I never did drugs. I didn't like altered states.

"Thank God you're not flying Aeroflot. Their safety record is deplorable."

I said nothing.

"And the radioactivity levels . . ."

"Mom!" I said. "Breathe. Do your relaxation exercises."

I had my own packing list, and in addition to the obvious ne-cessities (passport, visa, long underwear), it included Svetlana's letter and Jenny's book. I couldn't bring my full Jenny archive, but I took a few photos and clippings. I sealed them in a clear plastic sleeve and stowed it in my suitcase beneath my sweaters. By the time I set out for Dulles Airport in early autumn, most of the flow-ers in the Joneses' old yard were gone. With my mother's reluctant blessing, I finally boarded a Finnair flight bound for Moscow.

During my layover in Helsinki, I curled myself into one of the chairs near the gate and tried to sleep. I wrapped the strap of my carry-on around my leg, so that a thief couldn't wrest the bag away without disturbing me. But I couldn't drift off. It was the middle of the night to me, but it was morning in Finland, and the airport was stirring to life. I could hear the grind of espresso machines and the click of flight-attendant heels on the polished floor. The Finnair flight attendants impressed me with their efficient cool. On my flight from New York, their brisk offers of *"Kahvi? Tee?"* had the ring of commands. They had none of the painted-on charm I was used to seeing on the American airlines. I'd traveled a lot during college. I spent a year in Rome and made the requisite Eurail jour-ney across the Continent that summer, bunking at hostels and awaiting mail via poste restante along the way.

At the end of my trip, I spent a few days in London, where my father and Phillipa were installed in a large house in Holland Park. It was my first visit and the first time I'd met Sebastian. He was ten. They called him Sebby.

"Why does my sister have an American accent?" he asked our dad. We were in the breakfast room, and Sebby was spreading Marmite on his toast.

"Because her mother is American," my father said.

"Because *I'm* American," I said.

"So you are," my father said, as if this were news.

"I've been to America," said Sebby.

"Have you?" I said, and realized I was picking up their British inflection. My father had never mentioned bringing his son to the States. I'd seen my father just three times in six years. Business took him to New York sometimes. During college I met him once in Boston, when he shuttled up from La Guardia and took me to dinner at the Ritz Carlton, and once for a weekend in Manhattan, where he put me up at the Harvard Club. These visits retained the formality of job interviews; my father asked me questions, and I tried to come up with the most impressive answers. During one dinner I ordered a steak and he said, "You're not a vegetarian anymore?" But I was never a vegetarian. He had me confused with someone else.

"We went skiing," Sebby said. "On holiday. In Vail."

The girls at my school skied in Aspen and Vail; they'd return from Christmas and spring breaks full of stories of running into each other on the slopes. I'd never been to Colorado.

"There are no direct flights from London to Denver," I said.

"No," said my father.

"Did you fly through New York?" I said.

"Yes," said Sebby. What kind of name was Sebby anyway?

"I could have met you in New York," I said. "I could have gone skiing with you." I was not a good skier, but I wanted to be. Good skiers weren't afraid of speed. I was so nervous that I made wide, slow turns down the mountain.

"I didn't want your mum to worry," my father said.

"I'm in college," I snapped. "I don't live with Mom." I was startled by the anger I heard in my voice. I was tired of being lumped together with my mother in the same fearful box. I felt trapped.

My father registered surprise at my outburst, but his upper lip remained stiff. We hardly knew each other. "How's your mum's foundation?" he said.

The sneer in his voice made me jump to my mother's defense. I knew he thought her efforts were misguided, but I wasn't about to let him insult her. "Great," I said. "*Washingtonian* magazine profiled her on the fifth anniversary of Chernobyl." I didn't mention that the profile was really just a paragraph and that in the intervening four years there'd been no press coverage at all. The foundation hadn't sent an American student to Moscow since 1991.

"She's always chasing ghosts," he said.

"What kind of ghosts?" said Sebby.

My father ignored him. "Your mother does love a memorial. She would have set up a foundation for your sister if she could have done. If she hadn't been such a wreck."

"Do I have another sister?" Sebby said. It was the first time he had looked directly at me. I noticed that he and I had the same eyes.

"No," I said. It was astonishing to realize that my father had never told him about Izzy. I wasn't about to tell him; I didn't want to share anything—even my grief—with him.

"Do I have another sister, Dad?"

"No, Sebby, you don't," my father said.

My father had always been generous: he paid all my tuition over the years, and he never failed to send alimony. He didn't make it to my graduation because Phillipa had a riding competition, but he sent me a check. He was so enthusiastic about my plans that it was clear he was giving me money only because I was going abroad. *"You're young; you ought to be exploring the world,"* he wrote to me. It was the first letter I'd received from him in years. *"Don't let your mother keep you at home. You've got to live your life."* The check was for ten thousand dollars. All summer it lay on top of my dresser, pinned in place by a snow globe. An elementary souvenir from my first trip to New York. I still liked to stir the storm, watch the flakes fall over the Statue of Liberty. I didn't want my dad's money. It made me think of Phillipa, who inserted herself into everything with the determination of a tapeworm. I couldn't bring myself to cash the check until the day before I left for Moscow. I deposited it in my savings account. In Russia I vowed to use only my own hard-earned cash.

IT WAS EARLY AFTERNOON when my plane touched down in Moscow, and the Russians on board—many of whom had been drinking heavily throughout the flight—burst into boisterous applause. The clapping terrified me: celebrating the routine as miraculous didn't bode well. Inside, the airport was eerily quiet. I followed the mass of passengers down a flight of stairs to passport control. Outmaneuvered by seasoned Russians, I found myself at the back of an interminable immigration line. It must have been two hours before I reached the front. The officious woman who inspected my visa proved to be the warmest person I encountered that first day. At baggage claim I was amazed to see people smoking, flicking the ash from their cigarettes onto the floor and the rubber luggage belt. We waited for what seemed like an hour for the carousel to crank into action, but in the end our bags were carried in, two at a time, by a disgruntled handler.

"I hope you put a lock on your suitcase," I heard an American man say to the woman next to him. "They rifle through the bags, you know."

Thanks to my mother's precautions, my suitcase was locked. I retrieved it and made my way through customs. I had nothing to declare.

Sam's cousin Corinne was supposed to meet me at the airport. I finally identified her in the throng. She was the only one who didn't have a cigarette in her mouth. "Everyone smokes here," she said. "Even in the office. It's like living inside an ashtray. I quit after college, and now the smell of smoke makes me sick. I come home every day and have to wash my hair, like immediately. Otherwise my pillow *reeks*."

"I'm Sarah," I said.

"Right. Welcome to Russia."

The arrivals area was clogged with people. All the men wore

either Adidas tracksuits or leather coats. Most of the women were holding bouquets of flowers. Corinne threaded her way through the crowd. I followed her out to the curb and into the back of a gray Toyota Land Cruiser. "The magazine has a car and a driver. This is Boris," she said, gesturing toward the driver's seat.

The man behind the wheel turned around and smiled at us. There were dark, empty spaces where teeth should have been.

"He used to drive Brezhnev," said Corinne. "He pretends not to speak English, but I think he understands everything I say. I'm sure he was a spy. Maybe he still is."

Corinne was tall and broad-shouldered. Her eyebrows had been plucked in a severe angle that gave her face a merciless cast. She had wavy auburn hair and wore bright lipstick that exaggerated the downturn of her mouth. She was sheathed in black, with pointy heels. I soon learned that she always wore black. She said any other color was impossible to keep clean in Moscow. The whole city, she said, was coated in grime. I said she seemed young to be an editor, and she laughed. "I'm older than I look," she said, "and this place ages you fast, let me tell you. The pollution is doing a number on my skin. God, I miss New York." She grew up in Manhattan, then went to college at Vassar, she said. She studied Russian language and literature, then got her start as an editorial assistant at *Harper's Bazaar*. "I was the only person in the New York office who spoke Russian, so when they decided to launch the magazine here, they offered me the job."

As she talked, I could see Boris watching me in the rearview mirror. The car lurched onto the highway, and I looked up to see a

giant billboard. It was the only brightly colored thing in an otherwise grim landscape, and its presence was so jarring it was as if it
had been Photoshopped into frame. ПЕПСИ, said the sign. I
sounded out the word: "Pepsi."

"The choice of a new generation," said Corinne. "Pepsi was
the first foreign brand in the Soviet Union. They've been here
since like 1970. Cut some kind of deal with Stolichnaya: vodka in
stores in the U.S. in exchange for Pepsi here."

"Huh."

"It's a good thing you can read Russian. It'll make getting
around a lot easier."

"I'm rusty," I said. "I can only read really slowly."

"As long as you know the alphabet."

"Do you mind if I open a window?" I said. "I get carsick." The
numbing exhaustion of jet lag combined with a mounting head-
ache from all the smoke in the airport made me feel like I was
going to throw up. I cranked open a window, but the air that
rushed in wasn't fresh. I coughed.

"Terrible air quality here," said Corinne. "Whatever you do,
don't go running outside."

What struck me on the forty-minute ride into the city was how
run-down Moscow was. It was hard to believe that a country with
such exhausted infrastructure was ever considered a superpower.
The margins of the city were dotted with sad Soviet apartment
blocks, trapped in a 1960s version of the future. The avenues were
dirty—not with litter but with actual dirt, as if the entire city
needed a good scrub. And our car was one of the few on the road

that wasn't leaking exhaust. We were surrounded by ancient Ladas, some of them seemingly stapled together. "This is where the world's cars go to die," said Corinne.

"I thought Moscow would be . . ." I paused, realizing I wasn't sure what I had expected.

"More impressive?" said Corinne.

"Yeah, I guess," I said.

"The Metro is impressive. And the architecture in the center of the city, all the buildings from before 1917. But yeah, most of the country is falling apart."

I glanced at the front seat to gauge Boris's reaction. But if he understood, he didn't let on.

⌗

CORINNE'S APARTMENT was on Patriarch's Ponds, a location made famous by Bulgakov's *Master and Margarita*. A lot of expats lived in the neighborhood, she told me. The grand prerevolutionary buildings had been renovated to turn communal apartments into luxurious rentals for foreigners. The pond was in a leafy park, around which the gorgeous old apartment buildings stood watch. It looked a little like Paris. Boris pulled the car up in front of a pale yellow building. "No doorman," said Corinne with a sigh.

I removed my rolling suitcase from the back of the car and followed her to the front door. She unlocked it with an old-fashioned brass key, and then we were in a dank, dark stairwell that smelled of piss. "The elevator's broken," said Corinne, and so we walked right past the lift—it was the cage style that requires you to crank open the gate—and mounted a graffitied flight of stairs. At the top Corinne stopped in front of the only door. "I'm on the first floor," she said. "Or the second floor, as we'd call it in the States."

Corinne's apartment was a surprise after the dreary stairwell. I found myself in a large entrance hall with a parquet floor. The ceilings must have been sixteen feet high. French doors of elaborately carved wood opened onto a living room meticulously furnished in mahogany. It was like a Merchant-Ivory film.

"Shoes off, Russian style," she said. She removed her boots and stepped into the *tapochki* waiting by the door. "We'll have to get you a pair of your own slippers."

I took off my Converse sneakers. I was sure that my socks smelled foul after twenty-four hours of travel, so I peeled them off and opted for bare feet.

"My landlord is half Russian, half Italian," she said. "And his wife's American. They renovated the place with what they call 'Western standards.' There's only one bathroom, but it has a Jacuzzi tub." Moscow was still considered a hardship post. Companies lured expat employees there by paying for their housing.

"Beautiful," I said.

"When there's hot water," she said. "Don't get me started on that. Last week I went three whole days without it. I made the magazine put me up at the National Hotel." Corinne was fast and unwavering. Everything she said throbbed with the urgency of an ambulance siren. A real New Yorker, I thought. "I had the housekeeper make up your bed," she said.

I trailed her through the living room and down a short hallway carpeted with an Oriental rug. The doors at the end revealed two bedrooms. "You're on the right," she said.

The room wasn't large, but I couldn't get over the windows: floor to ceiling and veiled in brocade. I touched one of the drapes, and Corinne laughed. "Not much of a view, I'm afraid. The master bedroom looks out on the pond, but you're stuck facing the alley." Sure enough, when I pushed the fabric out of the way, I found myself looking at a dingy cluster of cars and two men in red tracksuits. Like tuning forks, they sensed that they were being watched and lifted heavy eyes to mine. They pinched their cigarettes between index finger and thumb, not with the nonchalance of dandies but with the obsession of addicts. I let the curtain fall into place.

"I have to go back to the office," she said. "Make yourself at home. The fridge is pretty well stocked. Just don't drink the tap water. There's drinking water in a cooler in the kitchen. But you probably just want to sleep."

I nodded.

"So you're okay if I leave you? My office number is on a pad next to the phone in the kitchen."

"Sure, thanks," I said. "I think I'll just take a nap."

⊞

I WOKE UP WITH TRAVELER'S DISORIENTATION: the curtains in the room were drawn, and it was so dark that I had no idea where I was. I fumbled for the bedside table lamp. I was in a brass bed with plain white sheets. In *Russia*. It was mind-boggling. I felt like I was underwater as I stumbled down the hall. The kitchen was large enough to accommodate a long table with six wooden chairs and an overstuffed, flowered sofa nestled by the window. Corinne was perched on that sofa, drinking a glass of scotch. The TV next to her was tuned to CNN.

"She lives!" she said, and muted the television.

"What time is it?"

"Midnight. I just got home. I was stuck at work waiting for a call from my boss in New York. Total nightmare. I'm working in two fucking time zones. Want a drink?"

I shook my head. "Just water," I said.

"You'd better get used to drinking if you're going to stay in Russia. Glasses are over the sink."

I filled a glass from the cooler and joined her on the sofa. "Thanks for letting me stay here," I said. "I brought you a few things, but I haven't unpacked yet." I'd brought her stuff you couldn't get in Moscow: good coffee beans and several bags of the Twizzlers that Sam said she loved.

"That's okay," she said. "Honestly, it's nice to have the company. It can get pretty lonely."

"I'm sure."

"So what's your plan for tomorrow?" she said.

"I guess I just want to wander around," I said. "See the city."

"First I have to take you to register your visa. Everyone has to register within three days. They love to keep tabs on us. The phone? I'm sure it's bugged. All the phone lines in foreigners' apartments are. Sometimes I hear this click when I'm talking, like whoever's listening got bored and hung up. I mean, it can't be very interesting hearing me talk about hemlines or whatever." She sipped her scotch. "Russians turn up their stereos really loud so that the listeners can't understand their conversations."

I couldn't tell if she was paranoid or self-aggrandizing or whether her fears of surveillance were grounded in reality.

"Are you hungry?" she said. "You must be hungry. I've got some eggs . . . and there's pasta in that cupboard. It's hard to get good fruit and vegetables here, though. You pay like eight dollars for a tiny bunch of broccoli. Oh, and I should warn you: I keep all my nail polish in the fridge. So don't be surprised."

I wasn't hungry. I couldn't even think about food. I asked if there was somewhere I could send an e-mail. "My mom's a worrier," I said.

"You can send e-mail from here," she said. "I have an account. There's a computer in the living room."

So while Corinne slept, I sat at her desk waiting for a connection. "Come on," I nagged the modem, but each time it dialed, it was busy. I felt terribly far away.

IN THE MORNING Corinne told me that her dial-up service was always spotty. "Just call her," she said. "You can use my calling card if you make it quick."

I got my mother's answering machine and was glad to know she was out of the house. After I went off to college, I worried that her loneliness would metastasize and corrode her completely. When she was home, she always answered the phone, and so every time I got the machine, I took it as a positive sign. It was proof that she had gone somewhere, and even though that somewhere was probably just the grocery store, I still clung to the possibility that she might meet someone, that she might fall in love in the produce section of Georgetown's "social" Safeway. She and some kindly widower might reach for the same grapefruit and their fingers would meet and she would find her way to happily-ever-after. I left a short, reassuring message for my mom. But I had only Svetlana's e-mail address. Over the summer I had promised to e-mail her when I arrived in Moscow. I studied the return address from the letter she'd sent me.

"Do you know where Petrovka Ulitsa is?" I asked Corinne.

She took the envelope from me. "DDBD," she read. "That's the ad agency."

"An ad agency?"

"Their headquarters are on Madison Avenue. Not sure when they opened an office here."

"And Petrovka Ulitsa?"

"Right next to the Bolshoi," she said. "Not far away. Who do you know at DDBD?"

"A friend of a friend," I said. "She offered to show me around."

———

I CAN'T REMEMBER how many days passed. I finally managed to send an e-mail to Svetlana, but I didn't hear back from her right away. In the meantime Corinne took me to register my visa at the local office of OVIR. It was my first time on the Moscow Metro. I was not prepared for the pushing and shoving: even seemingly feeble babushkas threw elbows in their efforts to enter the station. But Corinne was right: it was impressive. The stations were even deeper than in Washington, and the escalators were so long and steep that it took nearly five minutes to reach the bottom. I stood next to Corinne and watched the sad faces moving up the other side, grainy and slow as in a silent film. I didn't see a single smile. Underground, an ornate mini-civilization awaited us, marbled and chandeliered. All the stations proved resplendent. Each one had a theme. Arbatskaya looked like the lobby of an opera house. Ploschad Revolyutsii commemorated the Soviet people with soldiers, collective farmers, writers, and children sculpted in bronze. Mendeleevskaya was named for Dmitri Mendeleev, inventor of the periodic table, and its light fixtures resembled elaborate molecular models. Dinamo was a tribute to sports, with weight lifters and other Olympians carved into the walls. Digital clocks on the platforms showed how long it had been since the last train departed. They didn't tell you how long it would be before the next train came; it was as if the time were marked not for the convenience of commuters but as a way for the state to boast about its efficiency. The trains were never more than three minutes apart, said Corinne, and in most cases you waited for only one minute. We changed trains twice that day: I learned to push through the crush of people to get on and off. I have always craved personal space—even more so than other Americans, perhaps—but I learned I'd have to do without it. In Moscow, strangers compressed me into a tight, tense ball. I was always surrounded. Bodies were so uncomfortably close that I could see scales of dandruff on their scalps. The trains were quiet, though. There was no chatter, just the occasional "Are you getting off?" delivered in a low voice to anyone near the doors who might impede exit. Most people on the trains were reading. Not newspapers or magazines but actual books. Russians were famously literate, I knew—their reverence for literature is evident in all the writers' houses that are now museums—but seeing all the books made me happy. As a kid I'd been teased for being bookish.

"They think Americans don't read," Corinne said.

"Most of them don't," I said.

#

During those first few days, I made halting forays around the center of the city. I had a map, but I was self-conscious. Unlike in cities I'd visited in Europe, I didn't see other tourists. Every time I opened my guidebook, people stared. I'd never felt stranger. Most people were in dark colors—gray and black—and the smallest splash of something more vivid labeled me alien. I had a bright orange scarf, and though the wind was already brisk in September,

I often left the scarf at home so I wouldn't draw attention to myself. But even without it, my clothes set me apart. My wardrobe was decidedly tomboyish and collegiate—corduroys and cashmere crewnecks, mostly. I couldn't fit in.

I found my way to the lights of Pushkin Square—home of Moscow's first McDonald's—and down Tverskaya toward the Kremlin. Stepping into Red Square was like entering a movie I'd watched a thousand times. It looked exactly as it did on TV, and yet the scale of the place—bordered by the imposing walls of the Kremlin and the candy-colored onion domes of St. Basil's Cathedral—overwhelmed me. I stared at the armed guards outside the mausoleum. ЛЕНИН, it said. It was Lenin's tomb. Throughout history, Russian leaders—czars and then secretaries-general—had set out to make people feel small and powerless, and my insignificance as an individual was especially clear to me as I stood there. I could feel the weight of history. I wanted to take it all in, but I was afraid to stay still for too long, as though my freedom would be confiscated if I didn't keep moving.

I was afraid to go into a restaurant alone—I didn't trust my Russian, was terrified to speak—but in a fit of hunger one afternoon I managed to order a slice of pizza. *"Adin,"* I said. One. I pointed at the plain cheese pie. As I paid the girl behind the counter—the price glowed on her register, which was a relief, because I couldn't understand her—I sounded out the Cyrillic on the sign above her head. ПИЦЦА ХАТ. I was at Pizza Hut. I should have recognized the logo, but in a foreign alphabet even familiar signs were disorienting.

After only an hour or two, I'd retreat to Corinne's apartment, just to feel invisible again. Every time I got home, I felt defeated. I wanted to be a fearless, adventurous traveler, but Moscow intimidated me. At home I boned up on Russian grammar. If I could just master the language, I thought, I'd feel less helpless. I perused recent issues of the *Moscow Times,* trying to make sense of the place. In addition to the world-news stories, there were a lot of pieces dedicated to adjusting to life in Russia. I read reviews of bars and restaurants endorsed by expats, recommendations for inexpensive cultural outings (the opera and ballet were a steal!), and local news items that had been translated from the Russian papers. Most of the news was bad. Moscow, I learned, led the developed world in the number of fire deaths. The current grain harvest was the smallest in thirty years. President Yeltsin and his first deputy prime minister, Anatoly Chubais, were trying to reform the country's banking system in the wake of a liquidity crisis. Two American balloonists had been shot down and killed by a Belarusan air-defense unit. A government statement claimed that the balloonists were flying too close to a missile base. And Russia's nuclear-safety watchdog voiced concern about supervision of the country's military-industrial complex. In July, while in the hospital recovering from a heart attack, President Yeltsin had signed an order excluding civilian inspectors from military facilities. I decided not to mention this in my e-mails to my mother. I kept my missives upbeat. *"The architecture is amazing,"* I wrote. *"The women on the street wear super-short skirts even when it's really cold."*

The most harrowing news I read was about a nine-year-old

girl who threw herself in front of a Moscow train. Only a few lines were dedicated to the story, as if it weren't so unusual. Definitely suicide, the paper said. No known motive. I found myself thinking about that girl a lot, wondering what kind of pain could drive someone so young to give up on life.

One day I returned home to find the housekeeper in the kitchen. She was barrel-chested and smelled like mayonnaise. She lit up when she saw me. *"Amerikanka?"* she said.

"Da," I told her.

She clapped her hands. She wanted to visit America. She wanted to learn English, she said. She said something else I couldn't catch. *"Medlenno,"* I said. Slowly.

So she reduced her speed. "Nina," she said, and pointed at her chest.

"Sarah," I said.

She turned on the television set. There were two channels in English: CNN International and BBC World. She switched to the BBC, where a game show called *Ready, Steady, Cook* had just begun.

"Ya khochu ponimat," she said. I want to understand.

So I got my Russian dictionary and sat there on the sofa with her.

"Chto eto?" she'd say. What is it? She pointed at the ingredients, waited for me to unlock the mysteries of the recipe.

I flipped through my dictionary as fast as I could to find the answer. In some cases this required two leaps of translation, first into American English, then into Russian. The aubergine of the

Brits on TV—and of my father, I realized—was eggplant to me and *baklazhan* to Nina. Courgette was zucchini in American English, *kabachok* in Russian. Nina was avid and spirited; when I mispronounced a word, she leaned close to see the book herself. We were a good team.

Ready, Steady, Cook was on every afternoon. I began watching it even on the days Nina wasn't at the apartment. The premise was simple: Two contestants each spent five quid on food, and then the competing celebrity chefs had twenty minutes to turn those ingredients into something palatable. The contestants would carry their groceries onto the London set, thrilled to be on the telly, and when they emptied the contents of their bags out on the kitchen counter, the chefs would study the ingredients and feign distress. "What am I going to do with a pineapple?" they'd say. But they always came up with something. They had to make do with whatever they got.

⌗

IN THOSE BEWILDERING EARLY DAYS, I dreamed often of Jenny. Sometimes we were in her pool, playing Marco Polo. My eyes were closed, and I was groping around the shallow end, trying to find her. *Marco,* I called. *Polo,* she said, in a voice that barely suppressed a laugh. *Marco. Polo. Polo. Polo.* But the closer I moved to the voice, the farther away she was, and then I wasn't in a pool at all but in some kind of sludgy muck through which it was impossible to move. *Marco,* I called helplessly from the mire, but there was no answer, and I'd wake to find that my sheets were twisted around me because I'd been swimming in my sleep. It was embarrassing how unoriginal my subconscious was. But in the dream, she was so real that I could practically smell her. She was within reach, closer than I'd been to her in years, and her voice was urging me on—*Polo! Polo!*—as if she couldn't wait to be found.

7.

Svetlana agreed to meet me by Patriarch's Ponds. *"I will wear the red hat,"* she wrote. And on Saturday morning, at the appointed time, I found her sitting on a bench and wearing a red beret. She was slender and lithe, with the erect posture of a ballerina, and her legs looked especially long in her black miniskirt and tall boots. She wore a black wool cape with operatic proportions. In my corduroys and down vest, I felt crude. I felt a little better when I noticed a small hole in the left knee of her tights and observed that the elegance of her carriage was marred by her hair, which was brittle and streaked with peroxide. ("One thing the women here really need," Corinne had said to me earlier, "is conditioner. All these bad dye jobs have totally wrecked their hair.")

"So you are the Sarah Zuckerman," Svetlana said.

"Ochen priyatno," I said. Nice to meet you. It had been two years since my last Russian class, and the words felt heavy and hard to maneuver.

"Govoritye po-russki?" You speak Russian?

"A little," I said.

I tried to reconcile the face before me with the girl pictured in Jenny's book. The young Svetlana had been fuller in the face, and her eyes were brighter, more hopeful. She had a freshly scrubbed quality. This woman was narrow and gaunt, and her eyes betrayed nothing. She was beautiful in a damaged way. I stood in front of her, waiting for her to stand. But she pulled a pack of Marlboro Lights from her bag and lit a cigarette. She sucked in the smoke with vehemence, then raked her head and squinted at me. As she cataloged my features, I sat down beside her. I was careful not to sit too close; the foot of space between us was charged, tense.

"It is surprising," she said in English.

"What?"

"You are sympathetic girl."

"Simpatichnaya?" I said.

"Da."

"I think you mean pretty," I said. "Not sympathetic. Sympathetic means kind."

"You are not kind?" Her manner was abrasive.

"No. I mean, I am. I like to think so anyway. I try to be. But *simpatichnaya* isn't 'sympathetic' in English. 'Sympathetic' means 'kind.' *Simpatichnaya* is like the English for 'pretty.' Or 'cute.'"

"*Da,* okay, pretty. I did not think you would be such pretty. I have seen picture, when you were young girl. You were not so—"

I cut her off. "That was a long time ago." My awkward stage ended when I was about sixteen.

"*Nu, da.* How do you say? 'Ancient history.' But you were very plain," she said. She seemed determined to get a rise out of me. "Although you are not fat. I thought Americans were fat."

"Some of them are," I said.

"You are not the potato?"

"What potato?"

"Potato on couch." She blew smoke in my face.

"Couch potato," I said. "No, I'm not."

"But most people in your country are the couch potatoes. Lazy, fat . . ."

"Not as fat as Yeltsin," I said.

"Boris Nikolayevich," she said, "is the special problem."

I wasn't ready to drop the argument. "There are fat people everywhere. It has nothing to do with nationality. That lady isn't exactly thin," I said of a woman walking toward us with her dog.

The dog was scruffy and black, some kind of poodle mix, I thought. *"Malchik?"* Svetlana said to the woman holding the leash. A boy? It was strange to discover that Russians also asked each other the sex of their dogs. It was a practical question. Most dogs weren't neutered, so vigilant owners needed to keep the intact males away from one another.

"Devochka," the woman replied. A girl.

The woman had a stout peasant build and a weary face. She

might have been forty, maybe older. As Svetlana leaned over to pet her dog, the woman offered me a tentative smile. It was obvious I was foreign, but she didn't treat me as a threat. I smiled back.

"*Zdravstvuite,*" I said. Hello. Her head bobbed like a buoy.

The dog rolled over to let Svetlana rub her belly. I missed Pip. He was neurotic but comforting. Whenever I cried, he licked my face, and although I know he was drawn to the salt of my tears, something soulful in his eyes suggested genuine concern. He would lie next to me until I was okay. He lived until my first year of college. When I came home for Thanksgiving that year, the house seemed terribly empty without him. I kept hearing the ghostly echo of his toenails on the floor. My mother kept saying she was going to get another dog.

"*Zaichik,*" cooed Svetlana as she scratched the dog under its chin. *Zaichik* means "bunny," and I realized that it must be a term of endearment. Like honey bunny. The dialogues we had practiced in Russian class had not prepared me for actual conversations. *What did you do on Saturday?* our Russian professor would ask, stretching his words out like Silly Putty so that we could understand. We didn't know how to say, *I drank too much at a bad party,* but we could say, *I gathered mushrooms* or *I took a walk in the park.* Our textbooks implied that Russians spent a lot of time gathering mushrooms and walking in parks.

"You like the dogs?" Svetlana said to me as the woman walked away.

"I love dogs," I said.

"*Ya tozhe.*" Me, too. "I have the dog. His name is Pushkin."

"Like the poet," I said.

"You know Pushkin? I thought Americans were not so cultured."

"I was an English major," I said. "I've read a lot of poetry."

The truth is, I'd read only one Pushkin poem: "Ya Vas Lubil." I Loved You Once. We had to memorize it in first-year Russian. "I loved you once: perhaps that love has yet / To die down thoroughly within my soul." Apparently no English translation does him justice.

"The church where Pushkin married is here in center of Moscow," she said. Pushkin was from St. Petersburg, but Moscow had its share of monuments to him. A Metro station bore his name.

"Your English is good," I said. It was better than her letter suggested.

"I take the mistakes," she said. *"Nu, spasibo."* Thank you.

"You're welcome," I said. Then I said it again in Russian.

She deliberated, then said, "In Russian your accent sounds like you are from Gruziya, you know?"

"Georgia," I said. I knew that this was an insult. Georgians and other people from the Caucasus were looked down upon.

"Da."

"Like Stalin?" I wanted to remind her that someone from Georgia had once been in charge of the whole Soviet Union, even if it was with devastating results.

"Da, tochno." Yes, exactly. "You sound like Stalin." She laughed. Her laugh was a girlish confection, the sort of giggle induced by intense tickling.

On the pond, ducks made serene circles, and on the other side a young couple walked hand in hand. The man wore a blue Adidas tracksuit. I could hear him coaxing, *"Pochemu nyet?"* Why not? I wondered if he was trying to get her into bed.

"In winter this is for the skating," Sveta said. "The pond is frozen, the boys play hockey."

"Must be nice," I said.

"You will stay for winter?"

"Maybe," I said. "If I can renew my visa."

"You are married?"

"No," I said, shocked by the question. "I'm only twenty-two. Are *you* married?"

"Divorced," she said. Later I'd learn that many Russian women my age were divorced. They married at eighteen or nineteen, and the unions dissolved a few years later. To be unmarried at my age was to be an old maid.

"I have something to show you," I said. I pulled Jenny's book out of my bag.

Svetlana took the book and held it on her lap gently, as if it might break. With a sharp intake of breath, she extended a finger and traced the contours of Jenny's face. And then her other hand moved over her own youthful image. She fell into a sort of reverie as her fingers drew a frame around the two girls in the photograph. "She was first American I met," she said softly. "At first I was afraid, *ponimayesh?*"

"I understand," I said.

"Americans were supposed to be danger. But she was *ochen* . . . charming."

"Yes," I said. "Very charming."

"One night," Svetlana said, "I was permitted to stay with her in hotel. You cannot imagine how magical this was for me. A hotel! With the American! She removed her dress, and before she took the gown for sleeping—"

"Nightgown," I said.

"Nightgown, yes—before she put on the nightgown, I look at her and I think, 'This is *American* girl in her underwear.' Do you know she had flowers on her underwear? The little blue flowers."

I knew exactly which pair of underpants she was talking about.

"Soviet underwear was never so pretty. And I could not believe I was seeing American girl in her American underwear. She was like the . . ." She paused as she groped for a word. Then she mimed a horn extending from her head and looked at me for help.

"Unicorn?"

She smiled. "*Da.* Jennifer was like the unicorn."

She was, I thought. I'd felt a similar sense of joyous disbelief when she emerged in my life. "Have you seen this book before?" I said.

Svetlana shook her head. She was rubbing the tip of her finger on Jenny's pink cheek, as if the photo might release a wish-granting genie.

"There are more pictures of you in it," I said. I knew the book so well that I could have told her exactly which pages those pic-tures were on. I had it memorized. I watched her turn the pages.

"We were just girls," she said. "We believed everything they told us."

"Who?"

"Our parents, our governments," she said. "I believed in the party. I would stand when the Soviet anthem played on the TV. I had the picture of Lenin on my wall." She laughed.

"And now?" I said.

"Now I have the picture of Kate Moss," she said. "You know this British model?"

I nodded.

"After Jennifer returned to America, we promised to write the letters to each other . . ." she said. "But this was not possible. There were censors." She closed the book with a sigh.

"Did you ever hear from her again?"

"*Da,*" she said.

"When?" I said.

She returned the book without answering me. "*Ladno.* Now we will begin our tour. You don't mind to walk?"

"No," I said. "I like walking." I stood and awaited direction.

"*Krasnaya Ploschad,*" she said. We would start in Red Square.

⊕

SVETLANA LIT ANOTHER CIGARETTE as we walked along Bol-shaya Nikitskaya toward the Kremlin.

"The plane that Jennifer was on," I said, "was completely incinerated. No one could have survived that crash."

"How you know she was on the plane?"

"Because," I said. "The airport had a passenger list. There were names, there were official records."

Svetlana snorted. "Official records! Officials are bribed to change documents. This is absolutely normal in Russia."

"Do you have proof that Jennifer is alive?"

"Proof," she said. "Like geometry, *da*?"

"I came all the way here—" I said.

She cut me off. "And I will show you Moscow. Trust me."

⌗

As we entered Red Square, she said, "Unfortunately, is not possible to visit Lenin today. Mausoleum is closed."

Russians start a lot of sentences with "Unfortunately"; they are used to explaining what is not possible. But she showed me the plaques marking people buried in the Kremlin walls, including Brezhnev and John Reed, the American who wrote about the 1917 revolution in *Ten Days That Shook the World*.

"It's like the picture of Jenny," I said.

"Chto?" What?

"There's a picture of Jennifer standing right here, by these tombs," I said. "In her book. Are we allowed to take photographs here?" I removed my camera from my backpack and cast a nervous glance at the soldiers in front of Lenin's tomb.

"Is possible," said Sveta. So I showed her how to use my Nikon, and we re-created the picture from Jenny's book. I posed with my hands in my pockets under the plaque marking the grave of Yuri Gagarin, the first man in space.

We weren't the only ones taking pictures in front of the tombs. A bride fluttered in white next to her groom. It was customary, Svetlana explained, for newly married couples to visit a monument. It was hard to imagine a place less romantic than that wall commemorating the dead. But on our way through the Alexandrovsky Garden, we saw another pair of newlyweds by the even less romantic Tomb of the Unknown Soldier. The groom looked sour and rotting; the bride kept fussing with his tie, as if she could straighten his mood.

In Russian the word for "married" is different for men and for women. Married women are *zamuzhem;* if you break down the word to its roots, it translates as "behind the man." In college I had deconstructed Russian words as a mnemonic device. As a preposition, *za* can mean "behind" or "after," and as a prefix it begins verbs like those for "forget" (*To put the past behind you,* I'd tell myself as I flipped through vocabulary flash cards in the library) and "conceal" (*To put the facts behind closed doors,* I thought) and "envy" (*To see behind or look askance at*), to "fall silent," to "imprison," to "finish," and to "close." And yes, to get married. To get behind the man.

I asked Svetlana about this. She stopped and looked at me as if I were a curious specimen under a microscope. "You think too much," she said. "This American feminism is no good. Is not sexy."

I've never liked the word "sexy." In high school my friends tried it on as if it were a costume a few sizes too big. Before Valentine's Day they made stealthy trips to Victoria's Secret, in hopes that a shock of red or black lace under their well-mannered clothes would persuade them that they had wild sides waiting to be unleashed. The boys at our brother school ranked us according to "hotness," and as offended as we were by their rampant objectification of us as women, there was not a girl among us who didn't secretly long to be on their hot list. The boys even devoted a page in their yearbook to the girls they deemed worthy of pinup status. It was a predictable group: athletic and sun-kissed; the hair was long, the breasts pert. We knew the boys weren't worthy of passing judgment on us. And yet we had spent our lives chasing approval. We had been trained to get A's. We were good at taking tests. We abided by rules and honor codes. We underlined our books, made careful observations in the margins, aced our SATs. And so these sons of statesmen, uniformed in blue blazers—they pulled off their ties at the end of the school day and swung them around like weapons—became another jury for us to please. Before we walked across the Cathedral Close to play fans at the boys' lacrosse games, we brushed our hair, glossed our lips. They wore helmets; they brandished their lacrosse sticks like Vikings.

"I'm so relieved I'm not on the Babes page," I said, commiserating with the others who had been passed over, but cloistered in the bathroom at home under the magnifying lights I studied my deficiencies. My cheekbones were high, my lashes were long, but I was too pale, my boobs were too small. I counted every clogged pore. One nostril was smaller than the other. And I knew that the real flaws were inside. Jenny, I thought, would have been one of the "hot" ones. Not just because of the symmetry in her features but because of the easy harmony of her moods. She was open to other people, she was game. She assumed that people would like her, and so they did.

"This is why you do not have husband," Svetlana continued after a few minutes.

"You don't have a husband anymore either," I said.

She slit her eyes at me. "My ex-husband is Dutch," she said. "This was the mistake. I wanted to marry foreigner, the man with money. But the Dutch . . ." She paused before she made her pronouncement. "They are not passionate people."

"Van Gogh wasn't passionate?" I said.

"He was madman."

"Where is your ex-husband now?"

"Oh, he is still in Moscow. He has new girlfriend from Scotland. I have seen her once. She is fat and red." She flicked her cigarette onto the ground and returned the pack to her purse. "And now I live again with my parents. Until I find the new husband. I want an Italian this time. I am studying Italian. It would be nice to live in Napoli. I would eat beautiful pasta every day. I was traveling there last year. You know Napoli?"

I told her I'd been there for a couple of days.

"You cannot imagine how wonderful it is for us now, to be able to travel abroad. To finally see the world," she said. "This was best thing about perestroika. Life was good then. We were free to travel, but our economy was not so bad. Gorbachev was better than Yeltsin."

Svetlana proved to be an exacting guide. There was a lot to see, and she was not going to let me skip anything. She unspooled historical dates and facts without pause. "This is very old church," she said as we entered St. Basil's. Ivan the Terrible commissioned it in 1555 and then, according to legend, had its architect blinded so that he could never again build something so beautiful. That's Russia for you: there's always violence in the wings. After our visit to St. Basil's, Svetlana took me to GUM, which had begun its transformation from state-run department store to Western-style mall. The empty shelves of perestroika were now filled with foreign goods that few people could afford. The new tenants were Reebok and Benetton and Adidas, though the ubiqitous tracksuits sported on the streets of the city were mostly knockoffs. And the bathrooms, I discovered, were depressingly spartan and devoid of toilet paper.

Svetlana stopped to buy ice cream at a kiosk. It was wrapped in waxy paper; she peeled it away with a gesture that struck me as nostalgic. As she licked the cone, I saw traces of the eager child she must have been.

"What did Jennifer say about me?" I asked her.

"*Kogda?*" When?

"You said she told you a lot about me . . ."

"She said you were *grustnaya.*"

"That's sad," I said.

"*Da,*" she said. "You were sad."

She told Svetlana I was sad? Did she mean sad as in pathetic? Didn't she have anything better to say about me? Over the years I'd learned that some people are frightened by sadness, by intense feeling of any kind, and around such people I had learned to stay on guard, aware that revealing any vulnerability would push them away. I had other friends after Jenny, but she was the last person I completely let in, the last one to spend any time with my mother in our haunted house. I was sure that people would like me better if they didn't know where I came from. In high school I approximated an easygoing air, and in college I found a vaguely literary crowd in which a melancholy streak and bleak humor were practically required for membership. But the fact that Svetlana was dismissing me as "sad" seemed ironic given that she was Russian. Russians had a predilection for the tragic, didn't they? Surely this was a place where I wouldn't have to apologize for not being happy all the time. I liked reading the Russians—all those ill-fated love affairs set against desolate landscapes. I was partial to unhappy endings. Misery loves company.

THEN WE WENT TO THE KREMLIN. "*Kreml* means 'fortress,'" Sveta said. Like a game-show hostess, she gestured at the medieval walls that had kept people out for so long. There were two different admission prices: one for Russians, a much higher one for foreigners. This was typical, Svetlana said. All the museums also had a separate price for foreigners. I had no idea how many buildings the Kremlin complex contained. I would have been content to breeze through the grounds, but Svetlana insisted on a lengthy, formal tour. "Here is possible to see world's largest bell," she said of the Tsar-kolokol, which cracked before it ever rang and now sits, dormant, beside the bell tower. "Here is possible to see Assumption Cathedral," she said as we entered the building where heads of the Russian Orthodox Church were buried until the early eighteenth century. "Here you can see icons from twelfth and thirteenth centuries." This was not an interactive tour. She moved me from point to point like a toy on a factory assembly line. There were other groups of tourists being herded in similar fashion. Many of them clutched guidebooks as if they were security blankets. "Here is possible to see Annunciation Cathedral, built in 1484. Here you can see famous icons of Theophanes."

"So many cathedrals, so many icons," I said. So many onion domes, I thought. I was exhausted.

She studied me, trying to make sense of my comment.

"Religion's making a comeback, isn't it?" I said.

"What is this 'comeback'?"

"I mean, it's coming back. People are rediscovering religion?"

"Yes, well, Orthodox Church is suddenly very—how do you say it?—popular. You know, people followed the party, now they follow church. Unfortunately, I cannot say if they are true believers."

"So you came here with Jennifer?"

"What?"

"I mean, to the Kremlin. To all these churches."

"*Da, konechno.*" Yes, of course.

"Do you mind if I take a picture of you outside? By the czar's cannon, maybe?"

"*Pochemu?*" Why? Most Russians were understandably wary of cameras.

"My mother wants me to take pictures of the places Jenny visited when she was here . . ."

"When she was here?"

"*Da.*"

"You understand, of course, is possible she is here now."

"You've seen her?"

"Maybe," she said.

"If she's really alive, tell me where she is."

"I cannot tell you that. Not yet." Svetlana smiled. "Now we will see Armory. Many beautiful treasures to behold."

She had switched back into guide mode. Clearly I wasn't going to get any more personal information out of her that day. I followed her through the rooms of the Armory Museum in a daze. Sveta pointed at czarist regalia and Fabergé eggs, but I couldn't focus on the jewels. It was Jenny I was thinking about.

When we finally emerged from the Armory, it was nearly five o'clock and I was famished. "I'm hungry," I said in Russian. Actually, the construction I used translates as "I want to eat," which seemed appropriately insistent given how desperately my stomach needed to be filled.

Svetlana nodded. She said she'd take me back to Patriarch's

Ponds and resume our tour another day. "To be continued," she said. "Yes?"

"*Da,*" I said.

#

THAT NIGHT CORINNE TOLD me we were going out. I'd been in Moscow for nearly two weeks and had finally adjusted to the time difference. She told me I needed to get out and meet some people. It was Saturday, and Corinne said we'd start at Rosie O'Grady's, an Irish pub where all the expats went. It was already cold enough to require winter jackets. I wore the same navy peacoat that had shielded me from Vermont winters, but Corinne was in fur.

"I know, I know," she said when she saw me looking at her coat. "I was against fur before I came here. But then you realize that nothing else keeps you warm enough."

On the street she said, "We'll take a cab," and then stuck out her arm. I hadn't seen a single taxi since I arrived, but I soon learned that "taking a cab" was a euphemism for sanctioned hitchhiking. People just hailed any car that would stop, negotiated a price, and trusted that he—I never saw a woman driver—would take you where you had asked to go. It was a beat-up Neva that pulled over for us, and I was sure that my mother would be distraught if she knew I was climbing into a stranger's car, especially after dark, in a city where men were almost never sober. There were no seat belts in the back, and the driver's face was at best surly, at worst downright hostile, but I kept telling myself, *When in*

Rome . . . while Corinne began a rapid-fire exchange in Russian, most of which I couldn't comprehend. I don't think I let out my breath until we pulled up in front of the bar fifteen minutes later. Corinne passed some rubles to the front seat and then opened the door. We were out.

There was nothing remarkable about Rosie O'Grady's: it was a generic Irish pub, with signs for Guinness and wooden stools lining the bar. But as a foreign-owned bar in the city, it was to Moscow's expats what Rick's was to the denizens of *Casablanca*. Corinne seemed to know everyone: the *Newsweek* bureau chief who was complaining about his wife back in New York; the NPR reporter who kept twisting the resin bracelets on her arm as she spoke in a husky, smoke-filled voice; the economist from India who preached privatization; the Texan oil worker who bought me a beer and called me—without a trace of irony—"little lady." After a week spent struggling to piece together the conversations I'd heard in Russian, it was a surreal relief to be surrounded by voices speaking English. They were French, Swedish, Italian, British, Canadian, Australian, Indian, German, American, and Irish—the bartender took our orders with a brogue—and though they spoke with varying degrees of proficiency, it was English they conversed in. They traded stories of entanglement with Soviet-style bureaucracy. They bemoaned the lack of customer service. They diagnosed the ailing Russian economy and shook their heads about oligarchs. They told jokes about New Russians. (*New Russian #1: Nice tie. New Russian #2: It cost three hundred dollars. New Russian #1: You fool! You could've gotten it for five hundred around the corner.*)

And they were full of advice for me, the rookie in their midst. *Don't use credit cards*, they said. *Even at the fancy restaurants. They'll steal your card number and charge up a storm. . . . Beware of the Gypsy kids*, they said. *They'll descend on you around the Metro stations. They might look cute, but they'll pick your pockets clean. . . . Beware when someone shouts "Militsiya!" or "Police!"—it's just a tactic to divert your attention while someone else steals your money. . . . Be careful of making agreements with Russians*, they said. *Everyone lies*, they said. *. . . Russians are so xenophobic*, they said. *And racist. . . . Flowers*, they said. *Russians love flowers. Men and women. Give them flowers on their birthdays or when you visit their homes. But make sure you never give a bouquet with an even number of flowers. It's bad luck. Eleven flowers, thirteen flowers, but never a dozen.* I was learning a great deal about Russian superstition. *If you put a lot of salt in your cooking, it means you are in love*, Svetlana had told me earlier. *If you brush crumbs off the table into your hand, you will fight with your lover.* And she said, *Don't ever sit at the corner of a table during a meal, or you will never be married.* I said it was too late: I'd spent many years in corners.

"So what brought you to Moscow?" the expats asked. They offered their own history as pioneers: every story an epic with an adventurous hero. Their expat avatars were less timid, less awkward than the identities they inhabited at home.

"I don't know," I said, which has always been my answer when I don't feel like elaborating.

"She wants to be a journalist," said Corinne. She was on her third vodka tonic and getting louder and more strident.

They were all getting louder, actually. I hadn't been around so many drunk people since college. Their drinking was reckless and a little frightening, as each glass erased more of the evening's composition. *Is this adulthood?* I thought. *I graduated to* this? There were plenty of journalists there, from the *New York Times*, the *Washington Post*, CNN. They burped booze as they passed me their business cards and urged me to get in touch. Someone from the *Moscow Times* assured me he could get me a job as a copy editor. "You're obviously a smart girl," he said.

And then Corinne said, "We're going dancing," and I found myself carried by the flow back out into the street. There were two women with us—the husky-voiced NPR reporter and an Australian named Molly, who bent over to vomit right there on the sidewalk while Corinne hailed a car. "Propaganda!" Corinne said triumphantly from the front seat as the rest of us squeezed into the back. "Propaganda!" Molly said, with a hiccup. I cracked a window to get some air and hoped that Molly wouldn't throw up on me, and then I closed my eyes against the driver's dangerous maneuvers. It was only when the car slammed to a stop that I realized that "Propaganda" was our destination.

Propaganda was a nightclub, and it was dollars that Corinne and the NPR reporter shoved at the bouncer to buy our admission. Inside, techno music throbbed in the semidarkness, and both Russians and foreigners tangled on the dance floor. It was easy to spot the Russian women under the lights: they were much skinnier than the Westerners, and their skin—from years of poor nutrition, perhaps—was sallow. We took a table in the corner—"Not too close to the deejay!" said Corinne—and a petulant waitress took our order. When the shots arrived, I shook my head, but Corinne would not accept my refusal. "You're in Moscow," she said. "You have to drink vodka."

Three shots later I was dancing with the others. Corinne jerked around like a marionette. Molly wobbled back and forth like an inflatable toy. The woman from NPR, who finally told me her name was Leslie, closed her eyes in a sort of trance. Some of the people I'd met at Rosie O'Grady's arrived. Most of the men were grinding with bony Russian women—including the married man from the *Newsweek* bureau, I noticed—but I stayed close to Corinne and her friends, who agreed they wouldn't sleep with a Russian man for all the money in the world.

"Chauvinist pigs," said Molly, shiny with sweat.

"There must be exceptions," I said. The cocktail of smoke and disco lights was making me dizzy.

"I don't think so," said Corinne, her breath heavy in my ear. "The women are doing all the work in this country. The men are just getting drunk."

"The women here are strategic," said Molly. "Some of them get pregnant on purpose to make their American or European boyfriends marry them."

A Swedish banker split his pants trying to replicate an Italian's dance moves, and that's when Corinne decided it was time for us to go. We stumbled out into the cold.

"Let's walk for a bit to sober up," said Corinne.

The air was bracing. I wished I'd worn a hat. I trailed her along a quiet street, and then we were on Tverskaya and Corinne was marching down the steps to cross the street in one of the underground passageways. All the big Moscow avenues have crosswalks below the street, like the tunnels that connect New York subway stations, so that cars don't have to stop for pedestrians. I'd been in this very *perekhod* during the day, when human traffic shuffled through. But now it was four o'clock in the morning and empty except for prostitutes—I counted eleven of them—lined up against the wall like criminals waiting to be identified. Corinne and I stopped in our tracks. An oafish man stood in front of the girls, rocking back and forth on his feet, trying to choose. The girls were young—as young as fourteen, I'd say—and the one he selected reminded me of a rabbit: she had large, frightened eyes, and she stepped forward and then froze, twitching. I averted my own eyes. When I looked up, I could see the backs of her stockinged legs—a black seam slicing down each of her calves—as she disappeared up the stairs with the oaf. The lineup dissolved into the shadows. The other girls clustered in groups of three or four, passing around lighters as they fired up their smokes.

"That was horrible," I said when we were safely up the stairs on the other side of the street.

"You'll get used to it," Corinne said. "There's a terrible story about a foreigner who went home with a prostitute, had sex with her, and then realized her grandmother was in the other bed in the room and had been there the whole time. Maybe it's urban legend, but it's totally plausible."

"Yikes."

"You know what they call hookers here?"

I shook my head.

"Night butterflies," she said. *"Nochnye babochki."*

"Lovely," I said.

"And you know what the slang for 'pussy' is?"

"No."

"Bunker," she said in a Russian accent. "Means the same thing as in English. A bunker, where dicks can hunker down and feel safe."

"Until the postcoital fallout," I said.

"Exactly," she said. "Sam said you were funny."

"He did?" It was good to remember that I had friends who didn't just think I was sad.

"He sings your praises. Did you ever hook up?"

"With Sam? No. We're just friends." Sam and I had been friends since our freshman-orientation camping trip. He was a fixture of my campus life.

"I think he has a little crush on you. He talks about you a lot." She burped. "I've been drinking, so it's full-disclosure time."

It was nearly five when we got home. I'd never been so intoxicated and haven't been so since. I spent the next two hours stretched out on the bathroom floor, lifting my head every ten minutes to clutch the toilet bowl. Corinne drank two glasses of water and went to sleep. She had already built up a tolerance for Russia.

8.

ULITSA PETROVKA WAS A NARROW STREET. It was one of the places in Moscow that probably hadn't changed much in a hundred years, though its Old World charm was tarnished by chipped moldings and peeling paint. The entrance foyer of number 26 was in a state of aggressive decay. A uniformed *militsiya* man stood outside the booth that had been installed next to the elevator, his rifle on prominent display.

"*Pasport,*" he said. The word is the same in Russian and English, but he fired it at me in such a threatening manner that it took me a moment to understand. I felt like I was at Checkpoint Charlie and might be shot if I tried to get over the Berlin Wall. I shimmied my passport out of my bag—despite warnings about pickpockets,

I refused to carry one of the hidden wallets or fanny packs that so many Americans use—and handed it to him. He studied my passport while I studied him. He could not have been older than I was. His cheeks were pocked with scars, and his chin was corrupted by cystic acne. One pimple was particularly ripe; the pus was practically oozing out.

"Amerikanka?" he said. I nodded. Obviously I was American, not just because my passport had been issued by the United States but because my body's stiff, awkward simulation of deference revealed how unaccustomed I was to having my movements monitored. Sure, we had to go through airport security and show ID to buy beer, but we never questioned our freedom or our privacy. In 1995 I was not used to being watched. I was a privileged, white, American girl; I had never before worried that I'd be arrested or detained. The sight of this guard's gun changed that. He seemed tempted to punish me just because he could.

"Otkuda vy?" he asked. Where are you from?

"Washington," I said. *"Iz Vashingtona."*

"CIA?" he said.

"Nyet," I said quickly. *"Studyentka."*

I was not a student anymore, but I wasn't anything else yet. And I didn't remember the words for any other professions. He raised an eyebrow. I suppose my grasp (a tenuous grasp, but most Americans don't speak *any* Russian) of his language made him suspicious. Either that or I was so busy trying not to seem suspicious that I was especially suspect.

He picked up the red phone in his booth. *"Allo?"* he said, and then began talking so fast that I couldn't follow anything, except that he definitely said, *"Amerikanskaya devushka"* (American girl) twice. He paused for a long time, listening and interjecting an occasional *"Ladno"* while I tried not to gawk at the acne on his chin. He hung up the phone and regarded me. I waited. He didn't release me from his stare.

"Moy pasport?" I said, reaching for it. He stepped toward me and adjusted his gun. *"Nelzya,"* he said. It was forbidden.

I didn't know what to do. There were no cell phones then. The public telephones in Moscow were broken. ("I've never found one that works," Corinne had told me.) I was supposed to meet Svetlana upstairs in the DDBD office on the seventh floor at eleven o'clock. I was late. And it was clear that I was not permitted to move. This was a mistake, I thought. Jenny had been a guest of the Soviet government, so she saw only the best of Russia. But I was on my own in a city so crooked that you couldn't count on the law to protect you. I didn't know where the American embassy was, but I vowed to find out as soon as I got my passport back. My mother's anxiety about Moscow suddenly didn't seem so unfounded.

I stood there for what felt like hours trying to avoid the officer's gaze. I did not have the Russian vocabulary to ask why he was keeping me there. I could feel tremors creeping up my body and willed myself not to cry. *I'm going to end up in prison,* I thought. *I'll be put in one of those cages they lock the accused in during Russian trials, like a zoo animal in the courtroom. I won't even know why I'm on trial. I'll be sent to rot in Siberia.* My brain was stuck in these Kafka-

and Solzhenitsyn-powered circuits—*Gulag,* I kept thinking, *gulag*—and then I heard the feminine click of heels on the stairs.

"So at last you are here." I looked up to see Svetlana in a gray pencil skirt and a crisp white blouse. Mascara had caked in the corners of her eyes, but otherwise she looked very professional. She said something feisty to the guard in Russian, and he wilted. With stooped shoulders he gave me my passport and a curt nod. "Do not worry about him," Svetlana said to me. "He just needs to feel important."

"Lift ne rabotayet," he said, which can be translated as "The elevator isn't working (right now)" or "The elevator doesn't work (generally)." The latter seemed more accurate.

I was beginning to understand that elevators never worked in Moscow. "Soon it will be fixed," people said to save face, but as with so much of the infrastructure, one had the sense that they couldn't be fixed anytime soon. And so we began the long climb up to the seventh floor. The stairs were wide and dark—the bulbs in each stairwell were out—and despite the grand sweep of the entrance hall the successive flights narrowed. I was short of breath when we reached the top. There were piles of cigarette ash on the floor. Svetlana opened the door and ushered me in.

The office took up the whole floor of the building, and the walls had been knocked down to create one big, open space with large windows looking out at the Bolshoi. The carpet was an industrial gray, and wooden tables were plotted around the room, most of them crowned with desktop PCs. The people at these computers were smoking, and the air was gauzy with unfiltered cigarette smoke. A plate of glass separated two large, private offices from the main room. Blinds were drawn in one; in the other a bearded man sat at a desk and smiled strenuously as he held a phone to his ear.

"Our directors," said Svetlana, gesturing at the offices.

"So this is an ad agency," I said. I had never been inside an ad agency, but my impression had been that they were shiny places where the phones never stopped ringing. This smoky, sleepy room did not measure up.

"Come with me," Sveta said, and led me on a cursory lap around the room.

"Oleg," she said, indicating a heavy-lidded man playing solitaire on his computer. He held his cigarette in one hand and operated his mouse with the other. "He is art director." Oleg squinted at me, then returned to his game.

"This is Svetlana," she said as we passed a desk occupied by a plump, rosy woman in a green satin blouse. "She is bookkeeper. There are three Svetlanas in our company," she added.

"Volodya," she said about a lumpen figure in a sweater vest. He was bent over his desk reading a newspaper.

Then she marched to an empty desk in the center. She pulled an extra chair up next to her own and patted the seat, encouraging me. I sat.

"I am copywriter," she said. She handed me a business card. The word "copywriter" had been transliterated into Cyrillic: КОПИРАЙТЕР.

"That's the word in Russian?"

She nodded. It was one of many English words and phrases that had infected the language. Restaurants all over Moscow now offered a business lunch or, as the menus said in Russian, БИЗНЕС ЛАНЧ ("biznes lanch").

"I studied architecture," said Svetlana. "But you know, now the only decent jobs are at foreign companies."

"So you write ads?"

She nodded vigorously. "Why not? You think I cannot?"

"I didn't say that."

She lit a cigarette. Then she pointed at a framed poster on the opposite wall. It was a picture of the New York City skyline, with a giant Lucky Strike pack hovering above the Twin Towers. There was some kind of slogan in Russian on it. I sounded out the Cyrillic in my head.

"Does that say 'The American Dream'?" I said.

Sveta nodded. "Yes. To advertise Lucky Strike, we sell USA."

"And it works?"

"When Western brands came to Russia for first time, it was exciting. McDonald's, Nike, Levi's, Marlboro. People could not wait to buy. It was—how do you say in English?—status sign?"

"Status symbol."

"*Tochno.* Status symbol."

I'd seen the lines outside the first McDonald's on TV. It was crazy to imagine waiting hours for a Big Mac.

"Everyone wanted to taste USA. It was cool. It was taste of freedom. All you had to do was say something was American or

British and people would get in the line to buy it. *Bozhe moy!* The long lines for the free samples of Colgate toothpaste and Tampax. You know Tampax?"

"Too well," I said. All the smoke was making my eyes water. I surveyed the room. One Russian man I hadn't seen before looked about my age and was surprisingly preppy. He wore a blue oxford shirt marked with a Ralph Lauren polo pony. I smiled weakly at him and coughed.

"And now the attitudes start to change," Sveta continued. "People are tired of America. We were superpower and now? Our country is taking money from IMF? People abroad think our stores are empty, that no one has the bread to eat. People think Mother Russia is broken. Yeltsin is always drunk. He is the big joke. People are ready for Russia to rise up and become the superpower again." She seemed to be directing her aggression toward me.

"The Cold War is over," I said defensively.

"Da." She was emphatic. "But Russia is still great country. Russia is member of UN Security Council. Russia is champion. I am proud to be Russian. People want to be proud to be Russian. They do not want the shame."

"Of course not."

"During Communism we had no choice. We bought what there was. Now we have choice, so people want best quality. And the goods from the West were better quality. Better cigarettes, better toothpaste, better shampoo, better tennis shoes, and so on. Now: We must to make Russian products better. New standards. Competition. And so: Why must I smoke Marlboro if I want the quality tobacco? Why not Russian brand? Why must I drink Pepsi if I want the quality cola?"

She held out a can for me. It was white with a red-and-blue logo; at first glance I thought it was a Pepsi. But on closer inspection, I realized that the logo said CZAR. The letters were in Russian on one side, in English—in a font reminiscent of old Soviet posters—on the other.

"Czar?" I said.

"Our newest account," said a British voice. "We're spelling 'tsar' with a z because it's more dynamic."

The voice belonged to the bearded guy I'd seen through the glass of the director's office, the one who had been smiling on the phone. He was deflated and paunchy.

Svetlana stood at attention. "Richard, this is the American friend which I told you about. Sarah, this is my boss, Richard."

"I'm the creative director here at DDBD Moskva," he said, and rested his fists on his hips, in the ready posture of a superhero. I stood to shake his hand. His fingers were doughy and stained with ink.

"Svetlana here is a real go-getter," he said. "A real asset to our team."

Svetlana beamed like a teacher's pet.

"Taste it," said Richard, indicating the can in my hand. "I think you'll find it surprisingly good."

The can was warm, but there was no point asking for ice. Russians didn't put ice in their beverages. I popped the lid; the whoosh of released carbonation was convincing. It sounded as authentically American as Coca-Cola. I took a sip. It was sweeter than Coke—sweeter than Pepsi, even—with a metallic aftertaste that made me think of blood.

"Tasty, yes?" said Sveta.

"Ochen," I lied. Very.

"The brand won't launch for another year, but it's going to be brilliant. Finally a Russian cola that is good enough to compete with the Americans." Richard seemed more than a little eager to defeat the Americans.

I didn't tell him that I was half British. I was tempted to remind him that he worked for an American company but decided to steer the conversation out of nationalist waters. "Who are your other clients?" I said.

Richard was delighted to talk about the agency. They had opened its Moscow office in 1994. It was a joint venture with a Russian company. There was an American managing director, he said—"Mike is in New York this week"—and a Russian MD, who sat in the office with the blinds drawn. Their biggest clients were P&G and British American Tobacco. Svetlana lit another cigarette.

"We're growing fast," Richard said.

I took another sip of Czar. It was tolerable but still tasted like a knockoff. It was like those designer-perfume impostors from the 1980s. *If you like Coke,* I thought, *you'll love Czar.*

Richard burrowed a finger into his beard. His voice assumed the patronizing tone of a commencement speaker. He'd started in the London office but had worked for years in New York, and most recently in Prague, so he said he really knew the Eastern European market. Advertising, he said, was a wonderful business. A creative business. But this office was a special challenge, since advertising was a new concept in Russia. There were three expats in the office: two Americans, one Brit. The expats had a lot of industry experience, he said, and had been hired to teach the local staff how to run an agency. "The Russians don't know the first thing about marketing. They don't know about initiative. About competition. Or about hard work. We're teaching them how to be creative. How to be professional." He said all this in front of Sveta and in earshot of her Russian colleagues, and more than a few jaws clenched in response. Oleg the solitaire player looked especially vexed.

Much later I learned that because Richard could no longer get good jobs in London or New York, he had allowed a headhunter to lure him to Moscow under the premise that a stint on the "marketing frontier" would be a boon to his CV. Moscow was a plum assignment for journalists and diplomats, but for advertising creatives it signaled a career in decline. They weren't going to win awards at Cannes for Russian campaigns. When expats like Richard returned to their native countries, they hoped to find juicy offers waiting for them. In fact, their time in Moscow usually dulled their prospects. The bureaucratic red tape and mafia kickbacks exhausted them, and they eventually resigned themselves to getting drunk. Almost every expat I met had a serious drinking problem. And Richard didn't speak a word of Russian. He'd been there for over a year and hadn't made an effort to learn the language.

Richard seemed grateful for an audience. I was young and,

he must have thought, impressionable, and because I nodded and smiled as he pontificated about advertising, he proposed that I "brainstorm" ideas for the campaign.

"What campaign?" I said.

"Czar," he said. "You're American. You know about soft drinks. Maybe you can help Svetlana here come up with something."

"I don't know anything about advertising," I said.

"That's where you're wrong," he said. "Americans know everything about selling. It's in your DNA. I'm sure you can teach Svetlana quite a bit."

I couldn't tell if Sveta was annoyed that I was being encouraged to take her job away from her. When Richard wandered off, I turned to her. "I don't want to be a copywriter," I said. "I want to be a journalist."

"What is difference?" she said.

"In my country there's a big difference," I said. Even as I said it, I wasn't sure I could defend that position. Svetlana inspired knee-jerk reactions in me. With her I was an absolutist.

The Russian in the Ralph Lauren shirt ambled over to Svetlana's desk and asked her for a cigarette. She tossed him one, and he lit it, expelling the smoke from a sly corner of his mouth. *"Amerikanka?"* he said to me.

"Da," I said.

He asked me where I was from. I told him. He started to laugh. "I lived in Washington," he said in Russian.

"Tochno?" I said. Really? Then I wondered if I had misunderstood him. I looked to Svetlana for help.

"Andrei's father was the diplomat," she said. "In Vashingtone in 1980s."

The Russian embassy was a short walk from my house. Construction had started on Mount Alto—a controversial location, since it was one of the highest points in the city, an ideal place for surveillance—in the eighties, and even before the new embassy opened years later, its employees and their families were housed in apartments on site. In high school I used to see Russian men stumbling out of The Good Guys, the strip club a few blocks away on Wisconsin Avenue.

"How long did he live in Washington?" I said to Sveta.

Andrei answered me. His English was so devoid of accent that he sounded American. And I realized that he could have passed as American for another reason: he was so clean. He looked like a man who showered every day. Russians thought our American obsession with cleanliness was neurotic. "Four years," he said. "From 1985 to 1989. I was there when we discovered your tunnel."

The United States had built a tunnel under the Russian embassy in an attempt to plant listening devices, but the operation was exposed before any intelligence could be gleaned from it. Supposedly Robert Hanssen told the Soviets about it years before he was arrested for espionage.

"Not my tunnel," I said.

"Not *your* tunnel," he said. His eyes were teasing and blue. I couldn't tell if he was flirtatious or cruel. *"Spasibo za sigaretu,"* he said, and returned to his desk.

"Andrei is the account executive," said Svetlana.

She stubbed out her cigarette in the glass ashtray on the corner of her desk. It was from the Hotel Kempinski. When she saw me eyeing its logo, she said softly, "I took it from the room after I slept with a German. He was the guest there." I must have looked shocked. "What? You don't have the sex? Americans are such prude," she said.

I was getting tired of hearing generalizations about Americans. I wanted to explain that it was her unapologetically transactional attitude to sex that surprised me, but I changed the subject instead. "I thought you were taking me somewhere today," I said. I was getting impatient. Svetlana had lured me all the way to Moscow, and for what? To show me the promise of Russian consumer goods? "I thought you knew something about Jennifer."

"*Da,*" she said. "Our excursion. Come with me."

9.

I FOLLOWED SVETLANA DOWN THE STREET, where she paused for an endearingly wistful look into the window of a clothing boutique—"The Italians make such beautiful things," she said— past the grand façades of the Bolshoi Theater and the Hotel Metropol, and then we took a left. Sveta moved like a whisper: it was as if her feet didn't touch the ground at all, as if she were floating on her opera cape. She wasn't fast—I had to slow my natural gait to keep my pace with her—but she had a dancer's control and grace. We were heading toward Lubyanka Square, the home of what was once the KGB.

"Now there is museum at KGB," she said. She pronounced it the Russian way, Ka-Guh-Beh, the initials cloaked and thuggish.

When we entered Lubyanskaya Ploschad, though, the KGB building was far less imposing than I had imagined. Its Baroque exterior and mustard yellow walls suggested nothing more malevolent than impenetrable bureaucracy. After the coup, she told me, people descended like vultures and tore down the statue of Felix Dzerzhinsky that had loomed for so long in the center of the square. Dzerzhinsky founded the secret police (originally called the Cheka), and his statue had become a symbol of the culture of surveillance. The museum, she said, was not in the KGB headquarters but across the street, in the building that housed a grocery store called Seventh Continent. "Is very expensive market," she said. "Only foreigners shop there."

The museum wasn't marked; in fact, its glass entrance doors were hidden by heavy curtains, and when we stepped inside, I wasn't sure we were in a museum at all. It was a low-ceilinged space, with a few dusty display cases recessed against the walls. "Director of museum was colonel in KGB," Svetlana said, and on cue a man emerged from the shadows. He must have been in his fifties, and his hands were deep in the pockets of a limp, ill-fitting sport coat.

"*Zdravstvuite,*" said Sveta. Hello. And then to me, "He will give us tour. I will be translator." She handed a stack of bills to the man. Rubles reminded me of Monopoly money; they were made of cheap paper in pastel colors.

"*U vas dollary?*" he said, looking at me.

Everyone wanted American dollars. I turned to Sveta for direction, and she nodded. So I fished a ten from my backpack. He snapped it out of my hand like a shark.

The room was chilly and poorly lit. The man—his name was Anton, he told us—produced a pen from a pocket and with a sleight of hand the pen became a flashlight. He moved with reverence through the museum. It had been created in 1984, under Andropov, to house spy memorabilia but had opened to the general public only recently, and only by appointment. Anton promised to reveal secrets of the Cold War, but there was nothing revealing about his body language, and I was sure there were many secrets still being guarded across the square. The KGB had disbanded, but spies were still hard at work. The KGB's successor, the FSB, had more operatives working in Washington than ever before. Anton pointed his penlight at the display cases.

"Here is possible to see the equipment collected from captured American agents," Sveta translated. "These agents of CIA could speak Russian, dressed like Russians, but could not fool KGB. We knew their Soviet passports were counterfeit because..." Sveta paused and looked at me. "How do you call small pieces of metal that bind together the pages of the passport?"

"Staples?" I said.

"Yes, okay, the staples were made of the stainless steel. American steel, not Soviet, you understand? It was the gift away."

"The giveaway," I said.

Anton licked his lips as he waited for my reaction; he couldn't conceal his pride. The entire museum seemed designed to prove that the KGB had consistently outsmarted the CIA. We may have lost the Cold War, Anton seemed to be saying, but no one can beat us at espionage. He showed us KGB gadgets: a radio receiver disguised as a tree trunk, eyeglasses with poison hidden in their frames, a lipstick pistol, books with hollow centers, a *National Geographic* magazine with secret messages encoded in its print.

"Invisible inks," Sveta said. "Writing that can only be seen under light of the special wavelength. Messages were hidden in letters, in postcards. They could read—how do you say?—between the lines."

I'd forgotten, until that moment, that Jenny and I once experimented with invisible ink of our own. Someone—our science teacher, maybe?—had told us that messages written in lemon juice would vanish, only to reappear when the paper was exposed to heat. We sliced half a dozen lemons in her kitchen, squeezed the juice into a measuring cup, then diluted it with water. *I was saving those lemons to make a pie,* Mrs. Jones said with an exasperated sigh. *You girls had better not leave all those seeds on the counter.* We dipped cotton swabs into the diluted juice, and once we mastered the awkward task of writing with Q-tips, we filled a white page with random scribble. It was like writing with water, each letter disappearing as soon as it dried. The next morning we carried the blank page down to the basement laundry room and asked Mrs. Jones if we could use the iron. Under the iron's heat, the secret words appeared, the color of coffee stains. We must have been nine.

Anton fired his light at another case.

"And here is possible to see methods of concealment," Sveta translated. The light illuminated a gold signet ring. It looked like the ring that Mr. Jones used to wear.

"What is that?" I said to Sveta.

"That is concealment ring," she said. "For the microdots."

"Microdots?"

"Very small photographs," she said, pinching her fingers together as if to sprinkle salt. "Entire documents reduced to size of . . ."

"Punctuation marks," said Anton, finishing her sentence.

"You speak English?" I said.

"Of course," he said. "I am KGB."

Svetlana folded her arms and looked at me. *"Ponimayesh?"* she said. You understand? She had already started using the informal "you." She was talking to me as if we already knew each other quite well.

"What?" I said.

"The letter to Andropov," she said in English. "From your Jennifer Jones. What message do you think was hidden in invisible ink?"

"She was ten years old," I said. "She wasn't a spy."

"Nyet," said Sveta. "But her father was."

"That's ridiculous," I said. "He was a consultant." And then I realized how absurd I sounded. All spies, I knew, had covers. Some posed as diplomats—half the employees of the American embassy in Moscow were CIA operatives—others as businessmen. Washington was lousy with consultants—it was a word tossed around so often that I never thought to ask what sort of consulting was going on. "Edmund Jones couldn't have been a spy," I said.

"Absolutely he was selling the secrets to us," said Svetlana.

"You Americans," said Anton, "never want to believe that anyone could betray your country. You are patriot, okay, but believe me, there are many Americans who worked for KGB. Foreigners are all time asking me about the Rosenbergs. The Rosenbergs? Of course they were guilty. Edward Lee Howard? Without question. He is living in dacha right now, with protection of KGB." He paused for effect. Then smiled at me as if I were a grandchild who had asked for candy. "How is the expression? Don't insult our intelligence."

❖

"IT DOESN'T MAKE ANY SENSE," I said to Sveta that afternoon. We were at the Metropol, having lunch. She wanted me to see the interior of the hotel. "Art Nouveau," she'd promised. "Some of Moscow's most beautiful rooms." The dining room was sumptuous and empty. Though we were the only two patrons in the restaurant, I still felt compelled to whisper.

"What?" she said to me.

"Why would Andropov invite Jennifer Jones to visit the Soviet Union if her dad was in the CIA? And why would the CIA let him go? There are background checks."

"Did I say he was CIA?"

"You said he was a spy . . ."

"He was not CIA," she said. "But I can assure you that Edmund Jones was invited precisely *because* he could carry the information with him. The gifts for our party officials? The book of
Mark Twain for Andropov? What do you think was hidden inside
that book?"

The waitress arrived with our borscht. She couldn't have been
more than eighteen. She had sharp elbows and a lank, defeated po-
nytail. She set down the bowls without smiling. I waited to speak
until she walked away.

"He wasn't a spy . . . You have no proof . . ." I said, though
I could feel doubt gurgling in my stomach. My uneasy thoughts
returned to Mr. Jones on Martha's Vineyard all those years ago:
the way his face had turned, on a dime, into one I didn't know.

Svetlana offered me the basket of brown bread. "Russian
bread," she said. "Absolutely the best."

I took a piece. She watched me bite into it and waited for my
reaction. "Mmm," I said. She looked victorious, as if my apprecia-
tion of the bread were more evidence of her country's superiority.
Svetlana had pushed me to order a big lunch, though she'd opted
for only soup and a salad for herself. I knew that this was because
she was going to treat me and was making her own meal small to
keep costs down. I didn't want her to spend money on me, but I
was sure that I would offend her if I refused her hospitality. Russians were famously generous to guests.

"Why you think I was traveling with Jennifer?" she said.

"Because you were the epitome of Soviet girlhood?" I said.

"What is this 'epitome'?"

"Epitome . . . it means, like, the best example of," I said. "Like you were an advertisement for girls in the Soviet Union."

"Advertisement," she said. "This is funny. But no, we were together with Jennifer because KGB wanted to know if Jones was double agent."

"You were an informant?"

"In Soviet Union, comrade, everyone was informant."

I had no appetite. After just one mouthful of soup, I retired my spoon.

"It is not tasty?"

"I'm not feeling well," I mumbled.

"When Jennifer was here in 1983," she said, "all she did was complain about the food."

"Really?" Jenny's book made everything about her trip sound dreamy. I didn't know what to believe anymore.

"The only thing she would eat is the chicken Kiev. Very picking."

"Picky," I said.

"*Da*. Only Americans are so rich they can refuse food."

"Not all Americans are rich," I said.

"But Jennifer was rich, yes? And you are rich. You and Jennifer attend the private schools. She had the swimming pool."

"My house didn't have a swimming pool," I said.

"But you are still rich."

"My father is rich," I admitted. I was never comfortable talking about money. I knew that by world standards I was wealthy, but in the milieu where I was raised, most kids had trust funds.

"And your mother?"

"My parents are divorced," I said.

"I know this. Jennifer told me."

"Was this before or after she told you I was sad?"

"Of course you were sad," she said. "Your sister died."

I said nothing. I didn't like the idea of Jenny's using my family history as an anecdote.

"He gives you money, your father?"

I blushed when I thought of the enormous check he'd sent me for graduation. "Sometimes," I said.

"I give the money to my father," said Svetlana. "I have bigger salary now, at American company, than either of my parents. Average salary in Russia is eighty dollars per month. My mother works for Russian Olympic Committee for twenty-five years, but I am making more in one week than she is paid in whole month. My father is the chemical engineer. But I am supporting them."

"Wow," I said. I had been proud of myself for earning enough money for my trip to Moscow—I'd made the most of all those shifts at the coffee shop—but now I felt like a spoiled child. Maybe Svetlana was right about America. It was like kindergarten.

"Someday," she said, "I will be rich like you."

I moved my spoon to the other side of my plate. I felt so self-conscious that if Svetlana had offered me a cigarette, I would have smoked it just to have something to do with my hands.

"You must to eat," she said.

"I think maybe I should just drink a Coke or something. It will settle my stomach."

"I have something better than Coke," she said. She reached under the table and produced a can of Czar.

"You carry this around in your purse?" I said.

She shrugged. "Now we can brainstorm," she said. She tested the word as she said it, as if it were a melon she was examining before purchase. "Richard says whoever has best idea for Czar wins trip to New York. To work in office in Manhattan for a few weeks. It is incentive. I want to go to USA."

I poured the can into my empty water glass. The cola was flat. "You really think people are going to drink this instead of Coke? Instead of Pepsi?"

"And instead of kvass," she said. Kvass was a traditional Russian drink made from fermented rye. "Why not? We must to make brand stand for something."

"Stand for what?" I said.

"When you think of Russia, what do you think?" she said.

"What do you mean?" I said.

"First thing that walks into your mind when I say Russia."

"The KGB," I said.

"*Kak interesno*. This is what most Americans say," she said. "People come here and expect to see the spies. This is brand association."

"It's not a brand," I said. "It's your country."

"USA is brand," she said. "Your government is selling itself as

172

Land of Free, *da?* Here in Russia we must—how do you call it?—
reposition ourselves. So if Czar is Russian cola, what does this
mean? How is this cola different from American cola?"

"You said I should come to Moscow to learn the truth," I said.

"Ah, truth. You Americans love truth." She leaned back in her
chair and cracked her neck. "I think it is the favorite word—after
freedom, of course. You want the truth, and you ask for it like the
eggs you order for breakfast. Today I want my truth sunny side up!
And tomorrow hard-boiled. And then sometimes it is scrambled.
And you congratulate yourself for ordering this truth, because you
think asking for it is what matters. But what is truth? *Pravda?* No,
Pravda is a newspaper. We understand that there is not one truth.
There is your truth and my truth and yes, your Jennifer Jones's
truth."

"She's not *my* Jennifer Jones."

"No? You act like it. She is your obsession."

"I'm not obsessed with her," I said. "She was my friend."

"Obsession," she whispered theatrically. "Like Calvin Klein,
yes?"

"If she's really alive, tell me where she is."

"I can tell you where the defectors—how do you say?—gang
it out."

"Hang out."

"*Da*, gang out."

"She's a defector?" I said. My shrink was going to have a
field day.

Svetlana lit a cigarette and gave me a coy smile. "This would be very interesting truth. Front-page truth for sure. Is possible she lives in dacha outside Moscow, near Edward Lee Howard. KGB gave him apartment on Arbatskaya, dacha in country. Sure, maybe Jennifer Jones also has *kvartira* on the Arbat."

"Everything is maybe!" I said.

Svetlana smiled. "Exactly," she said. *"Babushka na dvoye ska-zala."* Literally, Grandmother said two things. Meaning no one can know for sure.

"I'm sick of maybe."

"Good thing come to those who wait."

"I can tell that you work in advertising," I said. "Everything you say sounds like a slogan."

"Richard gave to us the presentation of slogans."

"What presentation?"

"It was history of famous advertisements, from UK and USA. I know your Energizer Bunny. Your 'Ring Around the Collar.' I know your 'Good to the Last Drop.' Your 'Ultimate Driving Machine.' Your 'Breakfast of Champions.' Your 'Snap Crackle Pop.' 'Melts in Your Mouth, Not in Your Hands.' 'Takes a Licking and Keeps On Ticking.' 'Just Do It.' 'The Real Thing.' 'Where's the Beef?'—"

I interrupted her. "Did Richard give you a test?"

"Kakoy?" Which?

"You just memorized all those ads for fun?"

"I am learning to climb corporate ladder."

I studied her face for signs that she was joking.

"Capitalism," she said with a shrug. "You swim or you drown."

"Sink or swim."

"Sink or swim, *da*," she said. She pondered the slice of bread in her hand and sighed. "It is not only the maps."

"What maps?"

"The maps are always changing. Petersburg became Leningrad, then Petersburg again. And Latvia, Lithuania, Estonia, even Ukraine break away from Soviet Union. And the cathedral? The Cathedral of Christ the Savior? Right here in center of Moscow? Stalin tore it down, then Khrushchev built the swimming pool there, but now they have torn down pool to build again the church. Perhaps someday it will be another swimming pool." She waved her hand as if sweeping away cobwebs. "Everything is different. It is not the world we grew up in. Even our flag is new. *Ponimayesh?*"

"*Da*," I said. "I understand."

"Everything we were taught to believe in does not exist anymore. We cannot go back. So we must to find the new things to believe."

I admired her flexibility. She was too resourceful to sink. I looked at my watch and realized we'd been away from her office for two hours. "Aren't you supposed to be at work?"

"This is what you call working lunch," she said. Then she lifted a finger to silence me and held it in the air, as if it were a radio tower waiting for a signal. I listened. Finally she leaned in and whispered, "The truth is that Jennifer is not ready to see you. When she is, I will contact you."

"Does she know I'm here?" I said.

She sliced a finger across her neck to kill the discussion. Then she raised her glass and nodded at my glass of Czar.

I lifted it in a reluctant toast. Russians are fond of toasts. "*U menya tost*," they say. I have a toast. I waited for Svetlana's contribution.

"Up your bottom," she said.

I did not correct her.

The Moscow Rules, designed by CIA operatives
in the 1970s to outsmart the KGB:

1. Assume nothing.
2. Never go against your gut.
3. Everyone is potentially under opposition control.
4. Don't look back; you are never completely alone.
5. Go with the flow, blend in.
6. Vary your pattern and stay within your cover.
7. Lull them into a sense of complacency.
8. Don't harass the opposition.
9. Pick the time and place for action.
10. Keep your options open.

10.

I CALLED MY MOTHER that afternoon. It was early in the morning in Washington, and the phone woke her up. I knew she was sitting up in bed, fingering the telephone cord like a rosary. Her bedside table was always littered with apple cores—she ate fruit while reading at night—and the half of the bed that had once belonged to my father was a dumping ground for nuclear-safety reports.

"Sarah?" she said. I could hear the panic frothing in her voice. "Is everything okay?" [...]

Our conversation was fractured by a delay after each of us

spoke. The tenuous international connection turned the smallest pause for breath into something craven. I pushed my words into the first space I could find.

"I'm not in danger," I said. [...]

"This must be [...] costing a fortune. [...] Charge it to your dad." [...]

"I have a question," I said. [...]

"He can afford it." [...]

"My question" [...]

"Are you taking photos? [...] Going where Jenny went?" [...]

"I just want to ask you," I said. [...]

"Re-creating Jenny" [...]

Our conversation kept hitting speed bumps. "About Mr. Jones," I said. [...]

"Ed Jones?" [...]

"Yes. [...] What kind of [...] consulting" [...]

"Intelligence," she said. [...] "Intelligence operations. [...] They consulted for the NSA [...] the CIA." [...]

"The CIA?" I said. [...]

"The Defense Department." [...]

"CIA?" I said again. [...]

"Yes, the CIA." [...]

"Did he have access [...] to classified information?" [...]

"Classified?" [...]

"To secrets?" [...]

"Yes, all those guys do [...] at that level. [...] Not just government employees but the private sector [...] contractors and consultants [...] also. [...] Sarah? [...] Sar?" [...]

"I'm here." [...]

"Are you taking [...] the pictures? [...] The places Jenny" [...]

"Yes [...] but" [...]

"Be [...] careful." [...]

"Mom?" [...]

"Send me e-mail [...] so I know [...] you're" [...]

"Can you hear me?" [...]

But she was gone. There was a click.

⌗

I COULDN'T SLEEP THAT NIGHT. At two in the morning, while Corinne slumbered, I locked myself in the bathroom and filled the tub. The medicine cabinet was stocked with various vials and creams. ("I always get free beauty products at work," Corinne had told me. "Right now I'm totally obsessed with Clarins. It's the best.") Among the moisturizers and perfumes, I found a jar of bath balls. They were the translucent gold of amber and looked as if they were capable of suspending insects in their cores. Amber was big in Russia. Corinne said you could find beautiful amber jewelry at Izmailovo for almost nothing. I dumped two of the balls under the running water, watched them first dissolve into a viscous fluid like honey and then float into bubbles. The bubbles multiplied like cells, and the room filled with a strange, sweet smell. It wasn't lavender. It wasn't gardenia. And then as I sank into the water—so hot, so deliciously hot—it hit me: honeysuckle. "Honeysuckle," I said aloud, just to savor the tickle of the word. And then I turned on the Jacuzzi—such a 1980s luxury, I thought—and opened my legs around a jet. It had been seven months since I'd had sex. My last boyfriend was a philosophy major named Peter who announced one day, with the precision of a surgeon, that he was not in love with me. "I'm not sure I ever was," he said. "Though at one point I wanted to be."

"Don't do me any favors," I said to him.

"I deserve more," he said.

"More of what?" I said.

We had been together for eighteen months, and he'd declared his love for me many times, though in hindsight I realize he was really falling in love with himself. "You make me feel hot, and you make me feel loved," he said once.

Early in our relationship, he had called me a miracle. "I'm not a miracle," I told him. "I'm a human being with all kinds of flaws." He made fun of me for being so literal, but I had to set the record straight. If he thought I was perfect, he would be disappointed. The way my father was disappointed by my mother. The way Jenny was disappointed by me. I pressed myself closer to the water's source because I wanted to feel the rush, and I did, trembling in that hot, sweet bath until I was spent enough to sleep.

11.

EVEN BEFORE THE SNOW FELL, the color drained out of the sky. Everything was desaturated and gray. The horizon line vanished into the monotone. I could see how weather might calcify a person, how enough days without sun could make you hard. How your humor might get bleaker, how cynicism might take root. The air was glassy and sharp, and being outside made me feel ready to break.

I didn't hear from Svetlana for a few weeks. I called her office every day. The first few times, the man who answered just said *"Nyet"* when I asked for her and slammed the receiver down. I thought I had the wrong number and called back, only to be hung up on again. A few times I got her office voice-mail. I e-mailed her twice. Maybe she didn't get my messages. In those days e-mails sometimes took days—even weeks—to go through. So I fell in with Corinne and her expats. She spent most of her time with two other American women: Leslie the NPR reporter and a pale, willowy woman named Jane who worked at the embassy. Jane arranged to have mail from the States delivered to Corinne via diplomatic pouch. "It helps to have friends in high places," she said.

I joined them on their trips to the CD market to buy pirated music. We went to see American movies at the Radisson. One night we went to the American Bar & Grill for burgers (*gamburgery* in Russian) and beer.

"Is it true," I asked Jane, "that half the people in the embassy are spies?"

"All I know is I'm not a spy," she said. "I'm from Minnesota. We don't know how to keep secrets." Her hair was fair and fine as a duckling's; downy pieces stuck up around her temples, suspended by static. She wore glasses with frames the color of jade.

"And at the Russian embassy in D.C.?" I said. "Aren't most of the so-called diplomats spies?"

Jane swiped a french fry through the puddle of ketchup on her plate. "Are you one of those James Bond junkies who turns every coincidence into a conspiracy?" she said. And then, before I could answer, she said, "God, I love ketchup. It's embarrassing how much I love it. I'm such a stereotype. The midwesterner who loves ketchup. But I do. I put it on everything. Eggs, mac 'n' cheese, grilled cheese sandwiches. I can't help it. Sometimes I think I just eat fries as a ketchup-delivery system." She laughed at herself.

"And what's really annoying is you never get fat," said Corinne. "If I ate the way you do, I'd gain like twenty pounds."

"You'd never let that happen," Leslie said.

Silence fell over the group like a blanket extinguishing a fire. It was the awkward quiet of people who don't know each other that well, who still feel obligated to fill the spaces between them. Corinne, Leslie, and Jane were held together by the flimsiest of threads: they had nothing in common beyond nationality. In New York they might never have met. As a group they manufactured fun, but there was a sense that they were all settling for one another's company. All expat relationships are glazed with transience. You never get too attached because you know you're going to leave.

"Do you think that Dad always knew he'd go back to England?" I asked my mother once. I must have been nineteen, home for winter break. Our holidays were stunted and bare; some years we didn't bother to decorate our tree. We ordered Chinese food, as if we were actually Jewish. But it was Christmas Eve, and the public radio station was playing carols and my mother was singing along. She liked the old English ones: "The Holly and the Ivy" and "Lo, How a Rose Ere Blooming." She had a lovely voice.

"He didn't plan to fall in love with an American," my mother said. "But he didn't plan to fall out of love either. If things had worked out differently, we could have ended up in London with him."

Such a possibility had never occurred to me. It could have been me and my mom, not Sebby and Phillipa, in the house in Holland Park. Phillipa's Christmas card—a picture of Sebby on a horse—had arrived the day before. Over the years fewer and fewer people sent us cards. When my father was around, we received hundreds. My parents had friends all over the world. But after my mother stopped accepting invitations and going to parties, our names were crossed off correspondence lists. By the time I was in high school, the only card that arrived every year was the one from Phillipa and my dad. It was always addressed to me, as if my mom didn't exist.

"You would have had to take a plane to get to London," I said, and instantly regretted being so mean.

"I used to fly," she said.

My parents met when my father was in graduate school. My mother was an undergraduate—"a Cliffie," my father said—and he spotted her reading in Harvard Square and immediately asked her to lunch. "I was besotted," he said.

"What was she reading?" I wanted to know the first time I heard the story.

"I don't remember," he said.

"Emily Dickinson," my mother told me later. "I was reading Emily Dickinson. 'I felt a funeral in my brain.'" She let out a short, bitter laugh. "There was no false advertising, you know. I never pretended to be someone I wasn't. Your father just refused to see me for who I was."

✳

I CONTINUED TO VISIT the places Jenny had been, not just because my mother wanted me to but because I hoped to find some residue of Jenny's presence. I went to the Old Circus one night; it was full of children, and I realized that they were the first kids I'd seen in Moscow. I hadn't noticed a single playground. If children are the future, their absence suggested a lack of faith. But now I was surrounded by children—where did they all come from? They packed the sticky seats of the amphitheater, squirming and sniffling, their noses running with seasonal colds. Their giddy pink faces turned up to watch the acrobats. The costumes were tattered, with patches of fabric bereft of sequins, but if you squinted, the illusion was intact. *Jennifer Jones has taught us that children everywhere are the same,* said the opinion pages. *Innocence has no borders.* Jennifer Jones taught us that everyone, all over the world, loves a good show.

Meanwhile the *Moscow Times* ran a story about a traveling Russian circus that had been stranded, without money, in the Philippines for seven months. Despite charity donations, much of the troupe died of starvation. Just thirteen of the original thirty-seven performers and nine of the original animals survived the ordeal. "I'm sorry to laugh," Corinne said when we read the article, "but you couldn't make this stuff up if you tried."

Another night Corinne and I went to the Bolshoi for a performance of *Swan Lake*. The theater had seen finer days: it was a diva past her prime. The applause at the end of the ballet was the most remarkable thing about the performance. The dancers were summoned for curtain call after curtain call, and dozens of people in the audience approached the stage with bouquets. The clapping went on for half an hour, and by the end my hands were raw and the prima ballerina was holding so many flowers that we could no longer see her face.

I grew bolder about exploring on my own. I'd begun to make sense of Moscow's circular design, the concentric rings of its streets. The city had no grid; it rippled out from the Kremlin, vibrant in reds and yellows, but seemed duller the farther you moved from the center.

On the day I'd first met Svetlana, she said, "How do you like Moscow? Is it like Washington?"

"It's nothing like Washington," I said.

But I soon realized that wasn't true. Both cities loved monuments. Both had tombs dedicated to unknown soldiers and imposing statues of their founding fathers. In both cities there were too many one-way streets. You couldn't turn left anywhere in Moscow, so driving was infuriatingly inefficient. But the Metro was fast and cheap.

I went back to Lenin's tomb. Inside, the mausoleum was lit like a church, with a halo of light over the body. Americans told me that it wasn't really Lenin, that it was a wax surrogate entombed in glass. It did resemble a figure at Madame Tussaud's, I thought, but the guard whisked me and the other visitors through the room too quickly for us to get a closer look.

I visited the Tretyakov Gallery and the Pushkin Museum. I

learned the drill at museums: you had to trade your shoes for felt *tapochki* that kept sliding off your feet as you moved through the galleries. At the Pushkin I savored paintings by Matisse; at the Tretyakov I stood in awe of the Kandinskys and Chagalls. I walked past the White House—so different from the one in Washington— and the headquarters of the Soviet "news" agency, TASS. I strolled along the river by the beloved Red October factory, where the scent of chocolate in the air was cloyingly sweet. I ventured to Tolstoy's winter house, where everything had been preserved exactly as he'd left it. On the floor beside his desk were two tiny barbells. They must have weighed about one pound each. I wondered if he used them during writing breaks, if he was doing biceps curls right before he threw Anna Karenina onto the tracks.

I signed up for a Russian conversation class and started taking the Metro to Moscow State University every morning. There were ten people in the class, and all of us were women. Most were wives whose husbands' jobs had brought them to Moscow. There was a Chinese diplomat's wife, fine-boned and delicate; a freckled, middle-aged Brit married to someone at the BBC; a no-nonsense Dutch woman, whose elongated face reminded me of a Modigliani painting. Our teacher was Irina, whose pedagogy was inspired by the way children learn. She never spoke a word of English, but she repeated Russian phrases over and over again, trusting that meaning would be revealed by context. She stood in the center of the room, playing with props and exaggerating her expressions like a clown. The class was two hours long. It was baffling at first, but within three days I saw dramatic improvement in my language skills. I no longer constructed phrases in my head before I said them. Words were spilling out. I was picking up the speech patterns of the Muscovites around me. My vocabulary grew without flash cards.

I got used to the arbitrary scheduling of the *pereryv*—the break when shops, offices, and restaurants would close in the middle of the day, sometimes for an hour, sometimes longer. I got used to checking my coat everywhere (you had to check it, whether you wanted to or not). I learned that the main ingredient in "salads" was mayonnaise. I learned that Russians loved ice cream so much that they ate it on the street even when it was freezing outside. I got used to being bossed around by babushkas. Old Russian women didn't hesitate to scold people on the street. *Devushka!* they'd say. *Girl! You're not dressed warmly enough,* they'd say. Or, *Tie your shoe.* They always found something to wag their fingers at. Part of me resented the intrusion; part of me was sure I deserved the criticism.

I had always been quick to assume I was in the wrong. My perpetual sense of wrongness followed me into clothing boutiques, where I apologized to the clerks who maniacally refolded the sweaters I picked up from display tables; to hair salons, where I was uncertain about how much to tip; to shoe stores, where I often bought the first pair I tried on because I couldn't bear to trouble anyone to bring me another style or size from the back. There are some women—Mrs. Jones was one of them—who are comfortable being waited on. When she took Jenny and me to Saks Fifth Avenue, she thought nothing of monopolizing an hour of a saleswoman's time. Jenny and I sat on the floor outside the fitting rooms while her mother tried on dress after dress before their trip to the Soviet Union. "What do you think, girls?" she'd say, emerging from her stall. "Do I look like Jackie O?" And Phillipa was equally comfortable being served. On my visit to London, I was amazed to see that she actually summoned the housekeeper with a bell.

The babushkas working in Moscow's museums were quick to reprimand anyone who tried to take pictures without paying extra for a photography pass. There was a permission slip for everything, I discovered. If you wanted to swim in one of Moscow's pools, you first needed to visit a doctor—every pool seemed to have its own one-man clinic for this purpose—and pay to be examined as proof that you were not contagious with some kind of disease. Once you had your *spravka,* you could use the pools for six months, but even in the locker room the babushkas were there with unsolicited advice. On my visit to the Chaika pool—heated for swimming outdoors even in the dead of winter, when steam rose from the water as if from a hot spring—I was shamed in the shower by a babushka who stood uncomfortably close and pointed at my crotch until I had thoroughly scrubbed it.

I dropped off my résumé at the *Moscow Times.* They invited me back to take the copy-editing test. I began looking at the real estate section, at Western-style apartments. They were expensive, but I'd find a roommate, and if necessary I could dip into the money my father had given me. My mother wouldn't want me to stay, but I didn't want to end up like her, always taking the safe route, afraid to get on a plane.

One sunny afternoon after class, I strolled the Arbat, trying to be inconspicuous as I scanned the scene. It was a cobbled pedestrian street. A man in a withered tuxedo played the violin. I recognized the flurry of bright notes as a Mozart concerto and dropped a dollar into the velvet-lined case at his feet. Artists sketched caricatures in charcoal. Many of the drawings were of American celebrities; I saw David Duchovny and Cindy Crawford in the mix. There were some tourists, I noticed, and a lot of Russian teenagers, lurking in smoky packs. I don't know what I was hoping to find. Even if Edward Lee Howard still lived in an apartment on the Arbat, did I expect him to be milling around in the crowd? I don't know how I thought I'd identify him. What did defectors look like? Did regret linger on them like scars? Or, like my father, did they plunge into their new lives without looking back?

I saw *White Nights* a few months after Jenny died. Gregory Hines was an American defector who ended up in Siberia with his beautiful Russian wife, played by Isabella Rossellini. Baryshnikov starred as a Russian ballet dancer who had defected to America but ended up back in Soviet custody after his plane made an emergency landing on an airbase in the USSR. I sat in the dark wishing that Jenny could be there in the theater with me. *Is Russia really like that?* I would have asked her. It was 1985, and everyone in America loved Baryshnikov: he was gorgeous and talented, and he'd chosen *us*. He was like a lover who had actually left his wife, and America was his triumphant mistress.

Where the defectors hang out, Svetlana said, as if there were enough of them to form a club. As if they were assembled around a table, playing poker. Chips stacked in red, white, and blue, the colors of the country they left behind but also the ones of the place they now called home. There were two kinds of defectors: those who were running away from something and those who ran toward the Soviet Union for ideological reasons. The seekers of asylum and the true believers. Both were gamblers. Hedging their bets. Risking what they had in hopes of trading up. Reckless because they believed they were entitled to more.

Lee Harvey Oswald defected to the Soviet Union for a few years. When he returned to the United States in 1962, he brought a Russian wife and daughter with him. He assassinated Kennedy the following year. American Morris Cohen and his wife, Lona, were both KGB spies; they defected in 1969 and lived in Moscow on KGB pensions until their deaths in the early 1990s. The Cohens were awarded the Order of the Red Banner, the Order of the Friendship of Nations, and after the Soviet Union splintered, the Russian Federation issued postage stamps with their faces on them.

I considered the facts. Mr. Jones had access to intelligence secrets. He had opportunity: we gave him our letters, so he certainly could have buried messages in them. For the first time, it occurred to me that *he* might have been the one who hid my letter behind the bulletin board in Jenny's room. Maybe Jenny didn't know that it was there. Maybe she wasn't lying when she said she was sure Andropov would write to me. If Edmund Jones was a spy, then it wasn't my fault that Jenny abandoned me. There were larger forces at work.

Was it so improbable? Every true story about espionage was full of impossible-to-believe details. Georgi Markov, a Bulgarian playwright who moved to London and denounced his government through his work as a radio broadcaster, was murdered in 1978 by Bulgarian secret agents who stabbed him with an umbrella that had poison hidden in it. KGB colonel Oleg Gordievsky was smuggled over the Finnish border by MI6 when he defected to Britain. Edward Lee Howard escaped by diving out of his wife's moving car in the desert night; he planted a dummy wearing his clothes in the passenger seat so that when his wife drove back to her house, the FBI men watching her would assume that Howard was still there. What if the Joneses' plane went down with dummies on board? The more I thought about this scenario, the better I felt. I'd spent all that time on Martha's Vineyard holding a grudge, but maybe Jenny didn't do anything wrong. Maybe I was the one who owed her an apology. Maybe our friendship came to an end not because she preferred Kim, not because I was no fun, but because she sensed my pulling away.

❉

ONE NIGHT I asked Jane if the American embassy thought there were any unreported defectors. We were at Cafe Margarita, an arty den across the pond from Corinne's building. Some kind of jazz band was playing, and we'd all ordered red wine.

"What do you mean by unreported defectors?" Jane said. She pushed her glasses up on her head, and I noticed that she had almost no eyebrows. The absence of the green frames around her eyes transformed her face completely. It's funny how such a small change can make such a big difference. I thought of Pip. When he was wet, he looked like a completely different dog. With his usually fluffy coat flattened out by water, he was tiny and meek.

"I mean people who defected without ever officially declaring that they defected," I said. "People who were reported dead but didn't really die. People who chose to disappear."

"This is the problem," Jane said. "It's hard for us to build diplomacy with Russia when everyone's still holding on to these Hollywood clichés. Enough about defection and spies. This is a new era!"

"You know what this era is?" said Corinne. "It's the era of the Russian supermodel. Half the models on the runways in Paris, Milan, and London are Russian. All the scouts are flying in, wandering around these little Siberian towns looking for the next big thing. My boss wants me to find talent here."

"Do models count as talent?" said Leslie. She was the only smoker in the group. When warming up to make a point, she tapped her cigarettes on the table, ostensibly "packing" them, but with the vehemence of a judge's gavel. "How are they talented? Because they know how to walk?"

"Ladies," said Jane. "New subject: the Fourth of July picnic at the embassy. We're planning a really fun day for all the Americans here."

"You're already thinking about July?" said Leslie. "I have to survive this reporting trip to Chechnya first."

"Don't even joke about that," said Corinne. "War gives me the creeps."

"Then it's a good thing you work for a fashion magazine," Leslie said. "Your job is the polar opposite of public-radio journalism."

"Aren't you sanctimonious today?" Corinne said.

"Come on," Jane said. "Give it a rest. We're supposed to be showing Sarah a good time."

"You're having a good time, aren't you?" Leslie said to me. Her hair was short and spiky; she reminded me of a spider plant.

"Sure," I said. "I'm having a blast."

That night Leslie told me about Yeltsin's Truth Decree. In July 1994 the president had signed a decree forbidding false advertising. It was aimed at all the companies that were duping naïve Russians. "Billboards, TV commercials, newspaper ads telling people they'll get a thousand-percent return on their investments. These poor pensioners are sinking their life savings into these schemes without asking any questions. And then the companies just disappear and take all their money. Everyone wants to get rich, but no one really understands the realities of a market economy."

"My assistant lost a lot of money that way," Corinne said. "She invested her parents' savings, too. They lost everything. Can you imagine?"

"Con artists and crooks," Leslie said. "It's so depressing." Resigned, she lit a cigarette. "Reform is a pipe dream."

"The Truth Decree sounds like something out of Orwell," I said. "Did it work?"

Leslie laughed. "What do you think?"

⌗

SVETLANA'S OFFICE VOICE-MAIL MESSAGE was in English and Russian. I got used to hearing her say, *"Please to leave the message after beep."*

"It's Sarah. Zuckerman. Again," I said day after day. She didn't return my calls.

And so I waited and sifted through the information I had.

Mr. Jones had access and opportunity, but what was his motive? He had never struck me as an ideologue. He and his wife were so happy in Washington; why would they give that up? And even if he *had* been a spy, that didn't necessarily mean that Jenny was alive. If they weren't on that chartered plane, who was? The more I thought about it, the more absurd the idea of the Joneses defecting to the Soviet Union became. Because if they *had* defected, wouldn't we have heard about it in the States? Wouldn't the Soviets have called a press conference to announce their latest prize? YOUNG AMERICAN CHOOSES THE UNION OF FRIENDSHIP AND PEACE. CHILD DIPLOMAT MAKES HER HOME IN THE USSR. There was a public-relations frenzy when Stalin's daughter defected to the States in 1967 and then repatriated seventeen years later. TASS was quick to tell the world when the USSR granted Edward Lee Howard political asylum.

There was no reason to trust Svetlana. Jenny was invited to the USSR to prove that it was a peaceful, friendly place. For all I knew, Svetlana had invited me to further her own agenda, to demonstrate that post-Soviet Russia was still a "champion" capable of making world-class soft drinks. Maybe I was being used as a propaganda tool. Just because Svetlana was telling me something I wanted to believe, that didn't make it true. It was dangerous to get my hopes up. I steeled myself against inevitable disappointment.

I told Corinne that my Russian friend believed we hadn't walked on the moon. "A lot of people here think that," she said. "But they're just sore losers. They lost the Cold War, so now they're like, 'You cheated!'"

It was amazing to me that Russians and Americans still defined themselves in opposition to one another. Americans generalized about Russians; Russians generalized back. The Cold War was over, but the habit of drawing lines in the sand was hard to break. Corinne said that when she arrived, she wanted to make Russian friends. "But until about four years ago, it was illegal for them to spend time with foreigners. They're curious about us, but they're also still really suspicious. And it's so hard to get people here to be honest." Relationships with expats were safer, she said. But hanging out with expats seemed like a cop-out. I didn't want to be one of those foreigners who hid behind walls, the way the embassy people did.

"On my trip to the USSR, I learned about the importance of

friendship," said Jenny's book. In my room in Corinne's apartment, I flipped through the pages again. Jenny went to Pioneer camp, she visited a collective farm. She had lunch at the Soviet Women's Committee. She spent an afternoon doing gymnastics with the Soviet Olympic team. There was no point in trying to recreate her trip. Too much had changed. I had to find a way to break this to my mother, who thought a slide show of my photographs would be the perfect way to open the tenth-anniversary Jennifer Jones Festival. I returned to the title page, where Jenny's careful cursive waited for me. *"For Sarah, my best friend forever."* She wrote that in December of 1983. Just a few months later, she was spending all her time with Kim. Forever didn't last very long.

#

MOSCOW CONTINUED ITS STEADY march toward winter. Corinne screamed one morning when a mouse, driven inside by the cold, darted across the kitchen floor. It disappeared under the stove while we ate our muesli.

The days were getting so short. One Saturday I slept until almost two and then started to cry when I realized I'd missed most of the daylight. The sun wasn't completely up until nearly ten, and the light began to leach out of the sky by four. The darkness fell quickly and made me feel desperate, not just for light but for answers. There is something painfully honest about winter: the skeletal trees, the brutal repetition of the cold. There are no empty promises, no hazy, humid hopes. It's reality, lonely and stark.

What was I doing in this bleak place? My friends from college were having a good time cobbling lives together. My friend Juliet was rooming with two classmates on Ludlow Street. She e-mailed to say she kept running into people from school at neighborhood bars. *"Everyone in New York wants to know when you're coming home,"* she wrote to me earlier that week. *"We miss you. xoxoxo"*

I decided I'd finish my Russian class, go home for Thanksgiving, and never come back. I'd spend the holidays with my mother and then in January I'd move to New York, stay with Juliet on the Lower East Side. It was good to know I had real friends waiting for me. It was the safe route, but what was so wrong with that? I didn't have to make myself suffer. What was so awful about being like my mother? At least she was loyal. But a few days later, the *Moscow Times* offered me a job. I had aced the copy-editing test. They would even sponsor me for a new visa so I could come back after the holidays and start in January.

"We should celebrate," Corinne said that night.

"I guess."

"If you really want to be a journalist, make it happen. Start as a copy editor, become a reporter. Things are more fluid here—you can move up fast. You're welcome to stay here at my place for a few more months. Chip in a little for rent. Find your own apartment once you're settled into the job. When are you going to get another chance like this? We're on the vanguard here."

"Vanguard or abyss?"

"Isn't this what you came to Moscow for?" Corinne said.

I paused. I'd never told her about Jenny. The real reason I'd come to Moscow was too hard to explain, I thought, without sounding deranged. I liked Corinne, but she struck me as someone with no tolerance for ambiguity. She valued efficiency above all. She probably outsourced complicated emotions the way she sent out her dry cleaning. I could imagine her impatiently counseling friends through heartbreak, slamming the door on inconvenient feelings. *You just have to get over him,* she'd say, with a snap of her fingers. *Time to move on. There are other fish in the sea.*

Now she said, "You have to decide what you want."

I wasn't used to asking myself what I wanted. I was used to taking what was offered. What did I want? In what ways was I wanting? Wanting. Wanton. At times my behavior in college had certainly been wanton. I'd gone home with some guys just because they invited me. Just because it felt good to be desired, just because it was a chance to make heat on a cold night. For years I'd been replaying events in my head, looking for clues, for any foreshadowing of betrayal and abandonment. *I should have known better,* I'd tell myself after someone left me. I can't believe I thought I mattered enough to make anyone stay. I'd spent years thinking that I was "sad" like some people are French. I'd been telling myself the same story, branding myself as damaged and disposable. Easy to leave.

I liked the idea of becoming an investigative journalist, though. I liked the idea of having my name in the papers, not as the quoted best friend but as the byline. Corinne was right. It was time to focus on my future instead of trying to resurrect the past.

"Dear Mom," I wrote that night. "Most of the places Jenny vis-

ited don't exist anymore. I think we should forget about the tenth-anniversary celebration. People want to look forward, not back." I knew that her feelings would be hurt. She'd view this as a betrayal. But I couldn't keep carrying Jenny's legacy. I had to create my own. I tried to soften the blow. *"Maybe you can find a new cause?"* But I couldn't hit SEND. I couldn't take Jenny away from her.

12.

I WAS IN THE KITCHEN making coffee one morning in late October when the phone rang. It was the short ring of a local call. Corinne was at her office, so I answered.

"*Allo?* Sarah?" It was Svetlana's voice on the other end. *"Privyet,"* she said in a giddy singsong. I realized I'd missed her.

"I've been trying to reach you," I said. "Did you get my messages?"

"What messages?"

"There were a lot of messages."

She had a surprise for me, she said. A very big surprise. Would I come to her office today at eleven o'clock? She would meet me in the lobby, she said, so that the armed guard didn't bother me. I didn't want to miss my Russian class. There were only a few days of the course left. That week we had been practicing the subjunctive mood. "I would have gone to the film if I had had a ticket," our teacher, Irina, said. "I would have come to Moscow long ago," I said, "if I had been invited."

"What kind of surprise?" I asked Svetlana.

But she just said, "Eleven o'clock," and hung up.

❄

SVETLANA WAS WAITING when I arrived. She wore the same white blouse and gray skirt. I soon learned that most Russians wore the same thing to work every day. I produced my passport for the guard, but this time he returned it to me immediately and waved me past. On the way up the stairs, Svetlana said, "You brought your camera?"

"Yes," I said.

"Well, you cannot use it. This is the top secret."

In the office Svetlana led me to a door next to the kitchen. "Our conference room," she said. Inside was a long table on which nine forlorn cans of Czar clustered in the center. There was no one there. Just a large mirror on one wall and a framed noirish black-and-white print of Red Square opposite it.

"What's the surprise?" I said to Sveta.

"Focus groups," she said.

Richard appeared in the doorway behind her. "Today," he said, "we are doing consumer research. We've invited some people in for taste tests. A Czar challenge, if you will."

"What does this have to do with me?" I said.

"I thought you might enjoy it," he said. "Russian people your age . . . listening to what they have to say. And we could use a young American perspective. The Yanks in our office are much older. Of course, you'll need to sign an NDA. This is all highly confidential, but I know you've been helping Sveta with campaign ideas."

Svetlana was distributing plastic cups, placing three in front of each seat at the table. "I told Richard how productive we were at our lunch," she said, and gave me a knowing look.

"Yes, we were," I said, playing along. I realized that Svetlana must have expensed our meal at the Metropol. "We're full of ideas."

"Consumer research is a challenge here," Richard said. "Brits and Americans *want* to talk about themselves. Ask them one question about what laundry detergent they use and you get a whole monologue about their family. But Russians are tight-lipped. Afraid anything they say might be used against them. They'll tell you what they think you want to hear. Hard to get honest responses. But Svetlana here is going to moderate the groups. We've been training her, haven't we? Teaching her about market research."

Svetlana nodded. She was folding paper napkins into triangles.

"I thought you had a surprise for me," I said. "I assumed this was about our friend."

She didn't answer.

"I'm going to show you something," said Richard, like a magician ready to pull a rabbit from a hat.

I followed him out of the conference room and through the adjoining door. We were in a small, dark room in which six chairs had been arranged in two rows of three. One wall was a window that looked into the conference room. We watched Svetlana through that window as she arranged cans of Pepsi and Coke next to the cans of Czar.

"A one-way mirror," said Richard. "We can watch the groups, we can hear what the consumers say. They can't see us."

"Do they know they're being watched?"

"They do not." He crossed his arms over his chest. The gesture struck me as defiantly smug. "We're not legally obligated to tell them."

"You want Russians to get over their fear of being watched by watching them?"

"This is the way it's done," he said. "Advertising is about giving people *choice*. Consumers tell us what they want so that we can create products and campaigns that work for them."

"That work *on* them, you mean," I said. Through the glass, Svetlana was emptying a tube of Pringles onto a paper plate.

Andrei poked his head into the room. *"Privyet,"* he said in a tone that sounded like a taunt. He was wearing some kind of cologne with tangy citrus notes.

"Welcome to the front lines of the cola war," said Richard.

Andrei collapsed into a chair and lit a cigarette. Richard waddled out of the room. Through the one-way mirror, I watched him lean close to Svetlana and whisper something in her ear. Svetlana nodded and then hid all the cans of cola with a red cloth.

"For people my age, you know, Pepsi is almost like a Russian brand," said Andrei. "We grew up with Pepsi. Coke is seen as absolutely American, which helped them for a while. You know, they were the cool new foreign import. But they still have some catching up to do in this market. And our hypothesis is that America is losing its appeal as a selling point."

"I don't care about the cola war" I said. "I'm looking for my friend."

"What friend?"

"No one you know."

"Ooh, a secret friend," he said. *"Drug or podruga?"* A male or female friend?

Andrei reminded me of some of the boys I knew in high school. I'd cross the Cathedral Close every afternoon for swim practice—we worked out with the boys in their school's pool—and sometimes their campus felt like enemy territory. Some of the guys, out of faculty earshot, weren't afraid to hurl words our way. *Box,* they whistled. *Pussy.* They just wanted a reaction. Even a deferential greeting held the threat of mockery. I always darted up the flagstone path, head down, swim bag over my shoulder. I was on guard. *"Podruga,"* I said.

"So mysterious," said Andrei.

"My friend *died,*" I said.

"If she's dead, why are you looking for her?"

"It's not funny," I said. I was getting flustered. I could feel my cheeks engulfed with heat.

"Relax," he said. I've always hated being told to relax. It feels patronizing.

Richard returned. "Women in the first group, men in the second," he said.

Andrei crushed out his cigarette on the plastic arm of his chair, then swept the ashes onto the floor. "Come on," he said, kicking an empty chair my way. "This will be fun. We'll all learn something."

Richard pulled the door closed. We were in the dark. "No light in here," he said, "or they'll be able to see us through the mirror."

I felt a surge of claustrophobia. The older I got, the less I liked small, confined spaces. "I have to go," I said. "I don't feel well."

"You can't leave *now*," said Richard. "The consumers are coming into the room. We can't open this door again until after the first group." He stank of beer. The air was yeasty with his sweat.

Four women entered the conference room. They were all young—in their early twenties, perhaps—with hard, insolent faces. The hidden microphone wasn't on yet, so we couldn't hear Svetlana, but she must have asked them to sit down, because they all took seats. Sveta's back was to us, and I could see the sharp bones of her spine through her blouse. The other women faced the mirror. They were drawn to their own reflections. Hands moved to smooth stray hairs; mouths pursed to correct lipstick smudges. They performed these touch-ups with robotic precision. There were two blondes, a redhead—through her thinning hair I could see that her scalp was stained with dye—and a brunette. Suddenly we picked up the broadcast of Svetlana's reedy voice.

"What's she saying?" Richard asked in a stage whisper.

"She has asked them to introduce themselves," Andrei whispered back.

The woman on the far right began. She was the redhead. Her eyes were smudged with kohl. *"Menya zovut Natalia,"* she said.

"Her name is Natalia," Andrei said to Richard. "But Sveta is calling her Natasha." Natasha was the nickname for Natalia, just as Sveta was the nickname for Svetlana. In Russia, nicknames were standardized, along with everything else. We learned that Natasha was a secretary and that she was twenty-one.

The blonde next to her began to speak. *"Menya zovut Zoya,"* she said. Zoya had long, honey-colored hair with thick bangs that grazed her lash line and hid her brows. Finally, I thought, a Russian blonde whose roots weren't showing. Her hair actually looked conditioned. Too bad Corinne wasn't there to see it. Zoya said she was a teacher and that she was twenty-two. Then she said something about living in the States when she was a child.

"Did she just say she lived in America when she was young?" I said.

"No," said Andrei. "You misunderstood."

"We're trying to understand their perceptions of America," Richard said. "We're trying to understand how those perceptions influence their notions of soft drinks and their usage patterns. Is a cola inherently American? Do we have to traffic in American imagery?"

But I was sure I didn't misunderstand. She'd said, *"Ya zhila v Amerike."* I lived in America. Either Andrei wasn't listening closely or he was deliberately mistranslating. I couldn't see his face in the dark. Was he lying or lazy?

"We've lost the sound," Andrei said. We could see Zoya's lips moving, could see her head cock to the left as she listened to Svetlana's next question.

"Bloody hell," Richard said. "Sveta must have bumped her microphone. If it's not back on in a minute, you'll have to go in there, Andrei."

Zoya's attenuated fingers were stroking her collarbone. She had the high cheekbones and deep-set eyes typical of Russian women and the same haughty expression. But there was something about the way she leaned forward, the way she looked directly at Svetlana as if she were comfortable with interviews.

I stood up.

"Hey," said Richard. "You can't go in there."

"I just need a closer look," I said. I pressed my face to the glass.

Zoya sat back, tucked her hair behind her ears. There was something familiar in her gestures, an echo of a former self. It was like watching a silent film, like watching a home movie. It was Jenny I was projecting onto the scene. I filled the hollows under Zoya's eyes, dotted her nose with freckles, darkened her hair. Zoya looked nothing like Jenny. And yet.

"Is she Russian?" I said.

"Of course," said Andrei.

Then the sound came back on. The return of Zoya's voice—

husky, jaded, Russian—altered the scene. I could no longer see any trace of Jenny there. She shook her head dismissively. "I don't like American food," she said.

"She doesn't like American food," Andrei translated.

The next woman introduced herself. Her hair was the color of dishwater, and she nibbled on her bottom lip as she spoke. "She is Lyudmila," Andrei said. "She is a medical student. She is twenty-three."

"Who found these people?" I said.

"What do you mean?" said Richard. "The consumers?"

"Where did they come from? Did Svetlana invite them?"

"Svetlana helped with the recruiting, yes," said Richard. "We don't have a proper planning department. We have to work with what we have."

"Lyudmila says they used to pour Pepsi in wineglasses on special occasions," said Andrei. "When they were children."

I remembered New Year's Eve when Jenny and I drank Coke out of champagne flutes to ring in 1983. "Cheers," we said, uniting our glasses with a clink. "Not too much pop or you'll be up all night," Mrs. Jones warned.

"Now Sveta is asking them about colas," Andrei said. "About Pepsi and about Coke. What they drink. What they like. Their usage occasions. What do they think about when they see these brands."

"Too many questions at once," Richard said. "I told her, you've got to build the discussion slowly, let them open up, not jump right in with brand identities. Christ."

The women looked bored. The one named Zoya spread out her hands and scrutinized her manicure. Then she held her hands up on either side of her face and looked at herself in the mirror. Her nails were the color of scabs. And then she smiled. It reminded me of our elementary-school pictures. Once a year we were ushered into the gym where a photographer had set up a temporary studio on the stage. The photographer's assistant distributed black plastic combs so that we could neaten our hair while we waited for our turn in front of the camera. Jenny and I were always together, so when we reached the front of the line, I watched her pose. Her face was blank until the photographer said "Ready?" and then she switched on her smile. The dimples came out, her eyes lit up.

I moved toward the door before I knew what I was doing.

Richard grabbed my arm to restrain me. "Hey," he said. "There are rules. There are protocols." I noticed the puckered mark of a closed-up hole in his left ear and imagined the midlife crisis that had led him to pierce it years before. He had probably worked very hard to be hip. And now he was a fifty-year-old in a baggy sweater. A *jumper*, he'd call it.

"I think I know I her," I said.

"Millions of dollars are riding on this project," said Richard.

Who was the puppet master? Where were the strings? Had this whole thing been organized for my benefit? Was there really a cola called Czar?

Richard was out of shape and a little drunk. I wrestled out of his arms, opened the door, let the light compromise the research. And then I stormed into the conference room.

"I need to talk to you," I said. All four women at the table shifted their gaze to me. If they were alarmed, they didn't show it.

"May I help you?" said Svetlana in English. She stood, pressed her knuckles into the table until the skin blanched with the stress.

"This is the surprise?" I said.

"Please," she said to the women. "Help yourself to Pringles."

"Zoya," I said. "I need to talk to Zoya."

"*Ya?*" said Zoya. Me? Her tone was arch.

"*Da,*" I said. Up close, her eyes were a murky green. Not like Jenny's at all. Colored contacts, perhaps? I wasn't convinced.

"You are the interruption," Svetlana said to me.

"I know you speak English," I said to Zoya.

"Of course I speak English," Zoya said. "Educated people do." She had a Moscow accent. *But she's been here for ten years,* I thought. And Jenny was always good at accents.

"What's your real name?" I said. I felt like one of the bouncers at the Georgetown bars my friends and I used to frequent in high school. They used to quiz us about the information on our driver's licenses. The bouncers were right to be skeptical; our IDs were fake. But we were careful to memorize all the pertinent information. We lived in our false identities. We knew where everything was. In real life I was a Scorpio, but my cover was an Aquarius.

I heard the hiss of carbonation as Svetlana opened a can of Czar. She covered the can's label with her hand as she made her way around the table, filling cups. The perfect hostess.

The other women's eyes burned into me. I knew that Richard and Andrei were watching, too, from behind the glass. I glanced at the mirror but could see only my face staring back at me. They had obviously turned off the light. So the research was still under way, which meant that I was part of it now. I was another potential consumer under the microscope. Unless it wasn't real research at all. Maybe it was all staged and everyone was in on it, even Richard. Maybe he spoke Russian perfectly. Rule #1: *Assume nothing.* In the mirror all my uncertainty reflected back at me. My hair was neither blond nor brown but somewhere in between. My eyes were neither blue nor green. An indeterminate color. I wasn't sure what to write under "Eye Color" on my passport application. I finally settled for hazel, but that wasn't exactly right.

"What is this 'real name'?" Zoya was fierce, unyielding.

She looked so Russian. Until I traveled through Europe in college, I didn't understand how much physiognomy can give away. On a train from Paris to Rome, two traveling companions and I met an Italian woman who promptly categorized us as Jamaican, Czech, and Danish. "No, we're American," said my friend Kate, prepared to defend the Melting Pot. But the woman wasn't talking about nationality. She said it was clear from our faces where our ancestors had come from. Kate was in fact descended from ancient Bohemians, and Michelle's grandparents were from Kingston, but I protested that my ancestors were English until I realized that my forebears could be traced all the way to Jutland in what is now Denmark. All that emigration and assimilation couldn't totally erase our origins.

"Your American name," I said to Zoya. But I was running out of steam. *I'm losing my mind,* I thought. *I'm hallucinating because of all the smoke.* This was just some woman with a vague resemblance to Jenny. Russia was making me paranoid. Jenny had been dead a long time.

"Kto ona?" said Zoya. Who is she? She was talking to Svetlana. I was acting so crazy that they were talking about me like I wasn't there.

"She is a foreigner," Svetlana said, as if that explained everything. Or maybe she meant, "She is a stranger." It's the same word in Russian. A foreigner is a stranger. A stranger is foreign.

"I'm sorry," I said. "I made a mistake." I backed out of the room, hot with shame. My skin was prickly. I escaped to the bathroom and splashed cold water on my face. *Deep breaths,* I told myself. *Deep breaths.* My skin was blotchy, my eyes strained and bloodshot. I was washed out, uneasy. My skin is the sort that is often afflicted: sunburn peels like paint; mosquito bites pucker and swell. I'm quick to bruise. I break out in hives. A day at the beach leaves me raw. I don't look relaxed on vacation, but beaten down by the elements. How I longed to have the smooth, even-toned skin and doe eyes of someone who never had to try.

There was a knock on the door. "Just a second," I said. I needed to pull myself together.

WHEN I CAME OUT OF THE BATHROOM, Andrei was waiting for me. "What's wrong? You saw a ghost?"

I really was turning into my mother. Chasing ghosts. "Go translate your fucking focus groups," I said.

"Ooh," he said. "The pretty American talks like a sailor."

It was vaguely satisfying to debunk his idea of me as some kind of dainty flower. "She said she lived in the States when she was a kid," I said. "I heard her. Why didn't you translate that part?"

"You understand more Russian than I thought," he said.

"Answer my question," I said. "Why didn't you translate that part?"

"Richard wants typical Russians, okay? People who haven't been to the States, who have a very limited idea of America and American brands. That woman—Zoya—wouldn't have matched his recruiting specs, but Svetlana didn't have enough people for the groups, so she couldn't be too picky. Sveta obviously forgot to tell the woman not to mention her childhood in the States. I did not want Sveta to be fired." He was making eye contact with me. He wasn't blinking at an unusual rate. Nothing about his face suggested he was lying. "You're not going to say anything to Richard, are you?"

"No," I said. I didn't want Svetlana to get fired either. Especially since she was supporting her parents. "Did you know Sveta before you worked together?"

"Of course." I must have looked cynical, because he added, "You know, the intelligentsia. We're all connected."

"Is your father a spy?" I said.

"*Chto?*"

"Your father the diplomat, the one who took you to Washington . . . was he KGB?"

"*Amerikanka molodaya,*" he said. Young American.

"Was he?" I said. "Did he have an American contact named Edmund Jones?"

"Edmund Jones the spy?" he said.

"Edmund Jones was a spy?" I said.

"That's what you just said. I'm just repeating you."

"You should probably go back and translate. If Richard really can't understand anything."

"We're taking a break," he said. "Richard says we need to 'reset' their attitude and then start again in ten minutes. But don't worry, they will talk about you, and it will be a good place to begin discussion about Americans, about Cold War iconography."

"Great," I said.

"I'm kidding," he said. "You worry too much."

"So I'm told."

"Before you go," he said, "you need to sign this." He handed me a confidentiality agreement and a ballpoint pen. "Standard stuff," he said as I skimmed the page. "We can't have you selling our secrets."

⌗

AFTER I LEFT THE AGENCY, I waited outside on the street. I tucked myself behind one of the columns outside the Bolshoi Theater and kept my eyes on number 26. I just wanted one more look at Zoya. I knew she'd lived in the States; I needed to know if she lived in the house across the street from me.

After about forty minutes, she exited the building. She was

wearing a short wool coat and, like most women her age, a mini-skirt and black tights. She turned left and walked toward the Metro at Teatralnaya. I followed from across the street. I was a few feet behind her on the escalator as we plunged into the station; I was twenty yards behind as she crossed underground into the Red Line station called Okhotny Ryad. She never looked back. When she boarded the train, I slipped into the same car. She pulled a book from her bag. I was too far away to see what she was reading but close enough to see that it was in Russian. Zoya resembled all the other people on the train: sitting up straight, book open on her lap, taut as a wire.

As the train approached Park Kultury, she returned the book to her bag and stood up. In Russian she mumbled, "Are you getting off?" to the people blocking the door. The sea parted for her. I trailed her off the train and up the escalator.

When we emerged from underground, we were on the bank of the river. I followed Zoya over Krymsky Bridge to Gorky Park. She paid her entrance fee at the enormous stone gate. I did the same. The Central Park of Culture and Leisure was no longer the proletariat's perfect playground. The manicured gardens of Brezhnev's day had given way to cracked concrete littered with broken glass. Rickety amusements lined the riverbank: an old Soviet space shuttle; a roller coaster; a Ferris wheel. The Buran shuttle seemed especially dated, a trophy from another era. The Buran shuttles were designed in response to the American shuttle program but were never actually launched. Now this prototype was collecting rust.

Zoya walked with sharp, small steps. There was no suggestion of Jenny's easy stride. Her hands were shoved deep into her pockets. Was she meeting someone? There were other young people in the park, drinking and smoking, killing time. But Zoya marched toward the roller coaster. It seemed an odd choice on an October afternoon with just a couple hours of light left in the day. But when the coaster creaked into motion, I was two cars behind her.

I hadn't been on a roller coaster since a trip to Kings Dominion when I was nine or ten. Jenny's mother took us for the day. I remember the mounting dread as we waited in line for the Rebel Yell, snaking closer and closer to the ride's entrance, corralled by railings that made it impossible to turn back. My mother had alerted me to the dangers of roller coasters before we set out that morning. A sixteen-year-old girl had died after she fell from a coaster in Connecticut, she warned. A ten-year-old girl died after a ride in Orlando; apparently she'd had a heart condition that was triggered by the speed. Jenny squealed with excitement. I feigned enthusiasm. I wanted to be the kind of girl who was fearless and fun. When the safety bar came down, I clenched my teeth and shut my eyes as our car rattled up the first hill.

Now I kept my eyes open and saw Moscow spread out below us. We had a spectacular view of the river from above. If the coaster flew off the tracks, we'd plunge into the water and drown. I was sure that Russian safety standards were not up to snuff. A bribe slipped to an inspector was enough to cause catastrophe. I calmed myself by focusing on Zoya. I could barely see the back of her head. If she were actually Jenny, I thought, perhaps she came here to re-create her American childhood. The roller coaster was supposedly invented in Russia—that's why the French call them "Russian mountains"—but in Russia, roller coasters were seen as a foreign amusement. They called them "American mountains." The first coaster in Gorky Park was imported during perestroika.

Reasoning failed me and nerves took over when we reached the apex of the first hill. We seemed to hang in space for a moment, like a cartoon car whose driver has not yet realized he's gone off a cliff. Did I have an undiagnosed heart condition that was going to kill me? I had my passport, in case someone needed to identify my body. My poor mother. I clamped my eyes shut for a moment, but then I heard a delighted squeal—could it be Jenny's voice?— and I forced my eyes back open as we hurtled down the American mountain. I kept them open for every stomach-turning curve, every gravity-defying loop, and though I didn't hear any more Jenny screams, by the end of the forty-five-second ride I experienced the surprising alchemy that turns fear into thrills. I actually enjoyed it.

After the ride, Zoya nonchalantly lit a cigarette and walked toward the exit. Had she come all the way to Gorky Park for one roller-coaster ride? Was this her way of blowing off steam? Was this a typical afternoon for her? I suddenly realized I was going to throw up. The bile swam up my throat, and I spewed, leaving my motion sickness pooled on the cement. I studied the vomit as if it were a Rorschach test, and I swear I saw a hammer and sickle, and then an anchor, like the ones at the gates of the Naval Observatory on Massachusetts Avenue in D.C. And that made me think of the

British embassy, the brick monstrosity next to the Naval Observatory, and that made me think of my father, who escaped my mother because he thought he'd have a better life somewhere else. So much for vows. Jesus, I was so desperate for direction that I was looking for signs in my own puke. Surely this was madness. Was I destined to be like my mother, living in an emotional tundra with nothing but a library of memories, shelved by date, to keep me warm? I didn't want to spend my life replaying the same footage again and again. I wiped my mouth with the sleeve of my pea coat. When I looked up, I'd lost Zoya. She was nowhere in sight.

⌗

I SUPPOSE I THOUGHT that if Jenny were really alive, if we were ever reunited, that there would be some sort of instant click of recognition and that we would fit neatly together like old parts. But my encounter with Zoya—during the focus groups and then in Gorky Park—was so opaque that even hours later I wasn't sure what I'd seen. I could have sworn it was Jenny through the glass, but then inside the conference room nothing was certain. She thought I was a stranger. Surely Jenny would recognize me, even after all this time. I hadn't changed that much, had I?

As we get older, voices deepen. Wrinkles crease the skin around eyes. Teeth yellow. Hair turns gray. I'd seen how my childhood classmates changed over the years. Noses grew bigger in puberty, altering the way features lined up in a face. Cheekbones emerged from baby fat. Gangly girls became pear-shaped, stubby girls shot up, slouchers pulled their shoulders back. There were girls like Kim whose metabolisms betrayed them. And then there was me, who suddenly started getting noticed for reasons I couldn't explain and still didn't entirely trust. During college I ran into an elementary-school classmate on an Amtrak train somewhere between New York and Boston. Her family had moved away from Washington, so I hadn't seen her since sixth grade. "Sarah Zuckerman?" she said in disbelief. "You're . . . beautiful." She was nicer to me than she had ever been before.

In my room that night, I studied the photos of Jenny in her book. I tried to transpose my mental image of Zoya onto the pictures from 1983, to see if and where the bone structures lined up. It reminded me of *America's Most Wanted,* of the drawings speculating what criminals might look like long after escape. If you add ten years and twenty pounds and a mustache or a beard. If you change the hair color and the eye color and add glasses or bangs. The possibilities were infinite. Even something as simple as a hat or a scarf can change the way you see someone. I'd always thought of Jenny as typically American, but what did that mean? I could see now how deep her eyes were set and how high her cheekbones were. Her face was almost Slavic. What if she were really Russian? Maybe she and her parents had moved to Washington from Perm, not Dayton. Maybe they had been posing as Americans. It's amazing how our perspectives shift with time. It's like the drinking fountains at my elementary school. As a kid I had to stand on my toes to reach them, and when I went back to visit as an adult, I couldn't believe they were so low to the ground. I fell asleep with

Jenny's book open in bed with me. I was startled awake by the blare of a car alarm—they were everywhere in Moscow, erupting violently, reminding me where I was. A place seething with crime. A place of new money and ancient grudges. I went to my window. I don't know which car was the source of the noise, but it was snowing, and I watched the white swirl over the alley and cover the dirt.

13.

In the morning I called Svetlana again. I didn't reach her, but this time instead of leaving her a voice-mail message I decided to go to her office. I was tired of being strung along. I wanted more than focus groups. I skipped my Russian class and walked all the way to Ulitsa Petrovka. Inside her building, the guard demanded my passport as usual. I told him I was there to see Svetlana Romanova. "I was just here yesterday," I said in Russian.

He wanted to know if she was expecting me. I was proud that my Russian had improved so much that I could understand him. "*Nyet*," I said. She wasn't expecting me, but if he called her, I was sure she would be happy to see me. I smiled at him, as if I were a regular in a restaurant greeting my favorite waiter. But he remained impassive. I watched him dial the red phone, listened to him describe me as an "American girl." When he hung up, I expected him to wave me past. Instead he said that Svetlana wasn't there.

"Where is she?" I said.

"You can't stay here," he said.

"I'll wait," I said. "She'll come down eventually."

He told me I'd have to wait outside. I took my passport and returned to the cold. It was nearly eleven. I figured that Svetlana or one of her colleagues would step outside for lunch, that I wouldn't have to wait long. I was wrong. Two hours later I was still waiting. I jumped up and down to keep warm.

It was Andrei, not Svetlana, who finally came out of the building. He was wearing a suit—dark gray with pinstripes—and a navy blue tie, as if he'd been costumed to play a stockbroker. A camel-colored scarf gave him a dash of European flair. *"Nasha Amerikanka,"* he said. Our American. "What are you doing here?"

"I wanted to talk to Svetlana," I said. "She didn't answer the phone."

"She isn't here," he said.

"Where is she?"

"Yaroslavl."

"Why Yaroslavl?" I had only a vague idea where the city was. South, I thought, in the provinces somewhere. I imagined a grimy place with a colorless ache of sky.

"Sampling," he said. "Taste tests, on the street. Unmarked cans, to see what people say."

"When will she be back?"

He shrugged. "A few days. Why? You have the big idea for us? Sveta says you are helping with the Czar campaign."

"Not really," I said.

"You are still looking for your dead friend?" he said with a smirk.

"I'm not sure she's dead."

"Either she is dead or she is alive. Are there any other options?"

"That woman at the focus groups . . ." I said.

"Who?"

"Zoya," I said. "She reminded me of my friend."

"Zoya is *my* friend."

"Your friend?"

"Sure, we go way back. Our fathers worked together. I introduced her to Sveta. Now they are thick as burglars."

"Thieves," I said. "Thick as thieves."

"Ah, yes. Sometimes I forget these expressions."

"If she's your friend, why was she at the research yesterday?"

"They are paid for the focus groups. We needed people and she needed money."

"Let me guess: This is information that can't be shared with Richard."

He smiled. "You are clever girl. Walk with me. I am going to buy cigarettes."

I fell into step with him. We turned right onto Ulitsa Kuznetsky Bridge. Passersby carried plastic bags from designer stores—Gucci, Prada, Versace. These empty "packets" were sold on the street to people who could never afford to shop in such places but who wanted to tote designer labels. The bags were wrinkled and worn after being used again and again.

"You don't ever smoke?" Andrei said.

"I used to," I said. "Sometimes. In college." I always felt like I was faking it even during the six-month period when I smoked every day. It was an attempt at cool that never quite fit.

"You have the boyfriend?" He so rarely mixed up his indefinite and definite articles. The boyfriend, I thought, as if there could only be one for a lifetime.

"No," I said.

"Why not?" he said.

"I guess I'm defective," I said.

"What is wrong with you? You have an extra toe?"

"No," I said with a half laugh. "Just ten the last time I checked."

"You look like a normal girl to me. Absolutely normal American girl."

"You don't have much basis for comparison. How many American girls do you know?" I said.

"I lived in USA," he said. "I saw my share of Americans in Washington. Maybe I was looking through the fence of the embassy compound, watching the girls go by. Maybe I saw you in your school kilt."

"How did you know I wore a uniform to school?" How grown-up Jenny and I had felt at the start of fourth grade, when we started wearing those itchy tartan skirts.

"Lucky guess," he said.

"What about Zoya?" I said. "Where in the States did she live?"

"She was also in Washington."

"At the embassy with you?"

"Not with me," he said. "Our families were not there at the same time. She was already back in Moscow when I went to Washington."

"Was her father a spy?" I said.

"Sarushka," Andrei said. "You are an attractive girl, but this suspicion is not becoming."

"Doveryay, no proveryay," I said. Trust, but verify. It was Reagan's philosophy when dealing with the Soviets.

We had reached a kiosk near the Metro. Andrei asked for a pack of Marlboro Reds. The woman behind the counter reluctantly put down her magazine to fulfill his request. She shoved the cigarettes at Andrei.

"My friend Maxim is having a birthday party Friday night," he said. "You should come with me."

"I'm not sure I'm in the mood for a party."

"You cannot spend all your time with foreigners," he said. "Don't you want to see real Moscow?"

I did want to see the real Moscow, whatever that meant. But I hesitated. "It's only Tuesday," I said. "Give me a few days to think about it."

"Sveta will be there," he said. "She'll be back from Yaroslavl. You can talk to her."

"Okay," I said. He promised to pick me up outside Corinne's building.

✳

IN RUSSIAN CLASS THAT WEEK, we were expressing hopes and desires. "I would like to be a mother," said the Dutch woman. "I would like to visit Egypt," said the Chinese diplomat's wife. Irina waited for me to share my desire with the rest of the class. I hesitated, then said, "I want to find my friend."

"*Kakuyu podrugu?*" Irina asked. Which friend?

"*Podrugu myertvoyu,*" I said. The dead friend.

Irina looked frightened. So I pretended to have mixed up my vocabulary words. "I meant *podrugu kotoroyu ya poteryala*," I said. The friend whom I lost.

I could make a list of all the things I've lost over the years. Library books, parking tickets, swim races, my virginity, my temper. My grandmother's charm bracelet, which told her life story in gold baubles—a San Francisco cable car, a tennis racket, a tiny Eiffel Tower—fell off my wrist one spring afternoon while I was riding my bike around the neighborhood. My favorite jeans disappeared from the laundry room in my dorm sophomore year. And I lost a friend when my first serious boyfriend began sleeping with her—"an unexpected turn of events" he called it, as if he were as surprised as I was to find her in his bed. It was the only time I've been angry enough to throw something—an organic-chemistry textbook—at anyone. He ducked, but the book hit the mirror behind him and shattered glass all over his floor. "You fucker!" I said. And he, looking at the discarded condom wrapper on the bedside table said, "Well, yeah."

But with Jenny I had the nagging sense that she wasn't really lost, not for good. I thought of the Joneses' house after the plane crash. The grocery list, the casserole in Tupperware, the rugby shirt folded on Jenny's desk chair. They had gone away to Maine for one night; everything was ready for their return. Was it possible that they had staged everything to look as if they intended to come back? *You Americans,* Svetlana said, *believe everything you see.* In hindsight Mrs. Jones's grocery list seemed a little too perfect. Not a single item crossed out, no second thoughts. It was written in one color of ink, as if it had been composed on the spot. Was it a prop? And where was the cat? Had they taken Hexa with them?

I used to lie in bed at night thinking about what I would take with me if our house were on fire. Assuming my mom and Pip made it out on their own, what irreplaceable material object would I rescue from the encroaching flames? My priorities shifted year to year. When I was seven, I wanted to save the film reel of Izzy. When I was ten, it was my journal. Later, of course, I had my Jenny files to worry about. When the Joneses prepared to go to Maine, knowing they were never coming back to Cleveland Park, what did they take with them? I imagined Jenny in her room, ranking her belongings. She left her diary behind, I remembered, which made no sense. She wrote in it almost every night and was absolutely hysterical at the possibility that someone might read it. If they knew they were leaving for good, surely she would have taken the diary with her.

My rational brain told me there was no way she could be alive. Her diary was still there. There was nothing but circumstantial evidence that her father was a spy. And it seemed unlikely that the Joneses could have defected secretly. But I couldn't assume anything. I had to trust my gut.

⁜

ON FRIDAY NIGHT I found myself in the back of a car with Andrei on our way to the outskirts of the city. "These days only foreigners can afford to live in the center," he said. "And *novye russkie.*" New Russians were everyone's favorite scapegoat.

The car was a Lada, ashen and boxy, and there was a hole in the backseat's leather. I found myself nervously pulling out bits of foam stuffing. I wiggled my finger down far enough to feel the coils of the springs, and I imagined them rusted and tarnished like everything else in Russia. My fidgeting made me think of my mother. She could never keep her hands on the steering wheel. Buckled into the backseat (even when my father was no longer there to claim the passenger side, she insisted I stay in the back where it was safer), I watched her hands flit from radio knobs to her scalp— she'd scratch absentmindedly when stalled at traffic lights—to her lips, which she'd tap with two fingers in a three-quarter rhythm that suggested a waltz. I was used to her nervous energy, and in hindsight I realize that it kept her thin. She maintained a girlish figure without regular exercise. While my classmates' mothers embraced the 1980s aerobics trend, she worried herself into shape.

Andrei had a bottle of vodka and a bouquet of flowers. I'd forgotten to bring anything. My mother had always warned me never to arrive at a dinner party empty-handed. I was trying to think of some way to compensate for my bad manners when I felt Andrei's breath on my neck; he had scooted close to me.

"When was the last time you saw your friend?" he said.

"Which friend?"

"Your dead friend," Andrei said.

"Ten years ago," I said.

"That is a long time," Andrei said. "If she is still alive, will she be the same?" He was rummaging around in his pocket, and his arm kept brushing my leg. I shivered at his touch and slid over on the seat. "Sorry," he said. "I am looking for the lighter."

"Please don't smoke in the car," I said. "I swear I'll throw up."

"Ah, the delicate constitution! *Ladno.* For you I will wait." He removed his hands from his pockets and made a show of folding them in his lap.

"*Spasibo,*" I said.

"So you have ten toes and ten fingers," he said. "Do you have any extra parts I should know about?"

"No. Nothing extra," I said. "But I might be missing a few."

"You are a strange girl," he said.

The car came to a sudden stop in front of a dreary apartment block. Under the weak light of the streetlamps, I could make out a rusted slide in the courtyard, so out of use it looked like it had been abandoned by a civilization that was now extinct. *The land of happy childhood.*

"*Ladno,*" Andrei said again. He paid the driver while I got out of the car.

———

EVERYTHING IN MAXIM'S APARTMENT was dingy and brown. Even the walls were papered in a brown floral print. We removed our shoes in a cramped hallway and pushed into the living room, where a long table was piled with plates of cheese and various pickled things. Cucumbers had been sliced into stars that fanned across one plate. There were about fifteen people crowded around the table, and a scruffy man was playing the guitar.

"He is playing the songs of Vladimir Vysotsky," said Andrei. "You know Vysotsky? He was like our Bob Dylan. Folk music."

I nodded. Vysotsky's funeral was during the Moscow Olympics in 1980. Apparently a lot of people left the sporting events to attend the ceremony.

Andrei introduced me as *"moya Amerikanka."* My American. I blushed, but no one seemed to be laughing at me. Everyone seemed genuinely excited to make my acquaintance. Maxim the birthday boy offered me a clownish bow. I told him my name.

"Yevreyka?" he asked. Are you Jewish?

"Nyet," I said. "But a lot of my friends are," I added, afraid to seem like I was endorsing anti-Semitism.

"U menya tost!" Maxim said. Someone handed me a glass. His speech was too fast and elaborate for me to follow—lots of puns and wordplay, something about a bear, maybe?—but it must have been funny, because everyone was laughing. At the end I understood him when he said, "To America!" Maybe he was joking, but

everyone drank. I forced down a large swallow of vodka and then chased it with a pickle.

I pulled off my sweater and tied it around my waist. The room was stifling. The heat in Moscow's buildings was centralized; it was turned on at the beginning of October, and there was no way for individuals to control it. So outside you were freezing, but inside you were always too hot. It was especially stuffy on the Metro, where you were trapped in layers of clothing. Whenever I emerged from a Metro station, I could feel the sweat on my skin congeal as it cooled.

A balding guy in plaid bell-bottoms and a Brown University sweatshirt sidled over to us. "You are from America?" he said in English. I nodded. I felt like a doll on display. Wind her up and see the American drink vodka!

"You know Brighton Beach?" he said.

"This is Sasha," said Andrei. "He lived in Brighton Beach for a year in the 1970s."

It became clear that Sasha's English vocabulary was stuck in that decade. "I'm hep to the jive," he said.

"Lucky you," I said.

"Do you read *Cosmopolitan?*" he asked me.

"No," I said.

"Do you read *Playboy?*"

"*Nyet,*" I said. The Russian word seemed more forceful than "No."

"There are some very interesting articles about the joys of sex with older men." He raised his eyebrows. "Can you dig it?" Except it sounded like "Ken you dick it?" when he said it. He smelled of garlic. I swiveled away from him.

Suddenly Andrei pointed across the room. *"Vot ona,"* she said. There she is.

It was Svetlana. She wore a fitted red sweater with a plunging neckline. Her skin was milky and virtuous, and her breasts, I realized with a start, were large. My own body was girlish; I was still waiting for boobs. Maxim kissed her three times in the Russian fashion—left cheek, right cheek, left cheek—and then she spotted Andrei and moved toward us.

"We've been waiting for you," Andrei said.

"Privyet," Svetlana said. She lit a cigarette.

"Careful," Andrei said. *"Nasha* Sarah has the delicate constitution."

"Why is U.S. Constitution delicate? Because of founding fathers? They were not real men?"

"Not the United States Constitution," I said. "My personal constitution. Like my makeup."

"You need the makeup," she said. "You would look much better with the lipstick."

Andrei ignored us. *"U menya tost,"* he announced to the room, and glasses were refilled.

"Nyet, spasibo," I said, but Svetlana topped off my glass anyway. I didn't want to be rude. *This is how diplomats become alcoholics,* I thought.

The toast was to Maxim, and it was obviously affectionate.

The audience was rapt. It was like being at a wedding. Andrei concluded by wishing his friend happy birthday, and then everyone broke into clamorous song. On birthdays Russians of my generation sing a song from a beloved Soviet cartoon called *Cheburashka*. We had to watch it in college. In the cartoon a crocodile plays an accordion in the rain. "Let people stare," he sings. The song is cheerful, but the lyrics of the refrain ("Unfortunately, a birthday is only once a year") suggest that joy is fleeting. "Can't they just enjoy the moment?" someone in my college Russian class asked, "without reminding you how soon the fun will end?"

Andrei was at my side, pouring more vodka into my glass. He sang part of the birthday refrain, soft as a lullaby. *"Tolko raz v godu."* Only once a year.

Svetlana pinched my arm. "Sarah," she said. "Your birthday will soon be here."

"How do you know when my birthday is?"

"Jennifer told me."

"When?"

"On seventh of November."

"I mean when was she talking about my birthday?"

"She wanted to buy for you the gift," Svetlana said. "We with Jennifer were at the diplomat *magazin*."

"The diplomatic store."

"Da. It was day before she returned to America. I thought I would never see her again."

Did Jenny give me a birthday present from Russia? What I remembered most clearly were her rhapsodic descriptions of Svetlana that fall. I recalled, suddenly, her determination to learn the Cyrillic alphabet and her novice efforts to form Russian letters on the wide-ruled pages young children use.

"And you remember my birthday, even after all this time?" I said. I wanted her to confess that she had talked to Jenny about me more recently.

"Is easy to remember. It is our Revolution Day." November 7 was when the party marked the anniversary of the October Revolution; during Communism it was a day of military parades and marching Young Pioneers. Svetlana wandered off.

What did Jenny give me for my eleventh birthday? Sixth grade. Was that the year I celebrated at a bowling alley? Jenny, my mother, and me, with a lane to ourselves. A cake with cream-cheese frosting. It all came back to me. Jenny and I took turns penciling our scores into the squares on the sheet of paper provided. I got two strikes that day. I won both games and choreographed a goofy victory dance. I'd spent so much time inventorying my losses and rejections that I'd lost sight of the wins. How many other moments of triumph were buried in the archives of my brain? Jenny's birthday gift to me was wrapped in green and white stripes. I recalled tearing off the paper with uncharacteristic abandon. *A balailaka.* That's what she gave me. A Russian folk instrument, painted red with gold flowers. My mom strummed it right there in the bowling alley while she and Jenny sang.

"Who is Jennifer?" said Andrei.

"My friend," I said.

"The dead friend?" he said.

"Svetlana knew her, too," I said. "She visited Moscow when she was young."

"*Tolko raz v godu,*" he sang again. Only once a year.

I was already feeling muddled. The room was hot, and people were drifting in and out of frame, blurring in and out of focus. What the fuck, I thought. Might as well get drunk. I swigged the whole cup of vodka and shook off the burn. The man with the guitar shouted, "This is for our American!" and broke into the chords of "Hotel California."

"I hate the Eagles," I said under my breath.

⌗

LATER—I DON'T KNOW how much later, because I'd lost all track of time—Andrei had me pressed against a wall in the living room. His hands inched up my legs, but he kept his eyes on me, as if he didn't know what his hands were doing.

"I don't trust you," I said. My voice was unsteady.

"You're not supposed to trust me," he said. "I'm Russian. Your government *taught* you not to trust me. But you trust in God, yes? It says so on your dollars."

"I don't believe in God," I said.

"I thought all Americans believed in God."

"Not me," I said.

"What do you believe, Sarushka?" He prodded me with the diminutive; in his grip my name turned tender. He wrapped his hands around my throat, and I thought, for a moment, that he was going to squeeze the life right out of me. Instead he cupped my neck and pressed his thumbs gently into the knobs of my collarbones. "So skinny, Sarushka," he said. He bent forward, let his lips grace the triangle of skin between his hands.

"I think I'm going to faint," I said, but I was already falling as I spoke. I was on the floor without knowing exactly how I got there.

"You melted," Andrei said. He was crouching next to me, and I could see that he wore combat boots and that they were flecked with white paint. I tried to stand but couldn't.

"*Vsyo khorosho?*" he said. Is everything all right?

"I'm sorry," I said. Not because I'd fallen but because I was sorry to have caused a fuss. I didn't want him to worry about me. I've never been good at leaning on people. I'd had only two drinks, but it was on an empty stomach. And the room was so hot. And I'd been standing in one place for too long. My knees must have locked. I tried to explain this to him. I tried to tell him that it was nothing to worry about, that this was not the first time I'd fainted, but my words warbled. I was groggy. I didn't know what language I was speaking. I didn't see Svetlana; had she gone home? There were still a lot of people there, but the party no longer had a nucleus. Everyone was scattered in different corners of the room. One couple was making out on the couch, sucking at each other with gasping, gulping sounds.

"*Vsyo khorosho,*" Andrei said again, but it wasn't a question this time. Everything's okay. He repeated it again and again. And so I finally stopped trying to keep my head up and just let it fall onto his willing shoulder. Someone turned up the stereo. We sat against the wall with eyes shut.

"*The Wall,*" Andrei said to me in English. "Pink Floyd. That was an important album for us, before glasnost. It was so strange, you know. I went away to Washington, and when I came back, everything was different. In D.C. we hardly left the embassy grounds, so we were living in a miniature Soviet Union, but then we came back in 1989 and it was like a different country. We were raised to be like everyone else . . . But now . . ." He laughed. "Capitalism is all about individualism."

"In theory," I said. "We've got our share of joiners, too." I could feel how flushed I was. No doubt I looked awful.

As if reading my mind, he said, "*Ty krasavitsa.*" You're a beauty.

"*Ya?*" I said. I still wasn't used to hearing that I was beautiful. People started telling me that in college, when I had apparently completed my transformation from ugly duckling. When I got to college, I was considered sexy for all the things that had been held against me when I was younger. *You're hard to read,* said one guy. *You're disarmingly cool,* said another. And when their exploring fingers found their way inside my pants, they said, like metereologists describing tropical weather zones, *Here's where it gets really warm and wet.* I didn't trust those guys, with their undiscerning hard-ons, with their fumbles and grunts. One boyfriend fondled my breasts with the clinical detachment of a doctor looking for lumps. Their lust was fickle, careless. They were greedy. They would take what they could get, use you up, spit you out. But I liked the reductive nature of sex: in the moment's heat, affiliations fell away like clothing. You were left with skin and sweat, humanity's sticky essence.

"*Ty,*" he said. The informal you. He took my hand, then turned it over and studied my palm. "A long life," he said in English. "Many adventures. All over the world."

"I don't believe in fortune-telling," I said.

"The American who doesn't believe in anything. Come on," he said. "If not God, you must believe in democracy. Or the stock market. Or Coca-Cola."

"I've always been loyal to Coke," I admitted. "I've never liked Pepsi."

"Aha!" he said. "She believes in the Real Thing."

"I don't know what's real," I said. "And what isn't." *It's not that I didn't believe in anything, I thought; it's that I regretted believing too much. I believed in too many people. Like an idiot, I believed in forever.*

"I have something for you." Svetlana materialized next to me and yanked me up off the floor. Then she pulled a white envelope out from under her sweater.

"What's this?" I said.

"A special invitation," she said.

"You can't come all the way to Russia and not visit a dacha," said Andrei as he stood up.

"Your chance to see typical Russian country house," Svetlana said. "You will be our guest. We will have shashlik!"

"Shashlik is kebabs," Andrei said.

"Unfortunately, my family's dacha is only for summer," Svetlana said. "But we will go to our friend's house. Her dacha is ready for winter."

"Winterized," Andrei said.

"*Da,*" Sveta said. "Andrei will drive you."

"When?" I said.

She just pointed at the envelope in my hand. I opened it. Inside, the card read, "*Sunday. 12 o'clock. Our friend is expecting us.*" The words swam before me.

"I think I'm drunk," I said. "And I don't like being drunk. I need to go home."

"To USA?" Andrei said.

"Eventually," I said. "But right now to Corinne's. To the apartment I'm staying in."

"I will escort you," Svetlana said. "I am ready to leave." She touched Andrei's arm. "*Do zavtra.*" See you tomorrow. She went to get her coat.

"What are you guys doing tomorrow?" I said to Andrei. I was surprised to feel a jealous pang. Not of the sexual sort—though I did wonder if he and Svetlana had ever slept together—but the familiar sense that alliances were forming around me, that while I remained alone, others were teaming up. I felt comfortable with Andrei because his English was so good, because he had lived just a few blocks away from my childhood home. But he and Svetlana obviously knew each other very well. They were in league somehow.

"She meant Sunday," Andrei said.

"She said tomorrow," I said.

"She thinks today is Saturday," he said.

"If you say so."

"*Eto ya znayu.*" I know so.

"What else do you know?" I looked at him. He had a narrow, elegant face and short, reddish brown hair. His smile was tempting. I had a sudden urge to kiss him. I leaned in and let my mouth meet his. His lips were chapped and dry. I pulled back.

"I know you are very beautiful," he said.

"I'm not going to sleep with you," I said.

"*Nyet,*" he said. "Of course not."

"Sarah," Svetlana called from across the room. "*Davai!*" Come on.

#

IN THE CAR ON THE WAY back to the center of the city, Svetlana asked the driver to turn up the radio; it was techno music, and I could hardly hear myself think.

"It's so loud," I said. I could feel a hangover brewing. The night's events jostled in my head, and I was already having trouble separating fiction from fact. Did I really kiss Andrei? Did Svetlana really invite me to a dacha?

"I do not want him to hear us," Svetlana said.

I turned to look at her. I couldn't get a read on her face in the dark. "What?" I said. "Are you actually going to give me some real information? Or do you just like creating a sense of mystery?" I could smell the smoke from the party on my clothes and I couldn't wait to take a long, hot shower. "Smoke and mirrors," I said. "One-way mirrors."

"What did you think of our consumer research?"

"Sorry if I messed it up," I said. "But you promised me a surprise. I thought I saw Jenny in that room."

"Well, Richard thinks you are crazy, but it went exactly as I planned," she said.

"What do you mean?"

"You did see Jennifer. I wanted to get you in the room with her."

"What?"

"I wanted to see if you would recognize her."

"Zoya?" I said.

"She was not ready to see you, but I knew she would come to focus groups. You recognized her, she recognized you."

"I thought Zoya was Andrei's friend," I said.

She paused. Then she said uncertainly, "He told you that?"

"Yes," I said. "He said he introduced her to you."

"That is good," she said. "Jennifer would not want him to—how do you say?—blow on her cover."

"Blow her cover."

"*Da.*"

"She recognized me at the focus groups?"

"Yes, but she could not say anything. Not in front of Richard."

"That was really Jenny?"

"*Eto pravda,*" Svetlana said.

"But where is she?"

"She is living in dacha," Svetlana said. "Provided by KGB."

"I want to see her."

"This is why I arrange meeting. This is why we go to dacha."

"We're going to Jenny's dacha?"

"You must call her Zoya in front of Andrei, *ponimayesh?*"

"He doesn't know the truth?"

"He does not know that you know. He will report her."

"To whom?"

"She needs her father's KGB pension. It is not much, but she has nothing else, understand? If they think she wants to return to America, they will take it away. She will have nothing. She must be loyal to Russia because Russian government is supporting her. I told her perhaps you can help her."

"Does she want to return to America? Can't she just waltz into the embassy and repatriate?"

"She is always under the surveillance. She will explain to you. But remember: It is secret from Andrei. Promise me. You cannot tell him. He cannot be trusted."

"Was his father in the KGB?" I whispered.

She leaned close to me and placed a hand to my ear. *"Da,"* she breathed, as if blowing up a balloon with her secret. *"Yes. Of course."*

14.

IT SNOWED ALL DAY SATURDAY. Corinne and I made hot chocolate and popcorn and shuffled through her collection of pirated movies in search of something to watch.

"I'm sick of all of these," she said, "but it's too cold to walk to the video store." There was a small English-language video-rental place just off Malaya Bronnaya, near the church where Pushkin married, but it was a good ten minutes away. "Welcome to winter in Moscow," she said. "The key is to leave the house only when necessary."

We settled for old episodes of *Fawlty Towers* on the BBC. We sat together on the kitchen sofa, sharing the heavy wool throw. The usually unflappable Corinne was out of sorts that day.

"I told myself I'd stay here for two years," she said. "But sometimes I'm not sure I'll make it. It's good for my career, but it's killing me." She clutched her mug with both hands and stared into it, as if trying to read signs in the marshmallows. I'd never seen her so calm. She was still in her robe—it was creamy silk and printed with birds in flight—and without her signature red lipstick she looked frail.

"Are you okay?" I said.

"I'm just tired. I've been here almost a year, and we haven't even published an issue yet. We're just laying the groundwork for launch, greasing the wheels. I'm starting to wonder if it will ever happen. Most days I'm impressed if the phones work. I'm thirty years old, and I'm tired. Sometimes I just want to go home."

I envied her knowing where she belonged. "Maybe I shouldn't take this job," I said.

"Don't listen to me. I'm just cranky today. If you want to be a journalist, you should stay," she said. "There are big stories here."

"Do you remember Jennifer Jones?" I said.

"The old Hollywood actress?" she said. "What about her?"

"Nothing," I said. "She just popped into my head."

Corinne said I needed to figure out what I wanted. What I really wanted was to hear Jenny say, *I missed you.* But I knew I had inherited my mother's habit of holding on too tight. No one cared about my Jennifer Jones anymore. The Berlin Wall fell; the Soviet Union collapsed; I was no longer a wallflower. Why was I still obsessed with Jenny?

❉

LATE ON SUNDAY MORNING, Andrei picked me up in a large four-wheel-drive vehicle painted a dark green reminiscent of a tank.

"Is this yours?" I said. Very few Russians owned cars in 1995.

"I borrowed it from my father," he said.

I'd brought orange tulips—thirteen of them, purchased from one of the twenty-four-hour flower kiosks—and I put the bouquet in the back. There were two shopping bags propped on the seat. Through the plastic I could see the outline of soda cans.

"You want a Coke?" Andrei said. "I brought some for you."

"Aren't you supposed to be hawking Czar?" I said.

"Czar is owned by Coca-Cola."

"What?"

"They're trying to gain market share by launching a Russian brand. They're not going to tell people it's owned by Coke, but, you know, that's why one of Coke's roster agencies is doing the campaign."

"So an American company is using Russian nationalism to sell a Russian brand that is actually American?" I said.

"An American company with a British creative director and Russian copywriters," he said.

"That's insane." *Everyone is potentially under opposition control,* I thought.

"Eto biznes," he said. It's business. "Someday perhaps a Rus-

sian company will own Coca-Cola and Czar will be the flagship brand."

"How did you end up working in advertising?"

He shrugged. "My father knows Misha. The managing director. Every foreign firm needs a Russian partner to get started."

"You mean to handle the bribes."

"So many opinions, Sarushka," he said. "As if your country is not corrupt. It will take us about an hour to get there. You mind if I smoke?"

"I do, actually," I said.

"Okay," he said. "You're the boss."

"How old were you when you met Zoya?"

"I don't know. Thirteen? She was probably twelve. My parents took me to see her before we went to Washington, so she could tell me what it was like there."

So Andrei met Zoya about the same time Jenny died. It was possible that he met her right after she assumed her new identity. "And what did she tell you?" I asked.

"She told me about the embassy apartment building, about the school. She told me about your cherry blossoms."

"She went to the embassy school?"

"Of course. We all did. When she was there, the embassy office buildings were not yet open, but the school and the residential areas were complete in 1979, so . . ."

"You're sure she went to the embassy school?"

"I told you, we hardly left the embassy grounds."

"And her Russian?" I said. "When you met Zoya, how was her Russian?"

"Do you always ask so many questions?"

"I'm curious. And I'm practicing to be a journalist."

"Actually, the first few times we met, we spoke English. My parents wanted me to practice with her because she was fluent. My English was terrible in those days. My parents hoped that talking with Zoya would be like a—how do you call it? Crash class?"

"Crash course."

"Crash course, *da*. So I went to see Zoya a few times before we moved to Washington."

"Did she speak English with a Russian accent?" I said.

"No, she'd mastered American English. She taught me American slang. She told me about American television shows. *The Love Boat, Fantasy Island, Three's Company*."

These were shows I watched with Jenny. "And you're sure she was Russian?" I said.

He laughed. "As opposed to what?"

I changed the subject. I didn't want Andrei to get suspicious. For all I knew, there was a recording device in the car. "Where are we going?" I said. "Have you been there before?"

"To Zoya's? Sure. It's not so far from my family's dacha."

Russian dachas were handed out by trade unions, so each dacha community outside Moscow was defined by the profession of its inhabitants. The Writers' Union, for example, gave its members dachas at Peredelkino, where great Soviet scribes spent their summers. Scientists had dachas in one community. And I knew that KGB operatives had dachas in another one.

"Is it near all the KGB dachas?" I said.

"*Boltun—nakhodka dlya shpiona,*" he said. It's the Russian equivalent of "Loose lips sink ships," but literally it means "A chatterbox is a treasure for a spy."

I sank back into the passenger seat. Moscow was sprawling, vast. As the car rattled beyond the ring road, the city's main artery, I wondered if I was being kidnapped. During the 1991 coup attempt, the KGB held Gorbachev hostage in his dacha. I should have told Corinne where I was going. I should have told my mother. I should have e-mailed Juliet in New York or Sam in San Francisco. How long would it take everyone to notice I was missing? I didn't even know in what direction we were heading. Were we north of the city? East? West? *This is a fool's errand,* I thought. *I shouldn't have come to this crazy country at all.*

And then, the birch trees came into view: long white limbs lining the road like ghosts. And they were impossibly beautiful. Russians talk a lot about the soul. The *dusha.* The depth and mysticism of the Russian *dusha* can't be understood by foreigners, they say. The Russian soul is intuitive and fatalistic and strong. They believe in the incorruptible power of *dusha* no matter how much the material world disappoints. I pressed my nose to the window of Andrei's car and watched the birch trees flicker past, and I felt a stirring deep down. My soul was in there somewhere.

Finally we turned onto a dirt lane, rutted and crusted with old snow. Andrei slowed down, took the bumps with care. He hadn't said a word for nearly an hour. "We're almost there?" I said.

"*Da,*" he said. "*Gotova?*" Are you ready?

The dacha was a wooden cottage nestled in a grove of pine trees. It looked like it was made of gingerbread, with white trim like icing. Andrei cut the motor and reached into the back for the bag of gifts he had brought. We got out of the car. It was cold, but it was almost noon and the sun was bright on the snow.

"*Dobry dyen!*" Andrei called with exaggerated cheer. Good day! He knocked on the door with three quick raps. Was it some kind of code?

Zoya materialized in the doorway. "*Skolko let, skolko zim?*" she said. How many summers, how many winters? It was such a poetic way to say it had been too long.

15.

1983

IT'S THE DAY OF OUR CLASS PLAY. Our parents are arranged on folding chairs erected for the occasion, and the other lower-school classes—fourth-, fifth-, and sixth-graders—are cross-legged on the gymnasium floor. From backstage I spot my mother through a torn seam in the curtain. Her hair is hidden in a blue-and-orange scarf, and she's drowning in a cardigan that is far too big for her. She studies the program as if preparing for a quiz. In the front row, I see Jenny's parents. Mrs. Jones has dressed up; she's even wearing high heels. Mr. Jones is telling a story to the mother next to him. Or maybe it's a joke. The woman grins, captive to his charms.

Behind the curtain, Mrs. Gibson is whispering final notes. *Take a deep breath,* she says to us. *You know your parts, you're ready. Now just enjoy it. It's called a play because it's supposed to be fun.*

Jenny's ruby red slippers are on the prop table, awaiting the second act. They are patent Mary Janes, purchased at the little shoe store on Macomb Street, then smeared with glue and covered with glitter. Mrs. Jones made them. She volunteered her services; she loves costumes.

In a corner, Jenny is warming up her voice. *"To sit in solemn silence on a dull, dark dock / In a pestilential prison with a life-long lock. / Awaiting the sensation of a short, sharp shock / From a cheap and chippy chopper with a big, black block."*

Did you teach her that? It is Kim hissing in my ear. Was she actually the Wicked Witch, or is that just how I remember her? She raps my shoulder with her broom.

Teach her what? I say. I don't look at Kim, but I can see the ghoulish green of her face paint out of the corner of my eye.

That dumb vocal exercise, she says. *It's so depressing I figured it must have come from you. It's about jail and someone waiting to get their head chopped off. Gross.*

No, I say. *It didn't come from me.*

Jenny repeats the rhyme. Her alliterative consonants are defined and crisp. *Awaiting the sensation of a short, sharp shock.* She's not famous yet—her letter to Andropov won't be published for another three weeks—but she is already a star.

I hear the impatience of the audience: the squeak of metal as chairs inch back, the rustle of paper as programs are opened and closed, the wiggling girls who are glad to be out of class. And then Mrs. Gibson's voice from out in front of the house.

Welcome, she says. *We are so grateful you could all be here.*

My classmates and I cluster in a nervous swarm, and then Mrs. Gibson is there in the dark, hustling us into our places, and the lights in the gym go down, and when the curtain goes up, only Jenny looks ready to perform.

✦

EVEN AFTER ALL THESE YEARS, I remember the pungent smell of vinegar as we walked into the house. It was the marinade for the shashlik, Svetlana said. The kebabs had already been soaking for hours.

"It smells delicious," I lied.

Zoya was wearing a black turtleneck sweater and black jeans. She was shorter than I was, shorter than I thought Jenny would end up being, and curvier than I had imagined Jenny would be. "Welcome to a Russian country house," she said.

"This is Sarah," Andrei said. "Our American friend."

"The crazy girl from our office," Sveta said with a smile.

"I believe I saw you on the roller coaster," Zoya said.

"Really?" I said. I thought I'd been so stealthy.

There was something wintry in her expression. She wore small diamonds—or rhinestones? it was hard to tell if they were fake—in her ear and twisted them while she spoke. "I spent some of the money your boss gave me at Gorky Park," she said to Andrei and

Svetlana. "Those rides are expensive. It's hard to justify paying for them unless you get a sudden windfall. I decided to treat myself."

"What is this 'windfall'?" Sveta said.

"'Windfall' *eto kak udacha*," Andrei said. "Like a lucky break."

"Did you go on roller coasters when you were a kid?" I said to Zoya.

"We had no roller coasters in Moscow," Svetlana said.

"But Zoya lived in the United States," I said. "Didn't you?"

I waited for some kind of reaction. A half smile, a wince. Anything. Her face remained blank, serene as a mask. I inhaled deeply, as if the scent of her might give something away. If you asked me to describe what Jenny smelled like, I couldn't tell you, but I thought there might be some familiar note that would take me back to the Jones house. Zoya just smelled like tobacco. If regret had an odor, it would smell like an ashtray.

"*Da,*" she said. "But I gather their boss isn't supposed to know that." She handled her words carefully, as if they were made of glass. The Moscow accent I'd heard at the ad agency was gone. She spoke English like a native, with an American accent. But so did Andrei. It didn't prove anything.

I gave her the tulips. "*Spasibo,*" she said, and pressed her nose into the flowers for a careless sniff.

"Tulips smell like nothing," Svetlana said. "The Dutch have no passion, I tell you."

The room was crowded with various objects and competing patterns. The walls were papered in a dark red floral print on which dozens of oil paintings hung. The pictures were of ancient

Russian churches, mostly, with glinting gold domes. Three Oriental rugs had been arranged in overlapping squares, and the lamps were covered with patchwork shades. An antique silver samovar loomed on the sideboard, and among the books on the shelves painted lacquer boxes fought for space with dried flowers. I felt like I was stepping into a Chekhov play.

"This is a typical dacha?" I said.

"Dacha is where Russians go to relax," Svetlana said.

"Some dachas are much smaller," Andrei said. "And most dachas are only used between May and October. We grill shashlik outdoors. It is a little cold today, but we will manage." He held up a bottle of vodka and winked.

"Won't you sit down?" Zoya said. She indicated a leather recliner draped with an old quilt. "This is the most comfortable seat in the house."

I sank into the chair. Zoya and Andrei sat down on a sagging sofa opposite me.

"I will put flowers in the vase," Svetlana said. She carried my tulips away.

I ran my eyes over the room, looking for clues. On the bookshelves all the titles were in Russian. There were no framed family photographs, no evidence of the Joneses or of the United States of America. There was an acoustic guitar on the floor in one corner. An old turntable sat on a shelf with dozens of records stacked haphazardly next to it. An antique clock on the wall had Roman numerals on its face. A chessboard was set up on a small table near the window. What if, instead of MASH, Jenny and I had played a game called DASH, in which future home options were Dacha, Apartment, Shack, House?

"How long have you lived here?" I said.

"In this house?" Zoya said. She was doing math in her head. "Ten years, maybe. But my family also had an apartment in the city."

"On the Arbat?" I said.

"No," she said. "Chistye Prudy."

I kept waiting for her to give me some kind of sign, some nod of recognition. But the woman across from me remained detached. Her posture was remarkable: it was as if even her spine were unburdened by doubt. She had none of Jenny's softness; her edges were sharp. And yet I couldn't shake the feeling that I knew her. Under her icy shell, I could see a blueprint of the person she might have been.

"Where in the States did you live?" I pressed. "In Washington?"

"Yes, Washington," she allowed. She twisted a strand of golden hair.

"But your parents are Russian?" I said. Moscow Rule #8: *Don't harass the opposition.* I didn't want to push her. I'd play along.

"My parents are dead," she said.

The half-truth hung in the air between us the way, years later, I felt its presence between me and the man with whom I wanted to spend the rest of my life. "Is there someone else?" I said to him. We were sitting side by side on the sofa of the New York apartment we shared, and when I asked the question, he froze for a moment, then said—while staring straight into space or into the imagined face of the shrink who had coached him through the breakup rehearsal—"I just need to be alone. This is all I can handle." The unsaid words were suspended, as if from wires, and I knew that he had already transferred his allegiance, that another pair of hands was already guiding him inside her, that another conjured body fueled his masturbation, that another phone was receiving his flirtatious text messages. He couldn't look me in the eye. I could have said, *I can tell you're lying,* but he wasn't lying, exactly, just omitting the part of the story that would make him look bad. The result was the same, wasn't it?

He was withdrawing his affection; he was demoting me to the past tense. He thought his leaving me was unrelated to his joining her, but I knew he wouldn't have the courage to go without a destination. She was waiting with arms open, adoring and not yet disappointed. Because it's easy to love someone you haven't let down. In the beginning the promises are like fresh snow, not muddied by footprints, not yet trampled. You are a hero to the country you defect to, a traitor to the one you defect from. The face of the one you're leaving is crestfallen, biting her lip in an effort to stay strong, to believe, in spite of all the evidence, that you are innocent. "It just didn't work out," he said to me, as if he had no agency in the matter, as if it were chance, not choice, taking him away from me.

Would I have felt better knowing that there was nothing I could have done to make Jenny stay? Would it have been easier to let her go?

Svetlana returned with four glasses. "These are okay?" she said to Zoya.

Zoya nodded. In her presence Svetlana was deferential and

eager to please. I realized that Zoya was the sun who pulled Sveta into her orbit.

Svetlana placed the glasses on the coffee table and sat down beside Andrei. "Perhaps you would like to walk in the woods?" she said to me. "It is very beautiful place for walking."

"Also skiing," said Andrei. "Cross-country skiing." He opened the vodka and filled the glasses.

"It is not so cold today," Zoya said. "But better if we take a walk after lunch."

"*U menya tost,*" said Andrei.

"In English," said Zoya, "so our American guest can understand."

"*Ladno,*" said Andrei. "A toast to friendship between nations."

All our glasses met in the center of the table. "During a Russian toast," said Zoya, "you have to make eye contact with everyone." So for a moment my eyes locked on hers. They were impenetrable pools. I couldn't find my way.

"Now," Andrei said. "Time to grill shashlik. Come. I will show you how we do it." He beckoned to me.

I bundled up and followed him outside to a primitive grill constructed of a few bricks. He squatted to build his fire. "Svetlana is like schoolgirl around Zoya," Andrei said. He imitated her voice. "'Zoya says this, Zoya says that' . . . She would follow Zoya off a cliff."

"Svetlana told me I shouldn't trust you," I said.

He laughed. "That's because she is jealous. She knows I like you."

"Huh," I said.

"You like kebabs?"

"Sure," I said. "But I'm really cold." I wanted to talk to Zoya out of Andrei's earshot.

"I can keep you warm," he said.

I rolled my eyes. "I'm sure you can."

"You are very cynical for an American," he said. "You know that?"

"I'm going inside," I said.

＃

SVETLANA AND ZOYA were preparing lunch. I stood in the doorway of the kitchen and watched them chop vegetables.

"You like peppers?" Zoya said to me.

I nodded. The kitchen was a bright, charming space. Pots climbed the walls on hooks, and blue-and-white porcelain tiles made a flowery backsplash behind the stove. The table was draped with a yellow cloth and set with four china dishes in a green-and-white pattern. My tulips had been arranged in the center in a white jug.

Svetlana opened a jar of preserves and held it up for my inspection. "At dacha we gather the berries in summer and then make the jams."

Through the warped old window, I could see Andrei tending his fire.

"And mushrooms?" I said, turning back to face Sveta. "You

also gather mushrooms?" It seemed like a dangerous enterprise, separating the edible fungi from the poisonous. I wouldn't know how to tell the difference.

"Of course mushrooms," Svetlana said. "At dacha we live simple life."

I was about to tell Zoya I knew who she really was when Andrei walked into the room. "I am ready for the meat," he said, and clapped his hands.

Zoya passed him a plate piled with skewers of lamb. "I'll come with you," she said.

"When can I talk to her without Andrei?" I said to Svetlana after they had gone outside.

She just held a finger to her lips. "Shh," she said. "Patience."

I looked outside. Andrei caught Zoya's hand and pulled her close. The embrace was brief, but their bodies came together easily, as if by habit, and I wondered if they were lovers. I glanced at Svetlana. She was busy slicing bread.

❈

WHEN ANDREI AND ZOYA returned with the shashlik, we sat down to a feast. Soup, of course, but also beet salad, boiled potatoes, and the lamb kebabs. Even caviar, red and black. And vodka. Svetlana refilled our glasses as we took our seats.

"This is lovely," I said. "I hope you didn't go to all this trouble just for me."

"It was our pleasure," Zoya said. When she smiled, I saw the remnant of a dimple. I was following crumbs, trying to find Jenny's path through the woods. I sat across from her. Andrei was next to me.

"Do you like living here?" I said.

"I am a Russian citizen," said Zoya. "Where else would I live?"

"Why are Americans so surprised that we are happy? Russia is great country," said Svetlana.

"If Russia is so great," I said, "why are you trying to find a foreign husband so you can leave?"

"I keep the options open," said Svetlana with a shrug. I admired her honesty. I couldn't blame her for being pragmatic. Maybe she'd written to me because she thought I could help her find an American husband.

"You, too?" I said to Andrei.

"What?" he said.

"Are you also keeping your options open?"

"What do you mean?" he said.

"I wouldn't marry a foreigner," Zoya said.

"That's because you are still in love with Dima," said Sveta.

"I thought we weren't going to bring up Dima," said Andrei.

"Who's Dima?" I said.

"Dmitri is an asshole," Zoya said.

"Dmitri is her ex-husband," Sveta said.

"Does everyone have an ex-husband?" I said.

"I have an ex-wife," said Andrei. He laughed.

Maybe it was hard to commit to people when everything else was changing so fast. People seemed ambivalent about marriage and children. Russia had zero population growth. Women weren't having babies; they were having abortions. They used them as birth control. How could this woman—a divorcée, contemptuous of foreigners—be my former best friend?

"I don't regret my divorce," Zoya said. "I don't regret anything. I have a good life. I have friends. I have a vegetable garden. I swim every morning at the Olympic pool . . ." She ran out of items on her list. She raked her left hand through her hair, lifting the curtain off her face and exposing—for just a moment—a forehead that could have been Jenny's. "A toast," she said.

We all raised our glasses and awaited her speech. She looked directly at me and said, "To international correspondence."

We drank. We ate. We drank some more. By the end of the meal, I was quite drunk.

⁜

AFTER LUNCH I HELPED Zoya and Sveta clear the table. True to stereotypes about Russian men, Andrei remained in his chair and let the women do the work.

"How about a game of cards?" Zoya said. "We can wash the dishes later."

We all followed her into the living room and returned to our seats around the coffee table. She pulled a deck out of a drawer in the sideboard. The cards had pictures of Gorbachev on the back, but his famous birthmark had been airbrushed out.

"I saw Gorbachev once," I said. "When his motorcade was outside the Russian embassy. My mother and I were in the crowd. He waved to us."

The three of them looked at me as if I were a child whom they'd been forced to baby-sit. Clearly no one wanted to discuss Mikhail Sergeyevich.

"*Ladno,*" Zoya said. "We will play a Russian game called *durak.*"

Durak means "fool." Zoya explained the rules as she shuffled. The objective, she said, was to get rid of all your cards. The last player with cards in his hand was the fool. "There is no winner," she said. "Only a loser. The starting player is the attacker. The player to the attacker's left is the defender. Then we go clockwise."

Andrei continued. "The attacker turns over a card. If you can't defend, you must pick up the attacking card and add it to your hand, okay?"

"Aces are high. Trump always beats non-trump, so a trump six beats a non-trump king, *ponimayesh?*" Zoya said.

I didn't really understand, but I nodded. My motor skills were definitely impaired.

"Each player gets six cards to start," Zoya said. She distributed the cards with the stoicism of a professional dealer. She put the rest of the deck on the table and then removed the top card. It was a nine of spades.

"So," said Andrei. "Spades is trump."

Zoya attacked with a seven of hearts.

"You can beat that with any heart higher than six. Or with any spade. *Ponimayesh?*" Andrei said.

"*Da,*" I said. I was the defender. I looked at my hand, a blur of red and black. I was having trouble separating my diamonds from my hearts. I shook my head to restore focus. I had a five of spades. I slapped it down.

"*Molodets,*" said Svetlana. Good job.

"Now you are the attacker," Zoya said. I saw a glimmer of Jenny's competitive streak in her eyes.

I wanted to rise to the occasion, but my game was downhill from there. The vodka seemed to have had no effect on the others, but I felt like I was moving in slow motion. The fan I'd made of my cards kept slipping through my fingers, and I was struggling to keep the others from seeing my hand. Andrei, Svetlana, and Zoya easily defended my plays. I was the last one holding any cards.

"You are the fool," Svetlana said.

"The fool deals next," Zoya said. She pushed the cards at me. Then she lit a cigarette and passed the pack to her friends. Once again I was surrounded by smoke. I've never enjoyed feeling like a fool.

"Are we just going to keep playing cards and pretending we've never met?" I said.

The room grew very quiet. Svetlana and Andrei turned to look at Zoya. But Zoya kept her eyes on me. "We should take a walk before it gets dark," she said. "You must see our Russian forest."

"*Poshli,*" Andrei said. We're off.

"Andryushka," Zoya said. "Stay here and get the fire going, will you? I will walk with our American friend. Sveta can prepare our tea."

Zoya and I put on our coats and went outside into the winter afternoon. It must have been about half past three. I remember the silver light across her face; it made her skin look solid as stone. I walked with her into the woods, along a path that was nothing more than a dent in the snow. There were only a few inches on the ground, but it was perfectly white. I was right next to her, yet the distance between us still felt immense. Through the naked trees, I could see the roofs of other dachas.

"Lots of people are out here in the summer," Zoya said. Her breath hung in the air like an omen.

But on that early-November day, there was not a living soul around. The only sound was the crunch of snow beneath our feet. I was wearing the same L.L. Bean duck boots I'd had since I was fourteen. Zoya wore boots covered with fur and a heavy lambskin coat. Her head was bare, and her nose turned red and shiny in the cold. When we were about a quarter of a mile into the forest, she stopped.

"We couldn't talk inside," she said as she lit a cigarette. "It's always been bugged."

❖

THAT AFTERNOON ZOYA told me the story I wanted to hear.

"My father didn't start working for the KGB until we came to Washington," she said. "The CIA tried to recruit him at Yale in the 1960s—he was studying Russian—but he didn't want to be a spy. He was a scholarship kid. He just wanted to make money. But then he ended up as an intelligence analyst. In Dayton he worked on military-intelligence projects, but in D.C. he was working directly with the NSA and the DOD. He had access to all this information the Soviets wanted. And he was greedy. He wanted to pay off our mortgage, join the Chevy Chase Club. He needed cash for private school. He and my mom were living beyond their means. He thought he was smarter than everyone else; it never occurred to him that he'd get caught. It was supposed to be a onetime deal. And then when I wrote the letter to Andropov, it was like I handed him this grand plan. He didn't mail it—he took it to the Soviet consulate. It was on Phelps Place then, remember? He had contacts that made sure my letter reached the Kremlin and got it published. He knew we'd be invited to the USSR, because the invitation was his idea. The trip was good cover. We were sanctioned to travel there. We had all kinds of diplomatic protection. The press corps was traveling with us, so our every movement was documented. It wasn't like he could sneak off to meet with some KGB agent somewhere in Moscow. So I don't know when he handed off the information or how, but it was supposed to be the last time, you know, just one more big fat deposit for his Swiss bank account. Enough money for my college tuition. My mom didn't know. I didn't know—not then anyway. And he said he never passed any information to them after that, but in 1985 all these American assets in Moscow were discovered, and the CIA and FBI were hunting for moles, and everyone was getting suspicious. There was no evidence that my dad was even under surveillance, but he was really nervous, and the Soviets put all this money in escrow for him here and told him that they could give us a good life in Moscow. He defected on the condition that our family and friends would never know he was a traitor. He wanted to sneak away. He wanted to leave without looking like the bad guy. He was a coward."

"Why are you telling me this now?" I remember asking.

And her response was cryptic and profound: *"Govorish po sekretu, poidyot po vsemu svetu."* When you tell a secret, it travels the world.

She didn't learn the full story, she said, until she and her parents had been living in Russia for a year. She knew they had defected, but she didn't know why. She didn't know that her father was a spy. "Sveta helped me track you down. I wanted to contact you long ago," she said. "But I waited until my dad died."

"When did he die?"

"Last year. Heart attack."

"I'm sorry."

"Yeah, well. Living here depressed him. He basically drank himself to death. He sat in that leather chair and guzzled vodka and felt sorry for himself."

"And your mom?"

"The funny thing is that my mom really took to Moscow. She could always adapt to any situation. She started socializing with all these KGB wives, inviting them for dinner and teaching them how to bake apple pie. Her grandmother was Russian, so she embraced her heritage. She started a singing group and made the other women teach her Russian folk songs. She had a traditional folk costume and everything. She made the best of it. Until she got cancer."

"Is she . . . ?"

"Yeah. She died the year before my dad."

I wondered where Mr. and Mrs. Jones were buried. Had they been cremated? Were their ashes in an urn somewhere in the dacha? I shuddered.

"How's your mom?" she said.

"She's still around, still working for disarmament."

"I know. I've read about the foundation," she said with a short, sharp laugh. "Sveta says I should get a cut."

"A cut?"

"It's the Jennifer Jones Foundation, isn't it?" Zoya/Jenny said. "Without me it wouldn't exist."

"It's a nonprofit," I said. "There is no cut."

"It was a joke," she said.

"How come no one recognized you when you first moved here?"

"We didn't leave the house much the first year. We were out here in the country. A tutor came to give us Russian lessons every day, but otherwise we didn't have much company. By the time we were allowed to live in an apartment in the city, we'd learned to blend in. And besides, our deaths were reported here, too. It's not like anyone expected to see us."

"Why Zoya?" I said. "Did you choose your Russian name?"

She shrugged. "My dad always liked the name Zoe," she said.

"And the plane?" I said. "The plane that crashed? The one you were supposed to be on . . ."

"We weren't on it. The plane went down empty. The pilot

bailed out." She smiled as if she had just remembered something. "It feels good to speak English." Her voice was so much deeper. Even deeper than her mother's had been. I kept waiting for that moment when we would click. "When I do simple math in my head," she said, "I do it in English because I lived in the States when I learned arithmetic and pre-algebra. But geometry and calculus and statistics? I learned them here, so in my head the numbers and equations are all in Russian."

"Do you do a lot of math?" Jenny had been terrible at math; had she really made it all the way through calculus and statistics?

"Lately I must make many calculations."

Ten years in another country, speaking another language, eating different foods. Would she have grown taller if she had stayed in the States with access to more vegetables and less exposure to pollution? She went to Russian schools, was forbidden to travel abroad. It would change anyone.

"So you knew you were leaving," I said. "Long before you left."

"I knew a few days before we left," she said. "I couldn't bring anything with me. Not even my cat."

She was sculpted and cold, with none of Jenny's spontaneity and warmth. Doubt reasserted itself.

"What was your cat's name?" I said.

"Hexa," she said.

"What was your house number in Washington?"

"Three five zero three."

"When is your birthday?" I said.

"June eighteenth, 1972," Zoya said. "At least that was my old

birthday. All my Russian documents say I was born in May. I don't
have an American passport anymore. Everything from our old life
was destroyed. We had to start over."

"So you have no proof of who you were."

"I have you," she said. "You're my proof."

There are insects that have been suspended—lifelike—in
amber for 60 million years. Amber begins as resin, sticky and
sweet, trickling down the trunks of ancient trees. Mosquitoes,
scorpions, and ants are seduced by the smell, then trapped in the
resin and held, immobile, unchanging, as the liquid hardens and
the trees die and layers of sediment compress the resin into fossils.
Even after millions of years of pressure, the insects are preserved—
their legs and wings perfectly articulated—as if no time has
passed.

"What was my sister's name?" I said.

"Izzy," she said. "Short for Isabel."

"What about Kim?" I said.

"Who?" Her face drew an absolute blank.

"Kimberly Coughlin," I said. How could she forget Kim? For a
year they were inseparable.

It was possible, I suppose, that Kim had slid through one of
memory's cracks. There were certainly gaps in my memory. If Kim
didn't matter to Jenny as much as I thought, perhaps she had been
left behind. Jenny had more valuable memories to hold on to. I'd
like to think that I was one of the most valuable ones. Or perhaps
she didn't remember Kim because she wasn't really Jenny. After
all, Kim had never had a place on the official record of Jennifer

Jones's life. Even Hexa was mentioned in some of the interviews. Kim's name had never made it into any of the papers.

"You were my best friend," she said. The phrase had the hollow snap of a slogan.

"And now?" I said.

"Now I need help," she said. "I'm broke."

"I told you. The foundation is a nonprofit," I said.

"But your father gives you money."

"Svetlana told you that?"

"Last April," she began. "I had an investment opportunity. An oil concern. A chance to protect my savings from inflation. The money my father left—the pension from the KGB—I found a way to make it last." She drew nervously on her cigarette. "Oil. One thing this country has is oil. And the investment company's board of directors . . . . There were names I knew on the list. Names I recognized. Former government officials. I told Svetlana we would not have to worry about money anymore. The state is bankrupt, but the market, the free market, it will provide for us." She took another drag. "The minimum investment was one million rubles."

"You gave them one million rubles?"

She nodded, sadly.

"In April of this year?" She nodded again. I did the math based on the exchange rate in the spring of 1995. A million rubles was about two hundred thousand dollars. "And it's gone?"

"You think I'm very stupid, don't you? You think how very naïve I am, to trust these people. Their board of directors? All those official names? The fancy stationery with the letterhead? I know now it was false. These were common criminals. But you don't know what it's like to be here, with the ground shifting all the time under your feet, with the rules changing, with the food disappearing and the opportunities—so many opportunities! I thought I would be an actress!—slipping through your fingers. You see this house? This is all I have. I was going to be a movie star. I thought I was going to live in Hollywood. Now I barely have enough to eat. It's not fair. Do you know what it's like to lose everything?"

"You want money?" I said. I thought of the money from my father. Ten thousand dollars was nothing to him. He and Phillipa wrote checks of that size all the time.

"I wanted to see you again," she said.

It was what I'd longed to hear. But I'd always imagined hearing those words from the Jenny I knew. I'd been holding on to my fossilized idea of Jenny. The woman beside me—who claimed to be the former Jennifer Jones—seemed like a stranger. And it wasn't just Jenny I'd suspended in amber. I'd turned myself into a fossil, too.

"What about my letter?" I said.

"What letter?"

"My letter to Andropov," I said.

"I wrote the letter to Andropov," she said.

"You wrote the letter that he received," I said. How could she not remember? "Mine ended up behind your bulletin board."

"What do you mean?" she said. She looked genuinely confused. Maybe she never knew that my letter was tucked behind the bulletin board. Her dad could have hidden it and then told her he'd mailed both. Although I didn't understand why he wouldn't have destroyed my letter. Weren't spies in the habit of eliminating evidence?

The woman before me could have been Jenny. Or she could have been an impostor who'd been briefed by Svetlana. Jenny had told Sveta a lot about me in the summer of 1983. She told Svetlana that my parents were divorced, that my sister was dead, that I was sad. But she had obviously neglected to mention that I wrote a letter to Andropov, too. She never told anyone that the letter that made her famous was my idea. She never gave me the credit. I'd never told my story. Why would anyone believe me?

"Do you remember . . . ?" Zoya said. "The magnolia tree in your backyard? The way we used to touch the petals to see how fast they would turn brown?"

I had forgotten it until that moment. "Yes," I said. My mother had warned us that the oil in our fingers would ruin the flowers. *Don't touch,* she said. *Don't touch.* We couldn't resist.

"How much money do you need?" I said.

"For starters? Twenty thousand dollars," she said. "I owe the creditors . . . I don't know who to turn to. You're the only one who can help me."

"I don't have that much," I said.

"How much do you have?" she said. She dropped her cigarette and crushed it out with her left foot.

I didn't have to tell her, but I did. "Ten thousand," I said. "I have ten thousand."

She said I could deposit the money in a bank account she had set up. "I'll give you the account information." Then she hugged me. It was a hungry embrace. The appetite in her limbs—arms that held me for a beat too long, legs locked close to mine—was the strangest aspect of this Jenny. The girl I'd known didn't need me. I could feel her slide a piece of paper into the pocket of my corduroys. "You are a lifesaver," she whispered. She released me from the hug and clasped her hands together, the way Jenny's mother used to do. "You are saving my life. Do you know that?"

"Are you really happy here?" I said.

"I dream in Russian now," she said. "This is home."

⁂

BACK IN THE HOUSE, Zoya resumed her cover.

"So?" Svetlana said, expectation cresting in her voice. "It was a good walk?"

"A very good walk," Zoya said.

Svetlana poured the tea and set a plate of cookies on the coffee table. Andrei claimed the leather recliner. I was next to Zoya on the couch. Our conversation returned to its stilted conventions.

"We wanted to make you a cake," Zoya said. "A birthday cake. But in Russia it's bad luck to celebrate a birthday early. You have to wait." It was November 5. My birthday was in two days.

"Perhaps you will come back," Svetlana said. She and Zoya exchanged a look.

"When I was a child," I said slowly to test their reactions, "my friend and I wrote letters to Yuri Andropov. We were worried that he was going to start a nuclear war."

"The newspapers never said anything about *you* writing a letter," said Svetlana. She shot Zoya a nervous glance.

"No," I said. "Newspapers are not necessarily truth."

"We were all writing letters," said Andrei. "Post for Peace, we called it. Children here were urged to write to President Reagan. We thought you were going to bomb us."

"You wrote letters?" I said.

"Sure," he said. "Everyone did. Children were used for propaganda." And just like that, my experience was flattened into something generic, off the rack. Nothing about my story was special.

"Spasibo za kompaniyu," Zoya said when she showed Andrei and me to the door. Thank you for the company.

"Was it worth defecting for?" I whispered.

"What can you mean?" she said.

✤

ANDREI AND I DIDN'T TALK on the way back to the city. I was cold, and he handed me a blanket to spread across my lap. We were on a road without streetlamps; the headlights pioneered through the night. It was too dark to see the birch trees, but I could hear the wind in their branches. *"Tikha zoloto,"* he said. Silence is golden. I didn't answer.

When he finally pulled up in front of Corinne's building, he said, *"Chto ti dumayesh?"* What do you think?

"I'm still not going to sleep with you," I said. But I pondered what would happen if I did. Would I rifle through his wallet while he slept? It was hard to know who was in on what. I could seduce him for information, I thought. But I could picture the morning after, the awkward first look at each other in daylight. I'd play it cool while he pulled on his clothes and pretended he wasn't in a rush to leave. He'd pretend I mattered to him, and I'd pretend to believe it. He would tell me I was beautiful, but it wouldn't change anything. We'd still be pretending. I was holding out for the real thing.

His finger crawled up my arm. I pulled away. "Don't," I said.

"Have you found the friend you were looking for?" he said.

"I don't know," I said.

"*Ochen stranno,*" he said. Very strange.

"I'm a strange girl," I said.

"I like you anyway," he said.

"You don't know me."

"Let me get to know you. Have a drink with me."

"Not tonight," I said. "We've been drinking all day." Until I got to Moscow, I didn't believe the stories about how much Russians drank.

"Another night?" he said.

"We'll see," I said. "I'm starting a new job. I'm going to be busy."

"Americans love to be busy," he said. "So many to-do lists."

"You've got us all figured out," I said.

"What's wrong with you?"

"Nothing," I said. "Absolutely nothing."

———

IN MY ROOM THAT NIGHT, I pulled out the piece of paper that that Zoya/Jenny had folded into my pocket. It was typed, so there were no handwriting hints.

S,

As soon as I can pay you back, I will. But I need the money by December 1st. Please. I'm desperate. See account number below.

J.

P.S. Burn after reading!

I thought again of Zoya's hug. Did she feel that fierce need in me when we were kids? Did she feed off it until, like too much sugar, it made her sick?

I didn't need the money. I could transfer it into Zoya's account and pretend I'd never had it. It seemed fitting in a way, that the money my dad had given me should go to the friend who'd filled the space he left in my life. It was a relief to know that the money wouldn't be there, tempting me away from self-sufficiency. But that was assuming that Zoya really was Jenny.

There was only one way to find out.

16.

Z OYA SAID SHE SWAM laps at the Olympic pool in the mornings. So the next day I got up early and took the Metro there. I showed my *spravka* to the desk clerk, paid my admission fee. In the locker room, I soaped my private parts before anyone could yell at me.

I was out on the pool deck by a few minutes after seven. I wondered if Richard had watched the 1980 games. He said that Russians didn't know anything about marketing, but they were savvy enough to brand their games with Misha the Bear. The mascot was everywhere, even floating over the closing ceremonies as a giant bear-shaped balloon. On the wall of the pool, huge Cyrillic letters proclaimed the Olympic motto: БЫСТREE ЫСТРЕЕ ВЫШЕ СИЛЪНЕЕ. Faster, Higher, Stronger. I was about to get into the very pool the American swimmers were denied the chance to compete in because of the boycott.

Two old men were crawling down the lane on the far right, and in the center a flabby woman was breaststroking toward me. She wore a rubber cap with flowers on it, like the ones from the 1950s. The room was hot, and the suffocating smell of chlorine put me in a dreamlike state. I half expected to see Jenny emerge from the water in her yellow bathing suit. "Two out of three!" she'd say whenever I beat her to the end of her backyard pool. She couldn't bear to lose.

If I could see Zoya in a bathing suit, I could check for the birthmark. If the birthmark was there, I decided I'd give her the money, however vague her reasons for wanting it. I crouched at the edge of the pool and splashed water on my latex cap to make it slick enough to put on easily. I can't go into an indoor pool without thinking of my high-school team. Outdoor pools are for summer frolicking, but indoor pools I associate entirely with hard work. Sprints and drills. Sets on intervals. Only the truly dedicated swim indoors. I was a good swimmer. My old coach called me a stealthy competitor. He said I didn't look like a threat on the starting blocks, but once I was in the water, I was hard to beat. It was all about will. I snapped my goggles into place and slid into the lane.

I stuck to freestyle and counted the lengths with each flip turn. One hundred meters, then two hundred, then three. Jenny's book was full of pictures of the Soviet Pioneers competing in swimming races at camp on the Crimea. The sea was partitioned by lane lines. For the championships there was a red banner with the Olympic motto and bleacher seating for the crowd. "The water in the Black Sea is so salty," Jenny had said. "You float without even trying." I felt like I was in Jenny's wake, that with each stroke my fingers might catch her slippery toes. But it was the young Jenny I was thinking of. The person who didn't exist anymore. After five hundred meters, I could feel a burn in my biceps. My arms felt too heavy to lift, and my strokes became choppy. After one thousand meters, I stopped to rest. I stood panting against the wall of the shallow end, desperate for a drink of water.

That's when she walked out of the locker room. Unmistakably Zoya. She was wearing a red bathing suit and blue track pants. Her mouth was set in a furious expression, as if her teeth were clenched. I was in lane three. In my cap and goggles, I felt sleek and anonymous. She knelt at the edge of lane seven and stuck a tentative hand into the pool. Checking the temperature, I thought. I waited for her to take off her track pants so I could see her thighs. But she stood up and began stretching. She spread her legs wide, arced sideways, and extended an arm. In that position she looked so much like Jenny.

I pushed off the wall of my lane and stayed underwater so she couldn't see me. I'd reveal myself after another lap. I made it down half the length of the pool—twenty-five meters—before I needed to come up for air. That's what I've got going for me: strong lungs. The lungs of a nonsmoker. *Trust, but verify.* Is it really trust, though, if you have to fact-check it? Either you make the leap or you don't. You believe in spite of the doubt. You believe because you want to believe. Or you decide to put your trust in something—or someone—else. In yourself, maybe.

I switched to backstroke on my return to the other end of the pool. It felt good to swim. I felt invincible. *Faster, Higher, Stronger.* Of the Artek races, Jenny said, "Svetlana is a good swimmer, but not as fast as you." Jenny didn't watch the 1984 Summer Games with me. That was the year of the retaliatory Soviet boycott; she and I were already estranged.

I overtook a woman in my lane. She turned her head to the side and sucked at the air like a blind puppy trying to find a teat. Too much breathing will slow you down. About fifteen meters from the wall, I picked up speed. I wanted a strong finish. But I misjudged the distance and slammed my head into the wall. I was in the shallow end, so I stood up and pulled off my swim cap. My head was throbbing. When I touched the back of my scalp, my fingers came away warm with blood.

A babushka was reprimanding me in Russian from the next lane. "Be careful," she was saying. "You have to watch where you're going."

A drop of my blood hit the pool. I watched it separate as it moved through the water and thought, *If I were in the ocean, I'd attract sharks. I'd be prey.*

Zoya was thirty yards away, sitting on the deck, folded over her outstretched legs. Loosening up her hamstrings, perhaps. She could have been anyone.

Even now, in my thirties, whenever a romantic relationship

ends, I find myself saying, *He's not the person I thought he was.* From a distance a lover I knew so well becomes a man I do not recognize. I see him with his new girlfriend and even his posture is different. With her his stance is more solid, more aloof. I no longer see the cracks, the vulnerable places where he let me in. He is across the room at a party—with a little effort, an adjusted angle, our eyes would meet—but he might as well be on another continent. *Have you met X?* someone says to me, and I do not say, *I used to share his bed. I used to know his passwords and his whims.* Instead I say, in the same vague tone I reserve for elevators, *I think we met once a long time ago.* Because the person who he is with her is a stranger. A foreigner. Maybe the person he was with me was just a role he was trying on. And maybe the words he fed me were lines. But that doesn't mean the relationship was any less real. It felt true to me.

I hoisted myself out of the pool and stood there, dripping water and blood, knowing that my teeth would soon start to chatter the way they always did when I was cold. I felt woozy and wondered if I had a concussion. No one was going to sweep in and take care of me if I did. Even Jenny couldn't be counted on. She'd left me in the woods. If our roles had been reversed, she wouldn't have spent two hours looking for *me.*

When I asked my mother why I was the last to know the truth about Santa Claus, she said, "People believe in things until they don't need to anymore."

Suddenly I didn't want to see Zoya's bare legs. Even if the birthmark was there, Jenny was dead. My friend was gone. I didn't need her anymore.

Zoya never saw me. When I left the pool, she was still stretching.

✳

THE NEXT NIGHT I celebrated my twenty-third birthday by going out for Georgian food with Corinne and Leslie and Jane. They sang to me in Russian. Then Corinne said, "I don't think it's unfortunate that birthdays only happen once a year. I am in no rush to get older, thank you very much."

"Amen to that," said Leslie.

Jane insisted that we order champagne. It wasn't real champagne, though. Just the sparkling wine that the menu referred to as *shampanskoe*. We raised our glasses. "To your new job!" Jane said. "To your future as an ace reporter."

✳

THE FOLLOWING WEEK Svetlana would call me for the last time. "*Spasibo bolshoe,*" she said. Thanks a lot.

"For what?" I said.

"You helped us create the idea!" she said.

"What idea?" I said.

"For Czar," she said. "Now I will go to USA. To New York office. I will go to top of Empire State Building. I will walk on Brooklyn Bridge." She sounded like she might not come back. I pictured her triumphantly hailing a yellow cab.

"So what's the campaign idea?" I said.

"'Czar,'" she said. "'The cola worth defecting for.' The campaign will be tongue-in-cheek. We will use the Cold War imagery."

"That's good," I said. I didn't bother to point out that defectors were anachronistic with czars. "Congratulations. But you didn't need my help." When it came to marketing, she was an expert. I told her I was staying in Moscow to work for the newspaper.

"This is funny," she said. "You will be in Russia, I will be in America. We make a switch."

"It is funny," I said.

"When Jennifer Jones came here in 1983, I asked many questions about America. I never thought I would see for myself."

"I waited a long time to see Russia," I said.

"And?" she said. "You like what you found here?"

"Yes," I said. "I'm glad you invited me. Thank you."

"*Nichevo.*" It's nothing. "And our friend?" she said. "You will help her?"

"I can't," I said. "I don't have what she needs."

"You have everything she needs," she said. Her voice was drawn tight like a slingshot, ready to fire.

"I don't," I said. *"Eto ne pravda."* It's not true.

⁂

I TOOK A DIRECT FLIGHT to New York. I had a window seat, and as the plane lifted off early that afternoon, I looked out at the morose scene below. It was snowing gently, and as the runway lights streaked and blurred beneath me, I felt as if I were traveling through time. Going to Moscow was like stepping through a magic portal to a very different world. A world of superstition and shadows, of poetry and deadly icicles. Defectors and spies. Secret messages and invisible ink. Svetlana and Zoya and Andrei had served me the Russia of my imagination. It was hard to believe that it would take just ten hours to get back to the place where I began.

The seat next to me was empty, but across the aisle a toddler suddenly burst into hysterical tears. He writhed on his mother's lap. "I don't speak Russian," she said to me. "He's been crying for two days. I can't get him to stop." She rocked back and forth, and it was clear she was trying to soothe herself as much as the child. She told me that she had adopted the baby from an orphanage in Nizhny Novgorod and now she was taking him home to Nashville. She trembled as if the enormity of her decision to adopt this orphan had just hit her. On the flight to Moscow, she had probably been dreaming of nursery paint colors, and now she had the complicated knot of motherhood to face.

"I speak a little Russian," I said. Her eyes pleaded with me. So I began to coo, whispering sweet reassurances in the boy's mother tongue, and he watched me, with wary, watery eyes at first and then with increasing degrees of reverence, until we reached our cruising altitude and he went to sleep.

"Thank you," the mother whispered. She was so grateful that I was a little embarrassed. I felt like a tourist being asked for directions. I didn't know much, but this woman was so lost that she was willing to trust my expertise.

"No problem," I said.

"His name is Pavel, but we're going to call him Henry," she said. She clutched the child against her chest with the desperate love of someone who has been waiting a long time.

"Henry's a nice name," I said. I pulled the shade down and tucked my airline pillow against the window to cushion my head. I didn't realize how exhausted I was.

"It's my father's name," she said. "My husband wanted to name him after his father, but I said, 'If you can't fly over to Russia with me, you sure as hell aren't picking the name!' He couldn't really argue with that." And she kept talking, but I can't remember what else she said, because I drifted off. I slept for the whole flight. I slept through the beverage cart's debut. I slept through dinner and the movie. If Pavel cried some more, I didn't hear it. When I woke up, the cabin lights had been turned back on for landing. It was afternoon, and we were making our approach to JFK. The Russians on board applauded when we touched down.

"Welcome home," the man at passport control said to me as he stamped my documents.

"Thank you," I said, and some mixture of jet lag and patriotism caused me to tear up a little, right there in the airport.

On the other side of customs, I found my connecting flight to Washington. At National Airport my mother pulled me into a fierce hug. She was wearing a blue down jacket and a white wool hat with a pom-pom on top, an ensemble that made her look surprisingly young. "How was the flight?" she said.

"Easy," I said.

"You smell like cigarettes," she said.

"Secondhand smoke," I assured her.

✤

ON THANKSGIVING I TOLD my mother what I thought she needed to hear. We were in the kitchen, where she was, remarkably, preparing to stuff a turkey. She was rubbing a stick of butter over the bird, smearing its plucked, pimpled flesh with the same fretful drive she applied to everything. Her sleeves were rolled up, and her wrists were bony as a girl's, her fingers bare—no nail polish, no rings.

"You might want to sit down for this," I said.

"That's what your father said when he asked for a divorce," she said. She used the back of her left wrist to push a rogue strand of hair out of her eyes, then returned her greasy hands to the bird. "Whatever it is, I can take it standing up."

So we were standing when I said, "I think we should dissolve the foundation."

I don't know what I expected, but the news didn't send her scurrying to the bathtub. She took a moment to flip the turkey and then said, "I was afraid you were going to tell me you're pregnant."

"God, no," I said.

"Well, that's a relief. I'm not ready to be a grandmother. I don't bake cookies. I don't even know how to knit."

I helped her stuff the bird. I made the mashed potatoes. Our pie was store-bought, but we cooked the rest of our dinner ourselves.

In the end she was glad to let go of the foundation. "I kept it going for you," she told me. "Jenny was your friend."

"That was a long time ago," I said.

"To be frank," she said, "I always thought she was kind of self-centered. But she meant so much to you."

The next day she drafted a press release. The foundation was closing its doors because in the wake of the Cold War, its mission was no longer necessary.

#

As for my letter to Andropov, I read it one last time and then buried it in the Bishop's Garden. I had new stories to tell.

November 20, 1982

Dear Mr. Andropov,

Are you going to start a nuclear war?

My mother says that after a nuclear bomb, everything will be dark. She says there will be no sun, so it will get really dark and cold. She says that there will be ashes everywhere, so the world will be gray. Colors will be erased. Everything will die. Sometimes I wake up and wonder will this be the last day? And if it is the last day, should I do something different? Something special? But in my house it's already dark. It's already dusty and cold. Maybe the catastrophe has already happened. Maybe you think you can destroy us, but that is not true. We can destroy ourselves.

ACKNOWLEDGMENTS

The following works were essential to my research for this book: *Journey to the Soviet Union* by Samantha Smith and *The Spy Who Got Away* by David Wise.

I'm also eternally grateful to:

Bill Clegg, whose faith in this manuscript and brilliant notes helped me reach the finish line, and his incomparable assistant, Shaun Dolan; Andrea Walker, whose editorial insight made this book so much better, and everyone else at the Penguin Press; and Michael Cunningham, who has helped me in too many ways to count.

Elizabeth Bishop, whose poem "In the Waiting Room" inspired the title of this book.

Brooklyn College and Himan Brown, PEN American Center, the Sewanee Writers' Conference, the *Tin House* Summer Writers' Workshop, and the Corporation of Yaddo for support.

All the incredible writers I've had as teachers: Jonathan Baumbach, Charles D'Ambrosio, Stacey D'Erasmo, Joshua Henkin, Diane Johnson, Wendy MacLeod, Claire Messud, Mary Morris, Jenny Offill, Peter Rock, and Steve Yarbrough; the MFA program at Brooklyn College and my inspiring colleagues there, especially Marie-Helene Bertino, Adam Brown, David Ellis, Tom Grattan, Amelia Kahaney, Reese Kwon, Helen Phillips, Anne Ray, and Mohan Sikka.

Robert McFarlane and James Woolsey for answering my research questions; Sarah Corson for *knowing* I'd be a writer when I was in her second-grade class at The Potomac School; my former colleagues at Saatchi & Saatchi, especially Marcia Roosevelt; Hannah Tinti, Maribeth Batcha, and the whole staff of *One Story* magazine, where I learned so much about editing.

The editors of the literary magazines that have published my work: *Bellevue Literary Review*, *Guernica*, and the *Kenyon Review*, and the ones that honored my early stories with awards: *Zoetrope: All-Story* and *The Missouri Review*; Bill Henderson and The Pushcart Press; and Joel Whitney and Meakin Armstrong of *Guernica* for nominating me for the 2011 PEN Emerging Writers Award.

All my friends, especially those who offered encouragement at crucial points during the writing of this book: Laura van den Berg (who read early versions of the manuscript), Ann Marie Healy,

Kate Ryan, Meghan Kenny, Anne Kauffman, Catherine Despont, Hilary Redmon, Jennifer Vanderbes, and Colson Whitehead.

And finally, my amazing family. This book would not exist without the love and support of my sisters, Lizzie and Katie, who are both brilliant readers and generous hosts. I'm also grateful to my brothers-in-law, Will Darman and Reif Larsen; my nieces, Jane and Emma; Jonathan Darman; and Vicki Weil. My wonderful father has always believed in me, even when others doubted. And my late mother, who told me everything was material for my writing, was the one who first took me to Moscow in 1993. Thank you. I love you all.